A MAN OUT OF TIME
CHRISTOPHER LAFLAN

SEVERED PRESS
HOBART TASMANIA

A MAN OUT OF TIME

Dedicated to Sawyer & Colton, whose imaginations far exceeds my own.

CHAPTER 1

Sergeant John Crider raised his closed fist—a signal for the five-man unit of Shadow Company to halt. The bottom of his cloth facemask was thick with condensation, each breath cooled by the night air. He motioned twice to his left. Somewhere behind him, his team would be moving to their designated locations. Four days ago, recon satellites above North Korea detected an unknown power surge in an uninhabited area, east of Phungso. Within thirty-six hours, Shadow Company had boots on the ground.

John crouched and moved behind cover. He peeled back the protective covering on his watch face. Forty seconds until his team would be in position. Slowly, he raised his suppressed service rifle to his shoulder and peered through the scope. A bare yellowed bulb illuminated the front of a small brick building fifty yards away. The building was windowless, no bigger than a one-car garage, with a single rusted metal door below the light. Tire ruts cutting deep into the ground were a good indication the area was still active. The earpiece in his left ear clicked twice; a few seconds later, a single time. His team was in position. John began to lower his rifle when the metal door to the building opened. A bright white light flooded the area. Two figures, in military uniforms, stepped out into the night. One lit a cigarette while the other walked over and relieved himself on the side of the building. John pushed the communicator, around his neck, twice. Through his scope, he watched the soldiers simultaneously crumple.

"Advance," he said in a low whisper. The throat mic would carry the order to the rest of the unit.

John moved from cover and converged on the small building. Rodriguez and Zimmerman, from Unit Two, were already dragging the bodies into the nearby brush when he arrived. On the outside, the shed door looked weathered, but it hid a foot of steel behind it.

"Felts, you and Osborn stay sharp. A door this thick is hiding something," John said.

"Roger that, Boss." Osborn's voice echoed over the comm. "We'll keep your backside clean."

Rodriguez and Zimmerman followed John into the vacant, well-lit interior. Rodriguez walked the perimeter, examining the galvanized flooring.

"You think there's some sort of trapdoor here?" Rodriguez asked.

Zimmerman pulled the door closed. "I don't see any seams on the floor. The guards were definitely Kores, but they didn't seem too worried about security."

John walked, looking for anything they may have missed. "There has to be something—"

The floor shuddered and began to descend.

"Felts," John said into his comm. "It looks like this thing's an elevator. We may lose audio."

The communicator crackled. "We'll wait forty minutes before heading back to camp. Good luck," Felts's voice answered.

John took a defensive position by the back wall, facing forward. Zimmerman and Rodriguez followed suit, each taking a wall. There was no telling where the elevator would dump out, and this position would give each man three firing points with no blind spots. Fluorescents, recessed along the concrete walls, lit the platform as they descended. The platform slowed before opening into a large hallway. A single soldier stood at the lift control panel.

The operator's eyes went wide. *"Chim-ibja!"*

A muffled thud of Zimmerman's silenced rifle reverberated. The shot took the lift operator in the throat before he could fill his lungs again. John gave the signal, and the three advanced. The passage was quiet except for the soft hum of the industrial lights. A few doors lined either side. John knelt beside the first door. From a side pocket, he removed a two-foot piece of plastic tubing. He slid the small end underneath the door and put his eye up to the lens enclosed in the opposite side. The room on the other side came into view. Rotating the tubing, he scanned the adjacent room.

John retracted the tubing and glanced back at Rodriguez. "Storage."

At the next set of doors, John began to uncoil the tubing again but stopped at the sound of voices from the other side. Zimmerman took a position on the opposite side of the door. Flattening against the wall, Zimmerman drew his knife. John stowed the lens and did the same. Seconds passed, and the voice grew louder. The door handle twisted and opened inward. A man wearing a lab coat and black headphones stepped through the doorway, singing. John's left hand covered the man's mouth while his blade slid into the back of the man's neck, severing his spine. The man convulsed; a thin rasp barely escaped his lips. John pulled the body a short distance down the hallway. He wiped the knife on the man's shirt before clicking it back into its sheath.

"You guys need to see this," Rodriguez said.

John and Zimmerman joined Rodriguez at the doors. The interior was crammed with computer equipment, some carelessly tossed in piles around the room. At the far end, an observation window overlooked what appeared to be a larger room.

John pointed to a door across the room. "Zimmerman, get me eyes on the other side of that door."

"Got it," Zimmerman said. He moved across the room and knelt beside the door.

"These systems have to be at least ten years old. I mean look at this," Rodriguez said as he walked up to a computer screen. "This is old basic. Why in the hell would they be running basic?"

"It's the bloody Kores we're talking about. When have they ever made sense?" Zimmerman asked as he fished the miniscope under the side door.

John moved over to the observation window. The window overlooked a large rectangular room. They had to be a few stories up. Below, people in plastic yellow hazmat suits worked on a half dozen white cylindrical canisters.

"What does this look like to you, Rodriguez?" John asked.

Rodriguez pulled himself away from the computer screen and moved over to the window. "Looks like missile components to me. See those guys nearest to us?" He pointed at two men adding an electrical board to an inside panel. "Those could be guidance systems."

"But why six? They wouldn't be assembling this many in one place if they were nukes or biologics, and either of those would have given us a component signature by now," John said.

"What has me puzzled is the lack of substantial military presence," Zimmerman said, withdrawing the miniscope. "We've only seen three armed personnel since we arrived, and the stairwell on the other side of this door is unguarded."

John moved away from the windows. "If I wanted to make sure something was kept a secret, I would minimize the presence around it. Rodriguez, try and pull anything you can from the computers."

Rodriguez laughed a little too loud. "These things," he said, lifting one of the nearest keyboards, "predate USB drives. How do you suggest I get the information off?"

John turned. "I don't care how you do it, just get it done!"

"I thought you Mexicans could do anything with a little tape and some wire," Zimmerman said.

Rodriguez flipped Zimmerman the middle finger. "I'm Puerto Rican, *pendejo*! When shit hits the fan, I'll make sure to borrow your head scarf to wipe my ass."

Zimmerman grinned. "If I ate as many tacos as you, I might need it too." He opened the stairwell access door and started down the stairs before Rodriguez could reply.

John followed Zimmerman down. Rodriguez was still swearing on the comm when they reached the next floor. Despite outward appearances, the squad was close. Shadow Company was a special branch of the Combat Application Group, or CAG. Each of the five-man team John had hand selected was a certifiable badass, and each one a bigger pain in the butt than the last. It was a perfect family of misfits. Zimmerman and Rodriguez had come from the same unit. He had first met them in a shithole bar outside Raeford, North Carolina. At the time, they were diligently trying to out drink each other for the enjoyment of a woman, which could just as well have been a man in drag.

"Keep the comm channel clear," John said. There were a few more choice words from Rodriguez before the comm went silent.

"He was mad enough, he even slipped into Spanish," Zimmerman replied, clearly pleased with the results.

Systematically, they cleared each of the floors but found nothing except for more discarded computer equipment and storage.

"What do we have here?" Zimmerman said as they descended the last set of stairs. Unlike the other areas, this one featured a set of glass doors. There didn't appear to be any handle, just smooth panes of glass. John approached watching for movement on the other side. The panes opened, retracting into the walls. Lights in the ceiling illuminated a small room connecting the stairs to a larger area. Zimmerman followed John inside. The doors slid back into place. Behind them, the doors clicked.

John looked back at Zimmerman. "I don't like—"

The interior lighting changed to red, and pressurized gas expelled from the floor, filling the room.

"Hold your breath," John yelled, trying to shout over the sound of the valves. He took aim on the exterior glass door. The gas stopped, and the ceiling lights turned green. The doors to the larger room opened. John relaxed his finger on the trigger and released the breath he had been holding.

A nervous smile spread across Zimmerman's face. "Damn decontamination room."

They moved forward into the new area. A small wall separated the entry from the main assembly area they had seen from above. John moved along the edge of the wall and peered around. The workers in the yellow hazmat suits continued their work on the white cylindrical devices still unaware of the intrusion.

"Sergeant." Zimmerman had stepped in close to John. "Those men aren't speaking Korean."

Zimmerman was right. The men were practically yelling to one another to be heard through the enclosed suits.

"Sounds like Mandarin, but what would the Chinese be doing here? Thought they'd be too busy protecting Beijing from Allied Forces." Zimmerman said.

The communicator in John's ear crackled.

"I was able to access the mainframe, but all the data is in Chinese," Rodriguez said. "I'm a little rusty, but... holy shit!"

"Repeat," John responded.

"The thermal-electromagnetic pulse systems. They're right here!" Rodriguez replied.

"The TEMPs? Five years of fighting the Axis and the Chinese put the bloody devices in Korea. You have to be kidding me," Zimmerman whispered behind John.

John pulled away from the wall. "Rodriguez, we need to let HQ know what we've found, and do it fast."

Ever since the Chinese detonated the first TEMPs, every country on earth was scrambling to make their own, but none so far could recreate the results. Scientists working for the State Department believed the Chinese were using a newly engineered element. Without a sample, it would be impossible to recreate the effects. For John, the day the first TEMPs detonated in Cuba would always be burned into his mind. The electromagnetic fallout darkened a quarter of the southern United States. Without electricity, chaos erupted. The government was quick to react, enacting martial law, but it was only the beginning. The TEMPs not only damaged electrical systems, but the thermal wave sterilized millions of acres of farmland. It wasn't until two more devices were detonated in the United Kingdom and Turkey that World War III truly started. If these really were TEMPs, the mission had just substantially changed.

A few minutes later, Rodriguez came back on the comm. "We are to terminate and secure. Transport is on the way. ETA forty-five minutes."

John thumbed the firing mode switch on his rifle from burst to single. "We'll work from the back to front. We can't chance one of those things going off down here, so we need to keep it tight." He rolled his head popping his neck. "I counted seventeen. I'll take the left. You take the right. The faster trigger gets the last man. We'll go on three."

Zimmerman nodded.

John moved back along the edge of the wall. Zimmerman took position next to him. "One. Two. Three." He pivoted, stepping into view. He brought his sight down on his first target. Aim. Squeeze. The suppressed mechanical thud of the rifles sounded too loud in the oversized room. *Six, seven, eight.* The last man dropped to the floor.

"And that's nine," Zimmerman said, lowering his rifle. "You buy the drinks tonight."

Smug bastard, John thought. Movement on the floor caught his attention. An injured worker strained to reach a handheld device on a workbench. In one smooth motion, John raised his rifle and pulled the trigger. The worker arched backward and collapsed. "No. That's nine."

Zimmerman swore and strolled over to the worker's body. With his foot, he rolled the corpse over. The air filter attached to the front of the man's chest had a finger size hole in it. "Hit the damn filter."

John walked up and patted Zimmerman on the shoulder. "Let's go. I believe you have drinks to buy, and none of that cheap stuff this time."

CHAPTER 2

The flight back was always the worst for John. C-17s weren't known for their comfortable ride, but that's not what really bothered him. Around him, service members joked and laughed. A few flasks were being passed around. He rolled his finger on the smooth plastic wheel of his iPod, increasing the volume of Peter Frampton's "Show Me the Way." It wasn't that he hated the festivities, today the men did have something to celebrate. Finding those TEMPs could possibly end this war.

He closed his eyes and leaned his head back against the headrest. It was always after the mission was over that his mind turned to thoughts of Emily, the way a smile constantly seemed to play on her thin lips, or how her eyes sparkled when she laughed. The ache returned. Why did his memories always have to smell like that damn Florida hospital room? After the baby was born, they had plans to visit Emily's parents, but the TEMPs changed everything. In the blink of an eye, he lost half of himself that day. The better half. Only the tiny bundle screaming in his arms had kept him moving.

Someone flopped down into the seat next to him; a second later, a tug popped his left earphone out.

"I know what you're doing, John, and it has no place on this plane."

John sighed and opened his eyes. "I don't know how you always know, but I hate you for it, Jimmy."

Jimmy held John's loose earbud up to his ear. He made a face and let go of the bud. "I don't know how you can listen to that crap."

Jimmy Osborn. The only one on Shadow Company John had known personally. Only a year older than John, they had gone through boot camp together. At six four and maybe one-hundred eighty-five pounds fully clothed, Jimmy wasn't the typical recruit, but the man could fire a rifle like none other, and he was the best friend a man could ask for. When the rioting began after the initial TEMPs attack, Jimmy commandeered General Sorenson's personal sailboat to come and get John and his newborn daughter out of the city.

"Here." Jimmy held out a handkerchief and pointed to his nose.

John sat up and touched beneath his nose. His fingers came away warm and crimson. He took the handkerchief, not wanting to know how many times Jimmy had used it.

"Is it getting worse?" Jimmy asked. Even though Jimmy didn't look it, he was worried.

"Yeah," John said.

"Why don't you just take the medical discharge? God knows you could use a break from all of this."

John pinched the bridge of his nose to try and stop the blood flow. "They said it's growing too fast to do anything with," John said. "To be honest, I keep hoping I'll keel over at the end of a mission. At least that way Maddie will be set for life."

"Jesus!" Jimmy picked at the armrest.

"You know if something should happen—"

"Don't even," Jimmy cut in. "You know I can't stand the constipated look you get when talking about this. It makes you seem so... old."

"You're one to talk, Old Man."

"Hey now, watch it." Jimmy stretched and yawned. "Well, since you're a stubborn ass and won't do what you should, what are you and my goddaughter planning? It doesn't look like they'll be sending us out again anytime soon."

"What have you heard about the Alcor Cryo thing?" John asked, looking down at his iPod. Huey Lewis and the News had just come on.

"The freeze draft?" Jimmy snagged one of the flasks as it came by. He took a swig and grimaced. "Doesn't anyone like a good scotch anymore?" He held out the flask, but John shook his head. "That cryo stuff sounds like a bunch of bullshit if you ask me."

A year ago, Congress enacted the Cryonics Act. With the southern states off the power grid and the soil unable to maintain crops, the influx of people moving north became suffocating. Housing and other resources dwindled in less than six months. The government poured millions into searching for an answer. Alcor, which had been previously located in Scottsdale, Arizona, offered the best long-term solution: cryonics. At the time, it was deemed impractical, but substantial government funding saw the first human revived, with no long-term side effects. Unfortunately, these miracles of science did little to sway the American public. Not many wanted to be frozen, only to be woken to a world maybe worse off than the one they left.

John removed his other earphone and placed the iPod in his bag under the seat. "I don't know. Doesn't seem too bad to me. Hundred years in cryo and the government will pay you for your time. With the new house, I'm drowning in debt. How am I ever supposed to provide for Maddie when I can't even afford food?" He tilted his head, trying to relieve the pressure at the base of his skull. Another of the downside of illness eating him from the inside.

"We're all in the same boat, brother." Jimmy ran his hand through his hair. "That's why I'm living on base. I can't afford anything else, but the cryo shit just creeps me out."

"I know, Jimmy. All I want is to have Maddie grow up like we did. Not like this." John reached up and put his hand against his chest. He couldn't feel the picture in his pocket, but it was there.

"Easy to say for an Iowa farm boy. I grew up near Port Morris. Not sure we had the same childhood," Jimmy said.

"You know what I mean. A hundred years and they might even have all this cleaned up again. Maddie might be able to go to college one day. Who knows, they might even be able to fix me up too."

"Maddie did get her mother's brains, so of course she'll go to college." Jimmy relaxed back in the seat. "Look, I understand. Out of all people, I do, but it doesn't mean I have to like it. Who's supposed to watch your back when I'm six feet under?"

John shifted in his seat, trying to find a more comfortable position. He wiped his nose one last time and held the handkerchief out to Jimmy. "I'm hoping we'll have robots and unmanned aircraft doing all the heavy lifting by then."

"Yeah, you can keep that one," Jimmy said. "And that whole robot thing, can't see that going wrong, Terminator," Jimmy said in a terrible Arnold Schwarzenegger accent. He snorted when he laughed, causing a few of the other service members to take notice.

John groaned. Everyone always had to make some wisecrack about the 1984 blockbuster. "You had to go there, didn't you?"

"Sure did," Jimmy said.

John had been wrestling with the cryo decision for months. He often wondered what Emily would have done in his position. So much would change in a hundred years, and that really scared the hell out of him, but Maddie deserved so much more out of life than he could provide right now. Even if they couldn't do anything for him, at least, Maddie would still be better off. "You know I won't need my house when I'm a popsicle. The government payments will pay off the mortgage, plus it would be nice to know it was looked after while I'm gone."

"You know I can't do that," Jimmy said, fidgeting with the hole he had created in the armrest's pad.

"Sure you can. You're the closest thing I have to family, besides the in-laws. Look at it as my way of watching your back." He elbowed Jimmy in the side. "Maybe getting off the base might finally help you land a girl who doesn't swing around a pole."

"Hey, there's nothing wrong with a girl like that. They're so damn flexible and—"

John cut him off. He'd heard his share of Jimmy's adventures over the years. "Okay, okay. I don't need to hear it. Just promise me you'll look for a lifer."

"I'll try." Jimmy slapped John on the shoulder. "You know I could never repay you for this?"

"You already have, brother. You already have."

CHAPTER 3

The yellow cab turned down Railroad Avenue in Fairfax, a small suburb of Washington, DC.

John tapped on the Plexiglas, separating the front and rear of the taxi. "It's the second house on the right, the white two-story. I won't be long. Can you stick around?"

The cab driver nodded and pulled over to the curb. John swiped his debit card through the built-in terminal between the driver and passenger seat. He hated paying at every stop but understood not everyone came back. The cabby unloaded the two military duffels from the trunk and set them on the sidewalk. He would only have to reload them again, but it was better than the cab driver getting impatient and taking off with your stuff.

John slung a duffel over each shoulder, then took a long, slow deep breath. He had planted surveillance devices inside military compounds, rushed a machine-gun pillbox, even tossed back a live grenade once, and nothing scared him more than his in-laws, Darren and Beverly Westcott. Darren was a partner at McDaniel and Associates. His firm was the largest government-employed law firm in the United States. John's father-in-law had always believed his daughter deserved better than some military grunt. Beverly, on the other hand, was eccentric, to say the least. Her mix of pain pills and Xanax kept her blissfully unaware of the world most days. Really, the only reason John bothered at all was for his little girl. He stepped onto the porch and was about to press the doorbell when the door open. Darren, with his square-framed glasses and neatly trimmed graying hair, stood in the doorway.

"I see you made it back." There was an obvious tone of disappointment in Darren's voice. He stepped to the side.

"Good to see you too, Darren," John said, stepping into the foyer.

"Lucille is gathering Maddie's items. They should be down shortly," Darren said. "I'd offer you a seat, but unfortunately, we aren't prepared for guests."

Lucille was the Westcott's nanny. Darren had hired her because he thought his granddaughter could use a proper female influence in her life. More than likely, it was so Darren could limit his interaction with John, which was fine with him. Beverly entered the dining room.

"Jonathan," Beverly said, her speech slightly slurred. She had called him Jonathan since the first time they met, even though his name wasn't short for anything. Beverly's blue low-cut dinner dress looked a little tight, but she wore it well. She smiled and stepped up next to her husband, locking her arm through his. "Are you sure you won't reconsider, Jonathan? Maddie is no burden to us, and we could get her enrolled in Sidwell Friends School this fall. Just think of the doors that would open for her, and think of the friends. Little girls need friends."

John shook his head. Sidwell was one of the top private schools in the country, but with the influx of people from the south, tuition skyrocketed, pushing the cost to just under a million a year. Even if you could afford it, the chance of gaining admittance was about one in a million. "Thank you for the offer, but we are going to do this our way. You are always welcome to join us. Between your contacts and my government clearance, I know we could get you on the list at Alcor."

The lines on Darren's brow deepened. "You and this stupid plan. I told you last time, it's a pipedream, a get rich quick scheme. Are you really willing to break this family apart again?"

John clenched his jaw and tried to keep the anger from his voice. "I'm not breaking apart anything, Darren." His tone was sharper than he attended. "This isn't something I decided on a whim."

"And what if this plan of yours doesn't work? What if you're getting yourself into something so much worse? You have to think about Maddie." Darren said.

"I am. I may not be able to give my Maddie everything, but I'm doing the best I can, and I know if Emily were here she would say the same," John said.

Darren's face turned red. "You know we could stop you."

"Darren!" Beverly said, looking appalled.

John stepped in close to his father-in-law. He doubted the old man could be intimidated, but he'd be damned if he was going to back down. "You could try, but you won't."

A high-pitched squeal broke the tension.

"Daddy!"

A little dark-haired girl came bounding down the winding staircase. Lucille tried to keep pace with the five-year-old, but with a suitcase in one hand and coat in the other, she was doing the best she could to not fall down the stairs herself. Maddie took the last stair at a full run, her short legs propelling her across the wood flooring.

John reached out and scooped up the little pile of giggles. "I missed you, Green Bean."

"I missed you too, Daddywaddie," Maddie said. She grabbed his face and kissed him gently on the forehead. "Did you shoot anyone?"

"Madison!" Beverly said, clearly horrified.

John couldn't help but laugh. The things that came out of her mouth never ceased to amaze him—just another way she reminded him of Emily.

"You shouldn't worry about stuff like that." John set Maddie, along with his bags, down. "What you should be worrying about is who's going to help me eat this." Her eyes lit up, and she quickly grabbed the king-size Butterfinger he pulled from his khaki duffel. "We had better get going. Jimmy's going to meet us downtown, and I think he has something for you too. Now give Darren and Beverly a hug."

Beverly started to cry. "Grandma loves you." She squeezed Maddie tightly.

"Are you sure you won't change your mind, Darren?" John asked. "I know we don't see eye to eye on things—well, anything—but it would be nice to have us all together for Maddie's sake." He was serious. The Westcotts had no clue about his diagnoses, and there was a real possibility there would be no cure in the future either. Having Darren and Beverly with them would make certain Maddie would be well taken care of if the worst were to happen.

"Grandma, you're going to squish my candy bar," Maddie said, wiggling out from Beverly's grasp.

Darren smiled down at Maddie. "Come give your grandpa a hug too." He lifted her up and patted her on the back. "You take care of yourself, and take care of your dad. Lord knows he needs the help." After a few more squeezes, Darren set her down. He took the pink and purple coat from Lucille and helped Maddie into it. "If things had been different..." He zipped her coat, and never finished the sentence.

John waited for Maddie, outside the exam room. The interactive display in the corridor was tuned to one of the many twenty-four-hour news programs. Just one of the many reasons he didn't subscribe to entertainment programming at home. He tapped his bare feet on the cold tile floor. It was difficult to believe they were half a mile underground. At the onset of the cryonics program, the government tore down three city blocks, including the old International Monetary Funds property, to build the Alcor National Headquarters. For every floor above ground, they added ten below. With all the money poured into the place, they could have splurged for something a little more luxurious than the hard blue plastic chair he was sitting in. The upper levels of the Alcor building processed most of the program volunteers. Due to John's high-level clearance, and his connection to Emily's family, he and Maddie were processed with the political leaders and other upper-level officials.

A female nurse opened the exam room door. "Okay, Maddie, you're all finished."

"Look, Daddy! Your suit is the same color as mine."

Maddie turned in a circle, showing off the blue-and-gray hydro mesh suit. It mirrored his suit, minus the size. Stenciled in black on the front of each was first and last name, gender, date of birth, and date of entry.

John pulled her in close. "You look like a futuristic princess." He tweaked her nose playfully.

"Of course I do," Maddie said matter-of-factly.

"Miss Crider, don't forget your little friend." The nurse held up a little pink bear dressed in a matching hydro suit.

John could understand how this whole experience could be scary to a child, and the little bears were a nice touch. Maddie, like always, took everything in stride. She was so much like her mother. The nurse led them down the corridor and into an elevator. She let Maddie push the button labeled one-seven-five. The doors opened to another identical hallway.

"Sergeant Crider, we were able to get you and Maddie assigned to the same room," the nurse said, leading them down the row of doors. "Here we are, room fifty-two."

The nurse waved a card over the sensor, causing the door to slide open with a pressurized air sound. Thousands of metal and glass capsules lined the walls. A few attendants moved down the line checking information on small displays attached to each capsule. John had seen videos of the freezing process, but it was a little unnerving being this close to real people frozen in suspended animation. Maddie seemed unaffected and had not stopped asking questions, or giving improvement ideas to the nurse, since they stepped onto the elevator. He tried not to laugh when she told the nurse Kool Aid-flavored ice would be practical, and it would give people something to snack on as they thawed out.

"Here we are, Maddie," the nurse said. She accessed the terminal on the front of the capsule. The clear front door slid upward. "This will be your home for the next one hundred years. You want to give your dad a hug before we get you all connected?"

Maddie held out the pink bear. "You can take Princess Rose. She will keep you from being scared, Daddy," Maddie said.

John bent over, and Maddie latched onto his neck. "Are you sure you're okay with this?"

She let go and pointed towards the capsule. "Did you see all the cords in there?" she asked, unable to control her excitement.

John ruffled her hair. "I guess that's a yes."

"Go ahead and step up here, Maddie, and I will get you connected." The nurse strapped Maddie into the harness and twisted the hoses into the ports located on the suit. She fit a mask over her nose and mouth. "Okay, Maddie, when I close the door you will start to feel a little drowsy. When you wake up, a century will have passed."

John thought he heard her say cool. "I love you, Green Bean. I'll be right here when you wake up." He extended his index finger towards her, and Maddie met it with her own finger. "Sweet dreams."

The nurse pressed a button on the command terminal, and the lid clicked down in place.

Maddie's eyes slowly closed, and her head dropped to the side.

John's look of concern was met with the nurse's reassurance. "It's just the anesthetic. The neomorphic fluid needs to enter the lungs before the neuro freeze begins." The tank began to fill rapidly with a blue-tinged liquid. "It would be quite unpleasant if the subject was conscious for this part."

The liquid filled past the glass to the top of the tank. Maddie's dark hair floated like threads of dark ribbon.

"The neomorphic fluid will now be forced into her body. It won't hurt her, but it can be uncomfortable to watch," the nurse said.

Maddie spasmed as her body tried to keep the liquid from entering the lungs. A light turned green on the terminal. The nurse pressed a button on the tank, and the liquid inside misted and froze.

"Everything looks good. All activity is now entering suspension." The nurse moved the terminal back in place on Maddie's capsule. "Your pod is across from Maddie's," she said, moving around John. "Lucky for you the A-Personnel wing is filling slower than anticipated. I know if it were my daughter, I would want to be as close as possible."

John placed his hand against the cold, clear glass of Maddie's pod. *I'll see you soon, Bean.* He reluctantly turned. The nurse was already busy at the terminal. "I appreciate this. Just knowing I'm close makes me feel a whole lot better about all of this."

"No need to worry. This is the most advanced system in the world." The door to the capsule opened, and she smiled at John. "Okay, Sergeant Crider, are you ready?"

John nodded and stepped up into the pod.

"I'll have to store that for you, Sergeant," the nurse said, holding out her hand.

John handed her the pink bear. "Oh, right."

In a few moments, the nurse had the harness and all the cords connected to his suit. She handed him the mask, which he fastened over his mouth and nose. It had the same distinct rubber smell that most aviation oxygen masks had.

"Just relax, Sergeant, and breathe normally." The nurse moved back to the terminal and pressed something on the screen.

The pod door closed and pressure-sealed, making John's ears pop. After a few deep breaths, he started to feel his head getting heavy, and his eyelids fought to stay open. The nurse waved, and nothingness overtook him.

CHAPTER 4

John's heart hammered inside his chest. Alarms sounded all around him. He tried to open his eyes, but couldn't compel his body to comply.

"We need to get his heart rate down before he goes into cardiac arrest!" A male voice to his left said.

"But what do you give him that won't interfere with the INOs?" another voice asked.

"Regeneration at twenty-three percent," a female voice said.

Something sharp stabbed into John's left forearm. Bile forced its way up his esophagus, burning his throat. He retched, choking on the acidic vomit.

"He's awake! Quick, put him out before he suffers any permanent brain damage," the male voice ordered. "Who the hell is watching the monitor?"

John slid back into unconsciousness.

"Regeneration is at seventy-five percent."

That voice was the same flat female voice John had heard from before. The shrill alarms had been replaced by the rhythmic beeping of a machine. It took a moment for him to open his eyes. Everything around was a blurry mix of white and gray.

"He has regained awareness, Doctor Malcolm," the female voice said.

"Thank you, Alice," the doctor responded. The sound of footsteps moved towards John.

John turned his head towards the sound and groaned as the washed-out world around him started to spin. A hazy outline of a person moved next to him. The figure gently tipped John's head back and flashed a bright light into each of his eyes.

"Alice, give me a full diagnostic."

"Yes, Doctor Malcolm," Alice said. "Regeneration has reached seventy-five percent. Cell optimization appears to be stable, and all major organs are functioning normally. Muscular conditioning is progressing at fifty-five percent. Neurological acclamation has reached ninety-two percent."

John tried to move his left arm but found it restrained. "My eyes?" His voice came out as a raspy whisper.

"Alice, please put our guest back under. We're not going to rush things," Doctor Malcolm said. "Increase INO levels. Sorry, Sergeant, but you'll need some more time."

John panicked and pulled at his restraints. "No! Wait!" he croaked, but it was no use. The darkness pulled him under again.

The muffled sounds of voices pulled John from unconsciousness. Subconsciously, he focused his breathing, trying to allow his head a chance to reorient itself.

"Is he awake yet, Malcolm?" a deep, husky voice asked.

"He should be ready for a brief visit this evening, Minister," Doctor Malcolm replied.

"This isn't a daycare facility. Wake him up," the minister ordered. Heavy footsteps crossed the floor, stopping beside John. "So, this is the best the twenty-first century had to offer?" The minister grunted and cleared his throat. "Send in Oddum and Makenzie, I have an operation to run, and this whole damn bloody process has taken too long already."

"I really don't think you should rush him. His muscular system reconditioning is complete, but there are still some lingering repairs that will need to continue for the next few weeks, and I would—"

The minister cut him off. "Do you know how much money is tied to this little project, Doctor? If he's not ready, it will be your ass."

John moved his head, and let out a pained sigh. Slowly, he opened his eyes. It took a moment for his focus to clear. He was in a small room. It was void of anything but the bed he was in. Two men stood next to the bed. The first man was squat, with short-cropped gray hair. John guessed he was the minister. The minister was dressed in matching black trousers and top. A thin line of white accented the sleeves and the front of the jacket, which did nothing to hide the man's oversized gut. The second man was a stark contrast to the first. He was tall and slender and wore all white.

"Sergeant Crider, my name is Doctor Tayler Malcolm," the man in white said. "Glad to see you're with us again." The doctor made a vertical motion with his right hand in the empty space in front of him. A blue translucent screen materialized in front of him. "Any discomfort you are experiencing should be short term. Alice, read out please?"

"Yes, Doctor," a female voice said, from within the room. "Subject One, John Alexander Crider, is functioning at ninety-eight percent. The INOs are functioning at one-hundred percent."

The voice was the same one John had heard before, but no one else had come into the room.

"I can see you're a little confused, Sergeant," the doctor said, looking over top of the floating screen. "You will find technology has taken some big leaps since last you were with us. Advanced Local Intelligent Cybernetic Entity, or ALICE, is an artificial intelligence. In fact, without Alice, you wouldn't be with us today."

"That's well and good, but can I get some water?" John asked, his voice hoarse and forced. He rubbed his tongue against the roof of his mouth. "Feels like I just ate sandpaper."

The minister laughed and slapped John on the leg. "Ha! My kind of man. He doesn't give two shakes about all the gizmos and gets right to the point."

Doctor Malcolm touched the wall, and a drawer extended from it. He removed a vial and placed it in the back of an injection gun. "Alice, help our guest sit up." The bed gently moved until John was sitting upright. "Here, this should help with the pain and rehydration."

The doctor placed the smooth face of the injection gun against John's down turned hand, and pressed the button. John waited for the small prick of a needle, but he felt nothing. The liquid within the vial quickly emptied. He cleared his throat and was surprised to find the dryness gone. *Needleless injections. Maddie will love it,*

John thought. "Doctor Malcolm, when can I see my daughter?" He hoped her experience reawakening was better than his.

Doctor Malcolm looked to the minister. His expression was worried.

"Sergeant, I'm Minister Tate. I'm in command of National Defense." Minister Tate moved towards the foot of the bed. "We brought you out first because we need your help. Oddum, Makenzie, join us." The door to the room slid open, and a man and women entered. "Sergeant, let me introduce you to Commander Nathan Makenzie."

John snapped his right hand to salute.

"At ease, Sergeant," Commander Makenzie said, not returning the salute.

The commander was at least ten years John's junior. It was difficult to discern the commander's branch from his uniform, but then again, the uniforms could have changed a lot over the years.

"And this is Professor Rebecca Oddum, an expert in genetics and field biology," the minister continued.

Professor Oddum's long reddish-brown hair stood out against her black pantsuit. "It's a pleasure, Sergeant," she said, extending her hand.

"Ma'am," John said, shaking her hand. "I assume this isn't about the Axis since we're all still here."

The minister nodded to the commander. "Commander Makenzie, let's bring the Sergeant up-to-date."

The commander placed a small black device on the floor. "Sergeant, some of this information may be difficult to accept, but we ask you to hear us out." The commander waved his hand over the device. A screen materialized above it, much like the one the doctor produced, only bigger. "In twenty twenty-one, the United Nations was able to drive back the Axis by using their own TEMPs technology against them. This was in large part thanks to you and your men. Unfortunately, the TEMPs did more damage than we could ever imagine." The commander touched the floating display, and it morphed into a large rotating world globe. "This is the world you left." The globe darkened from Cuba to the southern United States, representing the first TEMPs attack. "By the end of the war," large portions of the globe went black, "sixty-five percent of the world was affected. Governments collapsed, people starved, famine and disease ran rampant. Not even the United States was spared. In a few short years, the population of the earth was reduced by half." The commander shook his head slowly. "The losses suffered at home were staggering."

John seemed like the only one in the room affected by the sheer magnitude of the numbers. "Couldn't they have expanded the Cyro Act until everything recovered?"

"The United States did expand the program, but there wasn't enough time. Some of the more robust nations implemented cryonic projects of their own with limited success, and others just died out." The commander touched the globe, changing back into a two-dimensional display. "Allies became enemies as resources dwindled, but this wasn't the worst of it. In twenty thirty, scientists discovered the TEMPs devices had destabilized global temperatures and directly affected the earth's atmosphere."

John rested back against his pillow. His head was still reeling from the cryo reawakening process, but this was too much to grasp. They had thought finding the TEMPs would have put a stop to the war, but not this.

"Cut through the shit, and get to the point, Commander," the minister said, agitated.

The commander's jaw tensed, his mouth forming a tight thin line.

"If you don't mind, Minister," Professor Oddum said, breaking the tension in the room. She stepped over and placed a hand on John's arm. "The short is this, Sergeant. We need your help. You are the first successful reanimation we've had in five hundred years."

Five hundred years? That couldn't be right. "Wait. No. It was only supposed to be one hundred. What the hell happened?"

"With the global issues, it didn't make sense to wake people to the chaos. Once they were able to stabilize the United States, they found there were complications with the cryonics process."

"Problems? Oh, God. Maddie!" John ripped off the blankets, trying to get to his feet.

Doctor Malcolm winced at hearing the name. "Sergeant, you need to take it slow." He put up his hands, trying to block John's path.

"Move!" He pushed the doctor out of his way. The force of the movement caused John's already unsteady legs to give out underneath him. "I need to get to Maddie!" When his legs wouldn't work, he crawled towards the door. He needed to find her. A gentle pair of hands clasped around his upper arm.

"Sergeant, your daughter's safe. Please hear us out," Professor Oddum said.

The fight flooded out of John. Her hands were warm on his bare skin. Everything in him urged him to find Maddie, but where was he going? He had no idea where he was. Maddie might not even be in the building. Reluctantly, he let Professor Oddum and Doctor Malcolm help him back to the bed. Fatigue pulled at him. It had taken more out of him than it should have. "It was only supposed to be a hundred years." He rested his hands against his face. "I promised her." It was all his fault. Why did he have to be so damn stubborn?

"As soon as you are rested we'll take you to see your daughter. I understand how you're feeling, Sergeant," Oddum said.

"Do you have children?" John asked, looking up at Professor Oddum.

"Excuse me?"

"Do you have children?" John asked again.

"No," the professor replied.

"Then how could you possibly understand how I feel?" Professor Oddum was taken aback by his comment, but right now John didn't really care.

"I don't think any of us could understand," Doctor Malcolm said. "Trust me when I tell you I will do all I can for both you and your daughter."

"Is she awake, like me?" John asked.

"Not yet," the Doctor Malcolm said.

"This is why we need your help," Professor Oddum said. "We believe it was espionage, but we can't be sure. The pods are all linked to the main hub. This system draws a microscopic sample of biological liquid and analyzes it. Somehow a contaminate was introduced to the hub and was able to infect every single pod resident."

"It must not be too bad if I'm awake," John said.

"The contaminate is unique. Within seventy-four hours of revival, a patient's cells begin to break down. Once the process begins, full organ failure is inevitable within days." The professor stepped over to Commander Makenzie's display. She touched it and brought up a microscopic view of blood cells. Red donut shaped cells rushed by the screen. A slight motion of her hand and the cells began to slow. The cells turned black and piled on top of each other until the artery became clogged.

"Is this happening to me?" John asked, trying to control his temper.

"It was." Doctor Malcolm adjusted his glasses. "We have been taking steps to prevent that very thing from happening to you."

"And my daughter?" John asked.

"Right where you left her," the minister said. It was clear he was agitated. "The process to keep you alive this long is unfathomable, and so far, we have yet to see the benefits!"

John started to try and get off the bed again, but his vision blurred and he almost passed out.

"Minister, please," Doctor Malcolm said, pushing John back down. "He wasn't ready. I told you he wasn't, but you insisted. A minute ago, you were asking for his help, but now you're insulting him."

John put his hand on the doctor's arm, interrupting him. "Is she alive?"

Doctor Malcolm turned and looked at him. "All of her vitals are strong. With your help, I hope I can do much more for her."

"Okay," John said. He released the doctor's arm and turned his attention to Commander Makenzie. "You said you need my help. I'm not sure what use I will be to you anyway. Five hundred years is a long time."

Commander Makenzie nodded and touched the screen next to him. An image of China came into view. "That is the precise reason we need you, Sergeant. After the Great Axis War, China, like most countries, pulled back within their own borders. Unfortunately, disease and famine reduced a population of over a billion to just over twenty million in twenty years' time. What was left of the population reformed down in the southern region of Guangxi. Most of China was left barren and lifeless. The Guangxi region was not much better, but a few years later, they erected towers throughout the area. These towers disperse an electrical signal somewhat similar to that of an electromagnetic pulse."

Small red dots appeared on the map with larger circles overlapping, representing the mock EMPs' areas of effect. "Military warfare has changed substantially in the last five hundred years. Artificially intelligent machines do almost all the work." The screen changed and began playing combat footage of drone aircraft and some sort of small oblong shaped machine clearing rooms of a building. "We haven't lost a human in combat in over a hundred years."

John repressed a shiver. They had made war into a game. Looking into a combatant's eyes before you pulled the trigger made the struggle human. Every decision on the battlefield had a consequence. Consequences weighed against cost, not only in resources, but human cost. The further removed a soldier is from the frontline, the less they care about these costs. "If your robots can't make it across the border, why not send in real ground troops?"

"We have, but none have returned," the commander said.

John looked over at the professor. "With a population of only twenty million, sounds to me like you just need to leave them be."

The minister's face turned bright red. He opened his mouth, but Professor Oddum beat him to it.

"We can understand your apprehension to leave your daughter's side, but we weren't able to cure you, and we can't currently bring your daughter back without the process killing her." The professor moved around to the side of the bed. "After the Axis War, China poured extensive amounts of money into its genetic and biological science programs. The Chinese were trying to create plants and animals that could survive the humid and rapidly changing conditions caused by the TEMPs. Over the next hundred years, the project led to a vast expansion of vegetated growth in southern China." Professor Oddum brushed a stray curl behind her ear. "The Chinese were able to do this in soils with almost nonexistent nutrient levels—somehow they found a way. Of course, we tried to gather intel, but the area is a dead zone. To date, we have lost fifteen specialty trained groups. We can't afford to lose another."

"I'm no genius, but how does a tower produce an EMP and not destroy itself?" John asked.

"They should, but they don't," the commander said. "Which brings us to you." Commander Makenzie touched the projected screen again. John's military record appeared, including A-Level sealed files. "Last year, China's electrical disruption systems went down for twelve minutes. We're not sure why this happened, but we were able to scan the area. From the scan, we were only able to detect a solitary electrical anomaly coming from the region. We believe this anomaly may be the location of China's main genetics facility. If it is, we want their research. This research could help us save your daughter and millions of others. We need someone with actual combat experience to help us get the data out. The government is willing to offer you anything for your help."

"Only one signal? You would expect much more from the population size," John said.

"One of the dozens of questions we can't answer," the commander said.

John sat there quietly on the bed for a moment. "How soon, if the information is there, can you revive my daughter?"

The corner of Professor Oddum's lip raised in a grin. "I have a team on standby. If everything goes as planned they can have her up and around before we get back."

"And if I say no?" John asked. It wasn't an option, but he needed to know what kind of people he was dealing with.

"Then you die," the minister said, a little too quick for comfort. "And I will personally make sure your daughter is never revived from suspended animation!"

John turned, focusing on the minister. "If you fail to keep your word, Minister, even the fury of God will not keep me from detaching your head from your fat torso."

The minister's face went pale. He stumbled, taking a step back from the bed.

The commander cleared his throat. "There's one more thing, Sergeant. This is the last communication we received out of China almost two hundred years ago. The dialect has been converted to English, and we cleaned it up the best we could."

The commander touched the screen again, and the crackling pop of static filled the air. A frightened voice came out of the distorted communication. *'We... unable to sustain... control... lost...,'* static hissed through the signal, *'... control... impossible. Everyone's... dead...'* The signal squealed. John was forced to cover his ears. A moment later, the squealing subsided, and crying could be heard over the static. *'I left them... couldn't help...'* A scream rang out. *'Goliath!'* and the signal ended.

CHAPTER 5

John placed his hand against the cold, clear window of Maddie's pod and tried to keep the tears at bay. There were no dreams while in the pod, but he hoped she had them. Happy, silly, crazy dreams, filled with all sort of adventures. God, he missed her laugh. Her hair was frozen in lifeless wisps above her head. She was so close, and yet he couldn't hold her and tell her it would be okay. He clenched his teeth. *I should have known better, Emily.* Her father had been right. It was his fault, and now it might cost him the only thing left in his life. He wasn't naive enough to believe some sort of magical cure would just be sitting on a desk somewhere waiting for him to find it. The mission was a long shot, but these were missions the Shadow Company was trained to handle. But there wasn't a Shadow Company, not anymore.

The door to the capsule room opened. "Sergeant Crider," Doctor Malcolm said, entering the room. "I wanted to catch you before the commander came to get you."

John turned. The doc had let him into the lower wing to see Maddie when the staff wouldn't give him clearance. All things considered, Malcolm wasn't such a bad guy.

"Don't worry about it. He's running late anyway."

"I know." A weak grin spread across Doctor Malcolm's face. "Alice is rerouting the elevator a few times, so we can speak privately."

"Forty-two times to be precise, Doctor," the disembodied voice of Alice chimed in.

The doctor cleared his throat. "Can't say he doesn't deserve more." Doctor Malcolm stepped up to Maddie's pod. "I have watched over her since I came here. You could say I feel I have a vested interest in her and your welfare." He removed a picture from his pocket and handed it to John. "I figured you may want this. The original was damaged, I saved what I could. I felt like it was something I would want to have with me."

John stared at the picture of Maddie and her big goofball smile. He turned it over, and his heart sank a little. Emily's picture was gone. "I've never left on a mission without it. This means a lot, Doc." He reached out and shook the doctor's hand.

"Doc?" Doctor Malcolm asked.

"It's something we called the doctors back home."

"I see," Doctor Malcolm said. "It looks like the suit I gave you fits well enough."

John looked down at the gray-and-black spandex material. In truth, the material fit so well he forgot he was wearing it.

"Doctor Malcolm," Alice's voice chimed into the room. "Project Shadow has been activated. All monitoring systems are currently being redirected."

The doctor's expression became serious. "We don't have much time before the main system overrides Alice. I need you to listen, Sergeant. Your suit looks like all the others, but I've redesigned it. The INOs in your system..."

John's eyes glazed over, and the doctor tried again. "The Internal Nano Organisms, or really tiny robots, are rebuilding your cellular structure as it decays. Hopefully, they will make things right. The typical functional life of an INO is thirty days. Without any new ones added to your system, your organs fail, and you die. Moreover, once you enter the anti-electrical field around the mission zone, the INOs energy use will triple, if they don't burn out first. If you're lucky, they will make the trip intact; if not you'll have less than seven days." He turned and looked at the door. "Update, Alice?"

"Three minutes until the system corrects itself," Alice replied.

John clenched his fists. They never planned for him to make it back alive. The projected mission was expected to last at least twelve days, and that was with no complications. "The information we're going after. Will it stop this?"

Beads of sweat rolled down the Doctor's forehead. "No, but there is something else you need to know. The contaminate, in the tubes, was intentional."

"I know. Commander Makenzie and Professor Oddum discussed what they believe happened in the briefing." John replied.

"That was a lie. The government sanctioned what happened to all those people."

John's jaw tensed. "What?"

"I know you must be angry, but the information the minister wants you to get could result in the death of millions. You want answers, but now is not the time. You can't allow them to get their hands on that data."

"How do I know you aren't lying to me too?"

"You don't, Sergeant. I only hope my actions in the days to come prove I'm on your side."

"So you want me to give you the information instead of the government?"

"Everything's not what it seems." He removed a large syringe filled with blue tinted liquid from his coat pocket. "They're betting everything on taking the electrical field down. If they're successful, they'll be able to upload the information directly from the site. To the minister, everyone is expendable. What I'm offering you is a bargaining chip. I'll help you intercept any uploaded information. For all they will know, the upload didn't work. That will give you time to decide what to do." Doctor Malcolm wiped his forehead with his sleeve.

"If I decide to give you the information, can you do the robot thing to my daughter? Can you get her out of there?"

"It's complicated, but I'll do what I can. We'll get your daughter moved so they can't use her against us."

"And if I decide to give the data to the government and not you?"

"I will still do what I can for your daughter. This is just the beginning, and we would rather have you with us than against us."

John looked at the syringe. The needle had to be at least two, maybe three inches long. "Who is this 'us'?"

"Us is us, and when you decide you're with us, you'll know," the doctor said, a sad smile on his lips. He removed the protective cap from the needle. "I placed an organic circuit in your neck. Over the last month, it has been fusing with your central nervous system." He turned to the door again. "Alice, please download the file labeled Phoenix."

"Five seconds to completion," Alice's voice responded.

The doctor tapped the syringe a few times to remove the bubbles. "The nano cells in this will essentially activate the circuit and hopefully give you more time. Are you ready?"

"I thought you guys didn't need needles for injections anymore," John said, eyeing the needle.

The doctor smiled and pulled down the suit material around John's neck. "We don't, but I need to penetrate the circuit membrane for this to work."

"Okay, I think I'm... Ow!" The needle stabbed deep into John's neck. It felt like molten lead spreading through his body.

The doctor withdrew the needle. "Sorry about that, but we are running out of time. Take care of her for me."

John rubbed at the burning spot on his neck. "Take care—" The door opened behind them, and Commander Makenzie stormed into the room.

"I want that piece of shit AI erased, Malcolm! I've spent over twenty minutes on the damn elevator," the commander said.

"She's just a little temperamental sometimes."

The commander grabbed Doctor Malcolm's lab coat and jerked him in close. "Does it look like I give a shit?"

Doctor Malcolm looked down at the floor. "I'll take care of it."

"I shouldn't have to remind you of what will happen if you cross me." Commander Makenzie shoved the doctor back and turned his attention to John. "Time to get you outfitted, Sergeant. Are you alright? You're looking a little pale."

"He needed a few more days, but overall he should be okay by the time you land," Doctor Malcolm said.

"I didn't ask you," the commander said, not bothering to look at the doctor. "You mess up out there, and people die. Can you live with that?"

John pulled the suit material back around his neck. "I've seen my share of death. By now I think the Reaper and I have an understanding. I take lives, and she leaves mine to me." He gave the doctor a short nod and turned around to Maddie's pod. "Hold in there, Green Bean."

CHAPTER 6

Seats lined either side of the transport's cargo hold. Holes in the carpet showed where seats were removed to make room the extra cargo. If John had to guess, the aircraft was never designed for soldier transport. The recently added directional lights looked out of place next to the fancier built-in lighting system. It bathed the holding area in a strange multi-toned white. The directional lights were trained on six gliders, secured in pairs down the belly of the aircraft. Their wings were tucked up next to their fuselages. The glider's flat triangular design was different from the cigar-shaped aircraft John was accustomed to.

John folded the black synthetic fabric swatch he had taken from a tray in his room and tied it around his head. The mission objectives were simple. Drop within range of the signal, infiltrate, acquire, and extract all within twelve days. Unless the doc's strategy worked, John would be a dead man by day seven. It was clear he was a pawn. There were too many unknowns, but once they were on the ground, he would get his answers, one way or another. He might be expendable, but it was clear they needed him. The thirty-five soldier unit the commander had assembled was more of a battalion than an infiltration team. A group this size would make it impossible to remain undetected for long.

John pulled his makeshift bandana down over his right eye and tried to ignore a young soldier, who had for the last hour tried and failed to reattach a section of leg armor that had come loose. If something went wrong, it would go in a big way. *Go big or go home, Jimmy liked to say*, John thought.

He wished he had the chance to see how the city had changed in five hundred years. He could hear Maddie's voice in the back of his head asking if there would be flying cars. Was his house still there? Did someone from Jimmy's family still occupy it or had he ever moved in? Guilt washed over him. None of these things had occurred to him until now.

He touched the side of his nostril with his thumb. It was a habit now. It had only taken a month, maybe two, after his diagnosis before the nosebleeds began. He looked down at his thumb. No blood. The same since they brought him out of cryo. Something else he should have asked Doctor Malcolm about. It wouldn't matter much if he never made it back. His hand moved to the top pocket of his black combat vest and touched the laminated picture. The vest looked clunky and old compared to everyone else's sleek dark-green combat armor. The new armor was lightweight and supposedly indestructible, but the movement didn't feel natural to him. It had taken the requisition officer the better part of two hours to find the items he had requested.

To John's right, a big, thickly muscled black man had started to snore. Unlike the other soldiers, the man's arms were bare. He had removed the arm plates from the armor and cut away the suit sleeves. He glanced at the rifle secured next to the man. The rifle had changed very little in five hundred years. These new Python Assault Rifles were lightweight, worked on compressed gas, and fired a thin four-inch, nail-like spike. From the short demonstration John had seen, the spikes flattened and bloomed out as they penetrated, creating a sizable exit wound. At five-hundred rounds per magazine and two magazines per gas cylinder, the combat feasibility of the weapon was impressive.

A sickening growl emanated from the seat to John's left. Professor Oddum's sweat-matted hair stuck to her airsick pale face. Her scaled-down version of military combat armor couldn't cover the angry sounds her stomach was making.

"It is hard to believe someone can be queasy on one of these," John said, tapping his foot against the floor. The professor didn't belong on this mission. It was going to be difficult enough with the large team already, but add babysitting to the list and the job becomes a logistical cluster fuck.

The professor managed a sickly smile. "Tell my body that." She belched and swallowed hard.

"First time in the air?" he asked.

She closed her eyes and nodded slowly. "It's my first time leaving the city. I mostly do lab work."

"But aren't you a field biologist?"

"A field biologist who prefers the lab to the field," she replied.

Commander Makenzie stood up and walked out in front of the troops. "Okay. Listen up, people! We are twenty minutes from the wall. Once inside, we're on our own. Satellite imaging doesn't give us much to go off except for a heavy canopy and extensive vegetative growth. Alpha Team, I want the LZ cleared and mobilized by twenty-two hundred hours. Keep it clean and tight— we only get one chance at this." After a few other minor details, the commander made his way over to where John and the professor were sitting. "You two will be with me, Gramm..." He slammed his hand into the chest plate of the man sleeping beside John. "Damn it, Gramm! Wake your lazy ass up!"

Gramm stretched and wiped a line of drool from the corner of his mouth. "Old lady kept me up late last night." He grinned, still half asleep. "Said it would make me come back safe and all."

The commander pointed to his own eye. "Look me in the eyes, Gramm. Does this look like the face of a guy who gives a rat's ass?"

"Well, you might, Commander. She has this thing she does with her toes," Gramm said, lifting his feet up off the floor.

"Shut your mouth and listen," the commander said, clearly disgusted. "You three will be with me, Nolan, and Marcus." The commander looked down at John. "You're here to provide field expertise, Sergeant, but let's get something straight. I give the orders, and you'll let my men do the heavy lifting."

"Commander, with all due respect," John said, tilting his head to better meet the commander's eyes. "This is supposed to be an in-and-out mission. There shouldn't be a need for any heavy lifting."

The commander's jaw tightened, and his brow furrowed. "You'll do your job—or did you forget we have your daughter?"

John was up out of his seat before the commander could react. His knife pressed against the commander's throat. The muscles in his forearm bulged as he held the commander's head close with his free hand.

"Let's get something clear," he said through clenched teeth. "I'm not one of your subordinates. In fact, the only reason I'm here is for my daughter. You use her to threaten me again, and I'll end you." The commander tried to pull free, but John tightened his hold. "Do we have an understanding?"

Professor Oddum stood, her legs weak beneath her. She placed her hand on John's forearm. "I think he gets the point."

John released the commander, shoving him away. He had made an enemy here, but if what Doctor Malcolm said was true, he couldn't trust anyone.

"What are you looking at?" The commander shoved a soldier who happened to be walking past. "Everyone, load up!"

Gramm stood up and strapped on his rifle. The rifle locked in place on the back plate of his armor. "Hey man, that was some cool shit." He offered John, his hand. When John didn't take it, he dropped it to his side awkwardly. "So, what's up with your eye? You lose it killing someone?"

John sheathed his knife on his vest. "It's night out, and the lights they put in here will make it difficult for your eyes to adjust to the darkness. It takes the eye forty-five minutes to adjust to a low-light environment. You cover your rifle eye and switch when you hit the ground. It's hard to shoot when you can't see." He turned and took hold of the professor's arm. "Let's get you secured in the glider, Professor."

The gliders had three separate two-man compartments. The pilot and co-pilot sat near the nose, with the other two compartments balanced near the wings. John helped Professor Oddum down into her seat by the wing. After fastening her in, he took the seat next to her. Gramm and a young man no more than eighteen settled into the seats across from them. The commander and an older gentleman sat in the cockpit. John reached up and pulled the canopy down, securing it into place. A short hiss of air pressurized the compartment. The large cargo bay door began to lower. A light flashed illuminating the sky outside the aircraft. John shook his head slowly in disgust.

"What's wrong?" Professor Oddum asked, her face looking even paler than before.

He couldn't bring himself to tell her the crazy bastards were doing a glider drop in the middle of a thunderstorm. "The overhead lights. They didn't bother to turn them off before opening the bay doors," John said, deciding on the lesser of two evils. "If anyone's watching, they'll know we're here now."

"We're not going to make it through this, are we?" she asked, trying not to look out the tinted canopy.

"I'll make you a deal, Professor." He looked at her and smiled. It was hard not to like her. She seemed just as much out of place here as he did. "You don't barf on me on the way down, and I'll do everything I can to get you back home."

"Deal," she said. "But what if I can't keep that promise?"

He reached down into the pack he had sat in his lap. "Then you show me how to do laundry when we get home. It was hard enough back in my day, and I guess it's only gotten more difficult." He removed a roll of adhesive tape, and a small flashlight with a piece of thin red plastic attached to the lens, from the pack. Clicking the light on, he taped it to the metal ledge in front of them.

"What's that for?"

"When we hit the anti-electric cloud, this will let us know." He reached back into his pack, this time removing a piece of gum. "I'm not sure what flavor ultra-blast is, but chew it and hum as loud as you can, it should help." Even if it didn't, it would occupy her for some of the freefall.

"Thanks," she said, putting the gum in her mouth. "If we make it through this, I'll personally acquaint you with the twenty-sixth century."

The glider lurched forward, causing the professor to moan in protest. The first two gliders dropped into the night, followed by the next pair two minutes later. As their glider edged up to the open cargo doors, John counted the seconds. Lightning lit up the swirling vortex of rain streaming from the tail of the aircraft. *Three, two, one*—the glider disengaged, dropping them into darkness.

Rain beat against the canopy cover, but the sound was drowned out by Professor Oddum's screams. As the wings extended, the aircraft heaved; unfortunately, so did the professor. After a few minutes of unrelenting turbulence combined with the pungent smell of bile, John's own stomach began to roll. A light prickling sensation at the base of his skull was steadily increasing and had started to spread down his back and into his extremities. The small red glow emitted by the flashlight flickered and went out, casting the compartment into inky blackness. They had breached the electrical cloud.

"Phoenix online," a female voice said.

John looked over in Professor Oddum's direction, barely able to make out her silhouette. She hadn't said much since getting sick. "Sorry, I didn't catch that."

The professor didn't respond. John reached out, searching for her arm.

Suddenly the interior of the cabin lit up, and he felt the shockwave before the sound reached his ears. Above them, the canopy exploded. The wind tore through the compartment as the glider shook violently. They needed to get out. John pulled his bag from below his seat and snapped the shoulder clasps under his harness. The groaning sound of metal tearing could be heard over the storm. He fumbled in the dark with the professor's straps, trying to pull them as tight as he could. There was still no response from her. He grabbed for his rifle, but it wasn't where he had set it. A piece of the wing tore away, sending the glider into an uneven spin. On the side of his seat, John's hand closed around the release latch. In the midst of the chaos, it occurred to him that he didn't know what would happen when he pulled the release.

With a tug, what remained of the canopy blew off, and Professor Oddum's seat shot into the storm. A heartbeat later, he was ejected into the night. The cold rain stung his face. After a moment, the seat jettisoned away, and a small disk with cords detached from behind him and expanded into a silvery translucent square shaped parachute. The material looked too stiff in the wind-driven conditions. The glider had disappeared into the folds of the storm. He strained looking for signs of the professor, but the conditions made it too difficult to see anything.

The air warmed as he approached the unending expanse of the forest below. A tree landing was something he had practiced in the Special Forces, but it wasn't something that became easier with time. The old paratrooper trainers were always a little too proud of their body scars. He tucked his closed hands in front of his face and bent his legs slightly. His left boot brushed a treetop. The parachute pulled him through and into the next tree. Thin branches flexed and snapped under his weight. It felt like someone was hitting him repeatedly with a yardstick. The metallic chute caught in the upper reaches of the tree.

John dangled for a moment, trying to get his bearings. Rainwater dripped from the sides of his face. In the dark, it was difficult to judge how far from the forest floor he was, but it had to be at least sixty feet. He reached out and grabbed a branch beside him. Slowly, he drew himself over towards the trunk; the last thing he needed was the chute to tear away. Once he found secure footing, he unclasped his pack and freed himself of the harness. The professor couldn't be too far away, but first he needed to get down out of the tree.

He clipped his bag on and climbed slowly from branch to branch. Ten feet from the ground, he ran out of branches. The tree's trunk was covered with woody veins. Maybe he could use those to get the rest of the way down.

"Your current course of action is ill-advised, Sergeant Crider," a female voice said next to him.

Startled, John lost his footing. If not for the branch behind him, he wouldn't have had to worry about how he was getting down. "Professor?" He checked the ground around the base of the tree and the surrounding limbs. Maybe the wind forced her down into one of the neighboring trees. "Professor Oddum," he called out a little louder.

"Professor Oddum's rate of descent and the atmospheric conditions upon ejection should put her within a half-mile of our general vicinity," the voice responded.

It wasn't the professor, but the voice was familiar. He scanned the branches again, looking for the source of the voice. "I can't see you."

"I believe you are correct in your statement."

"You aren't Professor Oddum."

"I am an Advanced Local Intelligent Cybernetic Entity."

That's it. John knew where he heard the voice before. "Alice?"

"Affirmative, Sergeant Crider," Alice replied.

"But how," John looked around the tree again, "how are you here?"

"I do not have a record of the event. I can only speculate somehow my consciousness was downloaded into your biological spinal circuit in the lab."

It must have been from the shot Doctor Malcolm had injected him with. There must be a mistake. Something had gone wrong. He didn't have time to sort it out now; he needed to locate the professor. Thunder rolled in the distance. The wind had calmed since he first started his descent down the tree. Crouching, he lowered himself down onto the branch he was standing on. "We need to find the professor, Alice. Think you can give me a hand?"

"I do not have a hand, Sergeant Crider. As stated before, your current course of action is ill-advised."

"Sorry, but I can't do that." He gripped one of the protruding veins on the tree tightly and wedged his foot into the narrow space between. Pain erupted throughout his torso and left ear. He cupped his ear. The agony was intense, and as quickly as it started, it ended. Unclenching his teeth. "What the hell was that?"

"I advised you, Sergeant, and you chose to ignore me."

John's temper flared. "You're holding me hostage!"

"I am not holding you hostage. You have a ruptured eardrum and numerous broken ribs from your impact with the tree. Your descent down the tree has already caused additional damage to your body. I am concerned about the additional damage you may cause, as well as internal hemorrhaging. For your comfort, I have temporarily blocked your pain receptors until I can reactivate the INOs within your system."

He slumped down with his back against the tree trunk, straddling the branch beneath him. If there were the possibility of internal bleeding, he wouldn't make it far before losing consciousness or going into shock. Around him, the driving roar of the rain continued its unrelenting assault on the surrounding vegetation. At least, he was shielded from the worst of the storm on this side of the tree. "How long do you need?"

"Based on my initial analysis, eight hours," Alice answered.

"We don't have that kind of luxury," he said. "What is the minimum timeframe?"

"I will see what I can do, but it will require your trust."

He seemed to hear that a lot lately. "Tell me what you need me to do."

"Nothing. I will need to put you into a catatonic state."

"And how am I not supposed to fall out of the tree?" John asked.

"I will take care of that, Sergeant."

Rain droplets rebounded off his vest and pants. At least his clothes looked water resistant. He took a deep breath. In a tree, in enemy territory, with no weapon, and he was about ready to take a nap. *It could be worse,* he thought. Professor Oddum would have to hold out until he could find her—that is, if she wasn't dead already.

CHAPTER 7

"I'm so cold, Daddy."

He pulled Maddie in close and tried to wrap his coat around her. "I know, Green Bean," John said. Her body was like ice against his. "Daddy will get you warm." He rubbed her back, hoping to force some heat into her little body, but the longer he rubbed, the more she shook.

Her teeth clattered together. "Why... Daddy... I can't—"

The tears were still wet on his cheeks when John awoke. He shivered despite the temperature. Rays of light streamed through the small openings in the canopy above. The air was already thick with humidity and smelled of decomposing plant matter. It wouldn't be long before the temperature became stifling. He leaned forward and eased the tense muscles in his back. His legs were stiff from straddling the tree.

"Do I need to speak aloud or can you read my thoughts?" he asked.

"Verbal communication is preferred, Sergeant. The complexity of the human brain makes the real-time conversion of data difficult, though I can analyze neuron-based memory clusters."

"We need to find the professor." Great, now he was referring to Alice as a person. "Can I get out of the tree yet?

"I was able to bring a few of the INOs back online and fully repair your ear. Your broken ribs should be mended by tomorrow, so long as you refrain from any strenuous activity."

John grasped the protruding, vein-like bark of the tree and tugged, testing it. "Sorry, Alice. I can't promise anything."

On the ground, he pulled the straps on his pack tight. He wished he had time to cut away some of the parachute material, but right now finding the professor was more important. "Any idea which way we should—"

A scream echoed in the distance. Closing his eyes, John waited, straining to hear it again. There! He moved as quickly as he dared in the thick vegetation. A broken ankle was just as deadly as a bullet out here. Another scream—he was close. Crouched down, he released his combat knife from its sheath. Methodically, he crept closer. A profanity-laced rant came from overhead. In the tree above him, Professor Oddum swung back and forth, still connected to her harness.

He stowed his knife and called up to her, "Professor."

She looked down at him with a hopeful expression. "Sergeant? Oh, thank God. Get me down from here."

Aside from a few scrapes, she didn't seem the worse for wear. She had made it through the trees in a lot better shape than he had. John didn't know if he was jealous or impressed—maybe a little of both. "Sit tight, and I'll have you down in a minute."

"And where am I supposed to go?" she muttered.

Ignoring the comment, he set his pack down and unfastened the length of cord attached to the bottom. He slung it over his shoulder and started to climb the tree. It didn't take long to secure the rope to a thick branch above the professor.

"I'm going to lower this down. Place the knot between your feet. You need to get the pressure off your harness before you pull the release."

After a few attempts, the professor steadied herself enough she could pull the release and climb down. "I was worried I was going to be stuck up there forever."

"I would have been here sooner if I wasn't having troubles myself." It wasn't a lie, but it was probably better to keep Alice to himself for now. "If you hadn't screamed, I'm not sure how long it would have taken to find you."

The professor's face reddened. "Uh... when I woke up, there was... an arachnid."

John cocked his head to the side. "An arachnid? You were screaming like that because you saw a spider?" A smile spread across his face.

"The thing was huge!" the professor said, holding her arms

out in frustration. "Besides, what are you still doing up there?"

"I'm going to try and cut some of the parachute down," John said, trying to change the subject.

"I'm not stupid. I didn't expect to wake up dangling from a tree, you know." She scrunched up her face. "I wouldn't bother with the parachute. You won't be able to cut it. It's made of the same material as military body armor and hardens when force is applied."

John climbed up higher in the tree. "First lesson in wilderness training: everything you can find may save your life."

It took a while to untangle the chute, but it gave him a chance to fill in the professor on what happened. Back on the ground, folding the chute proved more difficult than he anticipated. With some trial and error, a few rocks, and some rope, he was able to fashion a crude pack for the professor.

"Here." He held out the pack to her. "I think we need to try and reconnect with the main force."

"Rebecca."

"What?"

"My name's Rebecca. I think we can do away with the formalities. Don't you?"

"To be honest, Rebecca, I'm not much of a formal type."

She looked at him her expression difficult to read. "How are we supposed to connect with the others?" she asked. "We don't even know where to look."

He hoisted his own pack over his shoulder. "The landing zone is only two days from the anomaly. With the loss of our party and the commander, the main force will most likely hold that position for at least a day or two. When they do move out, a group that size tends to move slower. If I remember correctly, there should be a river not far to the north of us. We might be able to reach it by nightfall if we're lucky."

John led the way into the thick brush. "Without a guide or a commanding officer, the main force would have some hard choices to make. It should buy us a few days at least. If I'm right, a group of their size will move slower and should be easier to track."

The professor had a strange expression on her face. "How do you know you're right?"

"We crashed short of our destination, which means the river north of us will be the best indicator of how far off we are, and if we get moving, we might just reach it by nightfall." John wiped sweat from his forehead. The humidity was oppressive. "The two of us should be able to overtake the unit within a few days. Either way, we make for the target, and if we miss them there, we'll make for the extraction point."

The professor stared at the ground with her arms crossed as they walked. "What if they make it there first?" she asked, chewing on her lip.

He casually waved a large fly away. "Then we go to Plan B."

"What's Plan B?"

"I'm not sure yet, but I'll let you know when I figure it out."

Ferns grew thick in every direction, and the treetops stretched above, blocking most of the direct sunlight. The combination of the two made it difficult to see the extensive root and vine systems underneath and forced a slower pace than John would have liked. Rebecca hadn't said much since they began walking, which was okay with John. He needed a chance to think, to process everything, but in the end, he kept coming to the same conclusion. This was one colossal bad dream he couldn't wake from. Doctor Malcolm seemed like a trustworthy guy, despite the talking voice in his head, but would he be so inclined to keep Maddie safe if the mission failed? There were too many unknowns, too many questions he wanted to ask Alice, but right now he needed to focus.

Outside of the dozen or so problems he already had, he didn't know how he was supposed to find the file, disk, or whatever it was. There was no certainty the doc's plan would work. He pushed everything out of his mind. Simplify. One thing at a time, and the first was finding the river. John pushed through a thick section of vegetation and stepped onto a cleared path.

Rebecca grumbled as she stumbled out after him. She wiped the sweat from her face with her forearm. "Finally! I don't know how you walk through that stuff so easily." Sunlight seeped through the open expanse created by the exposed ground. For the first time, they could feel movement in the air around them. The trail extended in both directions as far as they could see. "A road.

This has to lead somewhere."

John bent down and picked up a leafy sprig smashed into the dirt. He rubbed his thumb over the split stem. "I don't think this is a road."

"Of course it is," Rebecca said. "Look how big it is."

A large indention caught John's eye. "The ground's too uneven for vehicles to travel on," he said, walking over to the depression.

Rebecca followed close behind John. "Maybe it hasn't been used in a while."

John knelt. The impression was the length of his arm and a few inches deep. An intricate pattern crisscrossed the bottom and edges. He pressed his index finger into its center. The soil was soft and retained the outline of his finger. "I think this is a game trail of some kind."

"This large?" She looked over his shoulder at the indention. "It's more likely something fell off a transport."

"You see a lot of this kind of thing?" John asked.

"Mostly in books, but my research is extensive in many fields."

John stood and scanned the tree line. "Your books have a lot of three-toed things falling out of trucks?"

"Three toes? Don't be ridiculous." Rebecca looked back down at the print.

Movement in the ferns caught John's attention. He reached slowly up and grabbed the professor's wrist. In a whisper, he said, "We need to get off the trail."

"I don't understand," Rebecca said, still studying the print. "The shape is all wrong. This has to be from more than one animal."

"Sergeant Crider, I have detected multiple threats within the area," Alice warned.

"You're a little late," John said, staring at the shadowed green expanse in front of him.

Rebecca looked up at John. "Excuse me?"

"I am not omniscient, and your body provides numerous inconveniences, which lower my expected performance," Alice replied to John.

John blinked away a bead of sweat, wishing he still had his rifle. "Course of action." He hoped Alice understood what he was asking. Rebecca was already giving him questioning looks, and the last thing he needed was her thinking he was crazy. Maybe he was. The thought had crossed his mind. Alice could be the final delusions of his mind slowly dying. Rebecca's gaze shifted from John to something behind him.

"Down!"

Alice's voice was like a gunshot exploding in John's mind, the pain was unlike anything he had felt before. His body was in motion before his mind could catch up. He collided with the professor, driving her to the ground. The ground shook and the light from above darkened. A high-pitched screech forced John back into motion. He rolled off Rebecca, and tore his combat knife free of its sheath, but stopped.

There were things in the world that terrified him, like losing his daughter and being alone, but this—this was something else. The creature standing above them was massive. The grayish-brown and green pattern on the monster's body blended it well with the surrounding trees. In its teeth-lined jaws, something struggled to escape. The creature shook its car-sized head back and forth until whatever was in its jaws went silent. Its mouth opened and the brown feathered body of an animal dropped to the ground a few feet away.

Rebecca wept aloud. The giant creature stepped onto the carcass protectively, with one of its two muscular clawed feet, and let out an ear-splitting roar. John slammed his hands over his ears. Somewhere in the back of his head, Alice was screaming at him, but his body wouldn't move. The creature tilted its head, displaying a bright red crest of plumage, and emitted a loud clicking noise.

"You've got to be shitting me," John said under his breath. He reached down slowly for Rebecca. The creature followed his every move with its enormous head. "Alice, anything you can do would be great."

The slight ache in his side disappeared. John hoisted the professor over his shoulder. She was surprisingly light. Slowly, he inched back. In the distance, came another roar, causing the monster to turn.

"Now run!" Alice said.

John took off through the brush. There was not a chance in hell he was going to be able to outrun something like that, but hopefully, it was more interested in its kill than chasing them down. He didn't bother looking back and just ran. Rebecca's head slapped against the small of his back. There was no weight to her on his shoulder. Was this Alice's doing as well?

Before long, John had to slow his pace. The jungle had thickened, making it difficult to maneuver the fallen timbers. For the first time, he noticed his labored breathing and the burning sensation in his side had returned. He had tried to talk to Alice, but she had become strangely quiet. They would need to stop soon. It would be dark in a couple of hours, and there was no way he wanted to be walking around this place at night.

CHAPTER 8

John awoke in a cold sweat. There was no hint of a dream, only the unease of something forgotten. A night sleeping in a tree was never a good night, but it was better than the alternative. A dull throb lingered behind his eyes. His fingers felt around his side for pain. Hoisting Rebecca into the tree had taken what little strength he had left, but now the burning sensation was gone, and he felt rested.

All around, the already warming air was alive with song. Birds flitted among the branches, busy in their morning routine.

"Alice, you back with me yet?" There was no reply.

The sharp crack of a twig grabbed John's attention. He leaned out over the edge of the limb. Below, two creatures foraged among the vegetation surrounding the tree. Large ridged plates covered the animals' backs, and spikes protruded from their sides. An oversized boney mass at the base of the tail bobbed lightly side to side.

"When you're done would you mind untying me?"

John turned. He had lashed the professor to the tree to keep her from falling last night. "Glad to see you're back among the living." A firm tug on the looped knot loosen the ropes.

She rubbed the sides of her arms where the rope left indentions. "Yeah, well…"

"Mind telling me what I'm looking at?" he asked, pointing towards the ground.

Rebecca looked to where John indicated. "It's true!" she said, covering her mouth with her hands. "I thought it was a dream, but they're real. Real life dinosaurs." She leaned forward to get a better view. "Those are ankylosaurs. Do you see the black, quill-like fluff around the boney growth at the base of their tail?" She squealed with delight. "It proves dinosaurs are more closely linked to birds than we ever believed. A thousand years of research and we had still only scratched the surface of prehistoric life. If only I could get a better look at the therapod from yesterday—I swear it had what looked like filament on its head and back."

"Hate to ruin your excitement, but that thing almost ate us, and who knows how many more are out there."

Rebecca scowled. "That thing, as you call it, was a tyrannosaur, possibly related to a tyrannosaurus rex. But the size— God, it was huge."

"I've never seen someone so excited about being lunch," John said.

"You know you could show a little more respect than that."

John crossed his arms. "Respect? Teeth the size of my forearm, trust me, I take something like that very serious."

"I doubt it was stalking us. I wonder what it caught?" Rebecca mused, ignoring John's statement.

"There was a movie when I was young, where the scientists were able to extract dinosaur DNA from mosquitos trapped in amber," John said.

Rebecca rolled her eyes. "Deoxyribonucleic acid breaks down over time. The environment, location, and events at the time of death influence how long its chains are viable. After seven million years, even the best-preserved DNA would be unusable."

John frowned. "Okay, genius, maybe you could enlighten me to what we're dealing with here?"

"You know, you don't have to get so touchy," Rebecca said. "To be honest, I'm not sure about any of this. We could be dealing with a few species or an entire mixed ecosystem here, but what I can't figure out is how."

John unclipped his backpack from the side of the branch and set it on his lap. "Maybe they were supposed to be the fast food of the future," he joked.

Rebecca looked up at John. "Actually, that's brilliant."

"Okay, the sarcasm isn't needed."

Rebecca adjusted herself on the branch. "I wasn't teasing you. Whatever the Chinese did to the sterilized soil they did with plants—plants straight out of the fossil record. Plants, animals, and insects are linked in a thriving ecosystem. Remove one, and the others suffer. It all makes logical sense. What better to put in an ancient environment than creatures that once thrived in it. Not only that, but you increase your food source with the animals you introduce."

John dug in his pack and extracted two flat plastic containers. "If this place is thriving, where are all the people?" He handed Rebecca one of the containers.

"They may be centralized around the signal." Rebecca turned the container over, looking at it. "What's this?"

The container made a slight hiss as he broke the seal. "It's a food ration."

Rebecca followed suit. "Thank you."

John chuckled. "I don't know if you want to thank me just yet. These things were horrible back in my time."

"No, that's not what I meant," Rebecca said. "I never got a chance to thank you for yesterday. If you hadn't been there…"

"I promised I'd get you back safe."

Rebecca smiled. "And I'm pretty sure I barfed on you in the glider."

"Nothing the rain didn't wash away." With his fingers, John scooped out some of the ration and tested it. At least one thing hadn't changed with time. Rations still tasted like crap. "You know, I'll still need someone to show my daughter and me around when we get back."

Rebecca's smile faded for a brief second. "I'd like that." She picked out a square piece of what may have been chicken from the ration and put it in her mouth. "This is horrible!" she said, spitting out the mouthful.

"Eat what you can. It's calories, and you're going to need the energy today," John said, grimacing as he took another bite. "That message we heard said something about Goliath. Do you think it was talking about the dinosaurs? Maybe one of the big nasty ones?"

Rebecca thought for a moment, while chewing another bite. "Possibly. If they could create a dinosaur, there was no stopping them from making other things as well. Frankly, I'm guessing there are a whole lot of things out there we may not want to stumble upon."

"That's a comforting thought," John said.

After finishing the rations, they made their way out of the tree. The ankylosaurs had moved on, and John was hoping to put a little more distance between them and the creature from yesterday.

Traversing the ever-thickening jungle proved tedious. Tensions ran high as every sound put them on edge. John had spent time all over the world while deployed with the Special Forces. Each place had its dangers, but this place was different. The air had a weight to it that was more than just the humidity. It was the sense of being watched.

The temperature under the canopy continued to climb as the day went on. Sweat dripped down from the bottom edge of John's saturated headband, but the rest of his body was remarkably dry, thanks to the suit Doctor Malcolm had furnished him with. From what he could tell, Rebecca's light body armor worked in much the same way. Suit or no suit, they would need to find water soon or risk dehydration.

"So, what was it like back in the twenty-first century?" Rebecca asked, pushing aside a vine.

"Before the war?" he asked.

"Sure."

"It was... nice."

"Wow, enlightening."

John sidestepped a fallen tree. "Sorry. I don't know enough about your time to even know what the differences are."

"You could at least humor me," Rebecca said.

"We didn't have those fancy computers screens that appear in midair."

"Come on. You can do better than that."

John stopped and turned to face Rebecca. "Fine. We had space."

"Space?"

"A person could load up the car and leave the city behind for a few days. It's hard to explain, but life just kinda slows down when you leave the steel and concrete of the city. The war took that all away." He wiped a droplet of sweat of the tip of his nose. "I entered the cryonics program to try and give Maddie something—hell, anything—that would resemble a normal life. But you know what eats me inside? When I asked my daughter about the cryonics program, she didn't ask about her friends, our house, or even her toys. She asked if it would make me happy." John swallowed down the large lump that had formed in his throat. "I live every day knowing how undeserving I am to have such a blessing in my life."

Rebecca smiled. "It sounds to me like you're more than deserving. One question though—what's a car?"

"You don't have cars anymore?" John asked, surprised.

Rebecca laughed. "Nah, I'm just messing with you. I couldn't have you ruin that tough guy persona by crying on me, now could I?

"You know I could leave you out here with the dinosaurs?"

"That would be rude," Rebecca said, sticking out her lip.

"Come on," John said, resuming their trudge. "We need to keep moving if we want to find the river." At least he was hoping they would find the river. As strange as it was to have Alice in his head, he could really use her help. Maybe she could tell if they were going in the right direction.

"Mass transportation," Rebecca commented, a little while later.

"What?"

"Most of the population uses mass transportation. Very few can afford anything else. I wouldn't get my hopes too high about this future, or reality may just disappoint you."

Over the next hour or two, as well as John could tell, they walked in silence. They could hear the river before they saw it.

"Water!" Rebecca said, running ahead.

"Wait!" John ran after her.

The river was larger than what John had expected. The slow-moving, sandy-brown water spanned a quarter mile from bank to bank. A thick layer of green algae covered the rock embankments.

"We need to survey an open area before rushing into it."

"You worry too much. Now help me down," Rebecca said, holding out her hand.

John pointed down the bank. A pair of biped dinosaurs pulled their heads from the water, at the disturbance of their new intruders. The water glistened off their yellow-and-green crests, which protruded from the dinosaurs' heads. A long trail of aquatic vegetation hung from the nearest one's mouth.

"Those don't look dangerous, but we don't know what else is out here."

"I guess I'm still getting used to this place," Rebecca said.

The larger of the two dinosaurs bellowed and lumbered out of the water and back into the jungle, with the smaller not far behind.

"I guess they weren't interested in company, but look there," John said. Not far away the river curved. A large land jetty stretched out at the bend. "It'll be easier to get water there, but we need to keep our eyes open. Animals, including the big ones, don't stray far from major water sources."

They moved down the bank and out onto the soft muddy outcropping. The land pier stretched well past the curve and was mostly bare of vegetation. John set his pack down and removed a small hand pump with two clear plastic tubes, one on each end. He moved to the edge of the water and knelt down "This should clean most of the contaminates from the water. I don't have anything to put the water into, but we can drink straight from the hose."

"At this point I don't care," Rebecca said. She knelt next to John. "Is there anything you don't have in that bag?"

John placed the bottom hose into the water and gave the purifier a few test pumps. The discolored water passed up through the lower hose, and into the main chamber. A moment later, clear water poured out from the top hose. "Go ahead. I'll keep it going while you get a drink."

Rebecca leaned over and started to drink from the end. The air temperature was noticeably cooler out from under the canopy. John continued to pump the handle and looked out across the river. A few smaller animals moved along the far bank. Really, this place was beautiful. After seeing the devastation caused by TEMPs, it was hard to believe this was even possible. He looked around at animal tracks in the mud around them. There were all shapes and sizes. Not far from where they were kneeling, the area looked like something had smoothed away all the tracks. Somewhere from the back of John's subconscious, an uneasy feeling crept over him.

John stopped pumping. "I think we need to move to—"

Behind them, something scraped against the rock. John wheeled around.

Commander Makenzie and the three others from the glider lowered their rifles.

"Look what we have here," Commander Makenzie said. "Guess I shouldn't be surprised you survived this far."

"Commander," Rebecca said. "You're alive."

"No thanks to you," the commander said. "We could have made it to the LZ, but your ejection from the glider caused the wing to tear away."

"The wing was already tearing away before we ejected," John said.

"It was you?" The commander glowered at John.

"Got lucky," Gramm said. The big man's arms glistened with sweat. "We crashed into the river not far from here. Lost most of the equipment, but saved the rifles. It was a good thing too. We ran into something big. Probably used half our ammo to bring it down, but not before another bigger one came in from nowhere. Just thinking about those teeth gives me nightmares."

John caught scent of something rank. "Is someone injured?"

Marcus, the glider pilot, turned. "It's probably this." He gestured to the thing hanging from his back. "Shot the thing this morning. I was hoping we could cook it tonight."

The creature looked like a cross between a brightly colored bird and a lizard. Dried blood had crusted around a hole in the thing's chest.

"You've been walking around all day in a hot jungle with a dead animal strapped to your back?" John asked in disbelief.

"Didn't have much of a choice if we wanted to eat," Gramm said.

"That's right. We have all we need right here," Marcus said, caressing his rifle.

Nolan walked around to John's left and spotted what he was holding.

"Look, Commander! Sergeant's got a water filter," Nolan said.

"Speaking of supplies," the commander said. "Let's see what else you've got in the bag."

John reached down, shouldered his bag, and tossed the water pump to Nolan. "I don't mind sharing, but I'll make the decision on when and where." The front snap clicked as he secured it across his chest.

A smile spread across the commander's face. "You're acting like you really have a choice in all this, Sergeant." The commander raised his rifle, leveling it at John.

Rebecca stepped between them. "Have you lost your mind, Commander? We all need to work together if we are going to make it out of here."

While the three of them argued, Nolan walked down to the water's edge to get a drink from the purifier.

"The way I see it is you need my help more than I need yours. We've all seen what's out there," John said, pointing to the jungle wall. "And if Gramm's right, you just wasted half your remaining ammunition taking down a single dinosaur."

Nolan started laughing. "Dinosaur! That was a monster plain and simple."

Right, John thought as he turned to see the young soldier, struggling to work the hand pump. "I'd move over to the other side, kid. Plus, there's a lock on the side."

Marcus walked over and snatched the filter away. "Give me the damn thing."

John scanned the water for the disturbance from before but didn't see anything. "I'd keep back from the water."

"I don't take orders from you," Marcus said.

John turned and started walking towards Marcus and Nolan. "You don't understand."

A low clicking sound sent a wave of fear through John. Rebecca screamed, causing the whole party to turn back to the forest. Standing at the tree line was a large tyrannosaur. Its reddish-brown and green body was the same as the one they had seen on the game trail. In the late afternoon light, a crest of red feather-like filament was clearly visible on its head.

Marcus dropped the filter in the river and pulled his rifle around.

"I'll try to draw it over to the right. When I do, get your men and the professor out of here," John said to the commander. "Save the ammo, we may need it later." The commander stood staring up at the creature. "Commander!"

The commander only slowly nodded. John readied himself. If he could make it into the trees, it just might slow the giant down.

The water exploded behind the group. Marcus shrieked in terror as the jaws of an enormous crocodile closed around him. The tyrannosaur roared and charged forward with frightening agility. Everything dissolved into chaos. The muffled repeat of Marcus's gas-powered rifle filled the air, until the crocodile pulled him beneath the surface. Nolan stumbled from the water, his eyes wide. Gramm and the commander fired at the tyrannosaur with reckless abandon.

John grabbed Rebecca's hand. "Run!" From the sound of Nolan's shouts and the repeat of the rifles, the others were close behind. John ran towards a close, dense grouping of trees. Maybe they could lose it there. If nothing else, maybe the close vegetation would slow it down. The tyrannosaur roared again.

"Keep running, we're almost there!" John shouted.

"Sergeant, I would advise adjusting your course twenty degrees to your left," Alice said within John's head.

The area Alice had indicated was away from the thicket and provided almost no cover at all. Every instinct he had told him to head for tree cluster, but instead, he angled to where Alice had indicated. The edge of a small concrete structure came into view, most of it covered with thick jungle growth, but an opening was clearly visible.

John pointed. "There!" He ushered Rebecca inside and turned, motioning to the others. "Run!"

Nolan had outdistanced Gramm and the commander and sprinted past John. Out of breath, he collapsed inside.

John waved the commander and Gramm on. "Run, damn you! Run!"

The tyrannosaur was too close. They weren't going to make it. John ran inside and ripped Nolan's rifle out of his grasp. He ran back to the entrance, set the rifle stock into his shoulder, and squeezed the trigger. There was almost no recoil as the thin metallic projectiles left the barrel. The cylindrical bullets rebounded off the creature's forehead. Like most large animals, the dinosaur's skull was likely thick, and the chances of penetrating it were unlikely, but he didn't need to kill it, just slow it down a little.

Nothing impeded the animal. The tyrannosaur's jaws snapped right behind the commander, the creature raised back for another bit. John took in a deep breath and took aim at the eye. He pulled the trigger. The brow ridge above the tyrannosaur's eye erupted in a spray of blood and tissue. The dinosaur slowed for a moment to bellow and shake its head, but was soon after the fleeing men.

"Come on! Come on!" John prompted.

The enraged beast closed the distance fast. Gramm and the commander dove for the entrance.

"Move!" John dropped the rifle and shoved the commander ahead of him, deeper into the building. The tyrannosaur smashed into the entrance. The structure collapsed around the group, thrusting them into darkness.

CHAPTER 9

John bent the transparent plastic tube until the thin glass vessel inside cracked. With a few shakes, the tube began to glow with a fluorescent green light. The air was thick with dust, and debris lay in piles everywhere. A large piece of broken concrete blocked the entrance.

John held the chemlight overhead, illuminating the area. There was no sign of Nolan's rifle. It was more than likely buried beneath the collapsed entrance.

"Is everyone alright?" John asked. He was answered with a mixture of coughs and moans. Aside from Nolan, who had taken a nasty blow to the forehead, everyone appeared to be uninjured. John untied his headband and secured it tightly around the young man's wound. The cloth was wet with perspiration, but at least it would stop the bleeding. After propping Nolan up against a chunk of concrete wall, he went over and knelt by Rebecca.

"You okay?" he asked.

Rebecca was staring at her hands. She kept curling them into fists. "I thought this trip would be the experience of a lifetime."

John sat down. "I entered the service when I was eighteen, following in my father's footsteps. In truth, I just wanted to have a good time. The Gulf War had ended nine years before I enlisted, and no one anticipated the United States entering another conflict anytime soon. We were all wrong. Two years later, I was in Iraq. I spent two tours of duty in that hellhole before being selected for Special Operations. A few years later, I was appointed to an elite tactical squad. With each step up I took, I told myself it would get better."

"And was it?" Rebecca asked.

John took off his pack and removed another chemlight. "I realized something out there in the sleepless nights. I realized I was a horrible father. Maddie never complained about my deployments. She only told me to come back soon. I wasn't around, and it was forcing my little girl to grow up faster than she should have. I was missing out on her life."

After Emily's death, each new mission was a way for him to escape the pain. Once the hurting was gone, there would be time for Maddie. It was a lie, but escape was his drug. At first, it was only a bitch of a migraine, then the nosebleeds started. The tests results came back a few weeks later. His file from the private clinic lay crumpled on the passenger floorboard of the Durango. It was the first time he had cried since Emily had passed. Cancer wouldn't rob him of his time with Maddie—no, he had done that himself.

John cracked another fluorescent tube and tossed it near the commander. "You don't realize how quickly a day is gone until there are so few left." He shrugged. "Maybe, it wasn't an adventure you were searching for as much as a change."

Rebecca looked away from him. "Perhaps."

John removed four rations from his pack and took a quick inventory of the remaining contents. There wasn't much but a coil of rope, two chemlights, an empty water bottle, a single gel fire starter, and two metal plates. He closed the bag and set it next Rebecca. Grabbing the rations, he stood. "It will be dark soon, and I think here is as good as any to rest and regroup. Tomorrow we can try to find a way out. This hallway has to lead somewhere." He handed out the ration canisters, setting the last one down beside the commander, who didn't bother to reach for it. "These are the last of my rations, and unless anyone else has anything, we'll have to forage from now on."

Gramm twisted the top off his ration. "Sorry, Sergeant. Didn't think we'd need anything outside the main forces camp."

John couldn't blame them. Most of the men he has seen on the transport had never held a weapon, let alone been deployed into a theater of operations.

"Wait," Nolan said. "We can't leave Marcus out there."

John looked down at Nolan. "I don't think Marcus made it."

"No... you don't understand." Nolan struggled to get to his feet. "His suit should have kept him safe."

John put a hand Nolan's shoulder. "Even if the suit protected him from the attack, it wouldn't have saved him from drowning."

"I just thought," Nolan started, before lowering his head. He sat back down.

"I'm sorry for Marcus," John said. "He must have been a good man."

Gramm laughed out loud. "He was an asshole, but he was one of us."

John understood that sentiment better than most, having served beside many of the same. Beside Gramm, the commander was examining his ammunition magazine.

"How many do you have left, Commander?" John asked.

The commander glared up at him. Even in the darkened corridor, the contempt was evident. He inserted the magazine back into the bottom of the rifle. "A few," he said with a smug smile on his face.

John released his clenched fist. He wasn't going to play this game. Out here beating your chest and acting like a fool would only get everyone killed.

Gramm cleared his throat. "I've got 'bout twenty rounds left myself."

John nodded to Gramm. "Let's all try and get some shut eye. I'll take first watch—couldn't sleep if I wanted." It wasn't completely true, but he needed to speak with Alice.

"Watch!" The commander snorted. "What's there to watch? We have a ton of concrete between us and outside."

"Did you see any doors when we ran in here?" John asked. "Are you willing to bet your life nothing else wondered in here before we did?"

The commander didn't reply and rolled on his side away from the group.

Gramm held out his rifle. "I'll take the second watch."

John nodded and took the rifle from Gramm. "Get some shut eye. We may need it tomorrow." He walked back over and sat on the other side of Rebecca. "You know that goes for you too."

Rebecca ran a hand through her tangled hair. "I can't figure it out. Alpha predators shouldn't cluster this close together, and yet we have run into a tyrannosaur twice, and Gramm said they shot one as well."

John leaned the rifle against the wall next to him. "Gramm also said another one came at them after they killed the first."

"I know. It doesn't make any sense." Rebecca grunted in frustration.

John settled back against the cold stone wall. "Seems to make sense to me."

Rebecca turned her body to face John. "You're kidding, right?"

"Not at all," John said. "Tigers are territorial and even have the mental capacity for vengeance. There are quite a few stories about it. A poacher once came across a tiger enjoying its latest kill. Doing what a poacher does, he shoots at it but only manages to wound it. The cat slips away into the forest before he can reload and take another shot. Not wanting to go away empty handed, the poacher takes the remains of the tiger's kill. Later, the tiger tracks the man back to a hunting cabin. After tearing apart the cabin and not finding the poacher, the tiger waits three days, inside the cabin. You can guess what happened when the poacher finally returned.

"It ate him?" Rebecca asked. She tried to feign a look of revulsion, but there was more interest in her reaction than anything else.

John nodded. "Another is a couple of teens were taunting a tiger at the San Francisco Zoo. A short time later, the tiger leaps the sixteen and a half foot wall and escapes. Instead of attacking the numerous other animals near its enclosure, or the hundreds of other patrons at the zoo, it tracks down and mauls the teens who had allegedly been teasing it."

"You're thinking the tyrannosaur is doing the same thing?" Rebecca asked.

"What I'm thinking is, the tyrannosaur we saw today is the same one we saw on the trail. The commander's group likely killed its mate. The dead animal Marcus had slung across his back led it right to the river."

"Do you think it's still out there?" Rebecca asked.

"It's got our scent now."

Rebecca looked down and sucked on her lower lip thoughtfully. "It makes sense." She looked back up at John. "You sure you're not some stuffed shirt professor?"

John smiled. "No. I just watched a lot of reruns on Animal Planet."

"Not sure what that is, but I'll take your word for it." Rebecca adjusted her position on the floor and rested her head again John's arm. "I hope you don't mind?" She yawned and stretched out further. "I didn't want my head in the dirt."

The chemlight cast a fluorescent glow across Rebecca's face. John could feel his face warm. She was pretty—not as much as Emily, but no one would ever be. His life had a clock attached to it, and the alarm would go off sooner than later. After a while, Rebecca's breathing slowed and deepened. Carefully, he lifted a stray hair that had fallen onto her face. He looked over at the others. Gramm was snoring, mouth open to the world, and was only partly disturbed when he choked on his own saliva. John waited for a good while longer before trying to speak with Alice.

In a hushed voice, he asked, "Alice?"

"I am here, Sergeant Crider," she responded.

"Where'd you go?"

"I went nowhere, Sergeant. I am implanted within your conscious."

"That's not what I meant. I tried to contact you earlier, and you didn't answer."

"Your body is in a continuous state of decay, and until I can reactive more of the INOs, it requires my full processing capacity to keep your body from shutting down."

It hadn't occurred to him she was working so hard to keep him alive. "I wasn't doubting you, Alice. I was just... worried something happened to you."

"Your worry is unfounded, Sergeant. I am a program, nothing more."

"Program or not, we are in this together. I'm a simple man, and I don't need to understand it; I'll leave that part to you."

"As you wish, Sergeant."

"I've meant to ask you something." John slowly turned his neck from side to side, searching for the pressure at the base of his skull. "Before I was frozen I was sick—not with a virus, but really sick."

"I removed all the abnormal functioning cells. Currently, there are no traces of illness or foreign contaminants, apart from your cellular degeneration."

John's eyes teared up, and he swallowed hard. "I was a little uncomfortable with this, still am, but I know without you I die here."

"I do see an unnatural trend in your reliance on me, Sergeant."

John smiled. "Was that sarcasm?"

"I do not know. Your emotions and memory segments are overwhelming. I am unsure of what optimal parameters are within this vessel."

"You're doing fine, Alice. Don't take over my body and destroy the world and I think we're good."

"I can make no promises."

"Very funny." John leaned his head back against the wall. "I can see we'll get along just fine."

"Would it comfort you more," Alice's voice changed, "if I sounded like this?"

A breath caught in John's throat. That was Emily's voice.

"Sadness surrounds your memories of Emily. I thought you would be happy to—"

"No." John's hand shook as he wiped his nose. "Emily is dead, and no matter how much I miss her, an imitation can't bring her back. I know you don't understand, but please leave those memories where they belong—as memories."

"I did not mean to hurt you, Sergeant Crider," Alice said in her normal voice.

"I know. Can I ask you a favor?" John asked. "We may be together for a while, and I would prefer it if you called me John."

"Affirmative, John. I believe continuing to call me Alice may be incorrect. I would now be considered a biological interface, and a more appropriate name would be BALICE, a Biological Advanced Local Intelligent Cybernetic Entity."

With his eyes still damp he had to catch himself from laughing allowed. Rebecca stirred against his shoulder. "I'm pretty sure I like you just the way you are."

"Good," Alice said. "I do not think I would have liked being a Balice."

"I think I like this new side of you, Alice. It's quite refreshing."

"I am glad, John," Alice said. "I think you would like to know that thirty percent of your INOs are now reactivated and under my subroutines, but I will need you to sleep so I can continue repairing your system. I can monitor this area while you sleep and will wake you if necessary."

"Okay, Alice. I'm all yours again." He adjusted his position against the wall and closed his eyes.

"John, I sense the others are beginning to stir," Alice said.

Slowly, John opened his eyes. He didn't remember falling asleep, but the weariness in his body was gone. It didn't feel like he had slept long, but the chemlights had dimmed considerably. Rebecca rolled over, and her head was on his lap.

"When we speak again, you must explain why your heart rate increases whenever Professor Oddum is near you."

John cleared his throat and tried to sit up a little more. "Er, it's... difficult to explain."

Rebecca rolled onto her back and yawned. She stretched her arms out and arched her back. With eyes still half closed she looked up at John; after a moment, realization kicked in.

"Oh!" Rebecca bolted upright, her face bright red. "I didn't mean."

"It's fine, really," John said. He was just glad she woke up before the others. "Really, it was probably my fault anyway. I tend to move around a lot when I sleep."

Before long, the rest of the group was awake. John cracked the remaining two chemlights and handed the one he was holding from last night to Rebecca. The lights from the night before were dim, but having them was better than feeling around in the dark. He tossed one of the new lights to Gramm.

"Sergeant, how come you didn't wake me for watch last night?" Gramm asked.

"Don't worry about it. You looked like you needed more rest than me anyway," John said. He tossed the second light to the commander, who snatched it out of the air. "Commander Makenzie, take point."

Makenzie's jaw tensed, but he didn't argue. He pushed his way past Gramm and shouldered John as he walked by.

Giving the commander orders would only make him more difficult to deal with, but a loaded weapon behind his back was worse. John bent down and picked up the chemlight he had given the commander last night and stored it between a snap on his vest. He flipped the rifle over and held it out to Gramm.

"Cover our rear, and don't shoot unless you have to. Better conserve what we've got left."

"You got it," Gramm said, shouldering the rifle.

The passage leading from the entrance was relatively short and ended in a junction. Commander Makenzie continued down the left hall without a word, removing any need to discuss which way they should go.

"What is this?" Nolan asked.

"Whatever it is, it gives me the creeps," Gramm answered.

Doors lined the corridor on either side. Picking one, John walked over and tested the latch. The metal handle broke off in his hand. "Rusted." The rest of the door looked to be made of a plastic-type material. If the latches were corroded maybe he could force it open. He squared his body and kicked where the latch had been. The door tore free, the noise echoing off unseen walls. "Let me borrow your light, Gramm. Mine's a little dim."

"Sure, take it," Gramm said, handing over the light.

John stepped across the threshold. The greenish light from the chemlights illuminated a room surrounded by cabinets and a countertop. A small table and chairs took up the center of the room. The air was heavy and tasted stale. He moved towards another door at the back. Unlike the bare walls of the hallway, remnants of decoration hung tattered and broken. He lightly touched the surface of the table as he walked around it. The layer of dust was thick. No one had been here for a while.

The door to the other room was slightly ajar. Slowly, he pushed the door open with the back of his forearm. The light slipped from his grasp and landed with a dull thud on the floor. A scraping sound came from within the room. John froze, his hand unconsciously already closed around the cold handle of his combat knife. He released the breath he had been holding, listening for the sound again. The knife released easily from its sheath. He scanned the shadows for any sign of movement. Nothing.

Crouching, he picked up the chemlight and lifted it above his head. The room wasn't much bigger than the other. A knee high rectangular shape filled most of the room. To his left, he noticed a small gap in the wall.

"John."

John jumped at the sound of Alice's voice.

"From the shape and items dimensions, I believe you are looking at habitation quarters," Alice said.

"Apartments," John said.

John moved around what he guessed was once a bedframe toward the gap in the wall. Something still didn't feel right. The gap appeared to be a panel of some sort—maybe a closet—and looked like it should slide into the wall. He slipped the light stick next to the other one on his vest. With the knife still in hand, he gripped the closet door and pulled. The panel gave slightly but caught on something. He palmed the light again and leaned his head through the opening. In the corner of the closet was a human skeleton. The thighbone was stuck in the door track, keeping the closet from opening fully. Small markings covered the bones.

Behind him, something crashed to the floor. John turned, his head banging against the closet. His heart hammered in his chest. On the opposite wall, half a vent grate hung loose, swinging slightly; the other half lay on the floor.

"You okay?" Rebecca's voice came from out in the hallway.

He was too jumpy, but then again maybe he had reason to be. "I'm fine." He backed out of the bedroom and made his way to the others, but he still couldn't shake the feeling something else was in there, watching.

"Anything?" Nolan asked as John emerged from the room.

John shook his head and handed Gramm's chemlight back. "I think people used to live here."

"Used to?" Nolan glanced around wearily.

John nodded. "I doubt we'll find much here."

"Where do you think they went?" Rebecca asked.

"Does it really matter?" the commander said, looking irritated by the stop He started down the hallway without them.

John frowned. "I'm not sure they went anywhere, but it would be best if we kept moving."

Gramm tightened his grip on his rifle. "I'm with you, Sergeant."

"This place is way too big to only have one way in." John sheathed his knife. "Let's catch up with the commander and see what's further down."

The group moved on but found the hallway ended at an oversized stairwell. They had likely passed elevators of some sort, but without power and regular maintenance they wouldn't be of any use.

"Well, down we go," John said. "We might be able to cross over to another section. With any luck, we'll find another exit."

The commander ignored the comment and started down the stairs. Nolan shrugged and followed. The stairwell crossed back and forth with each level ending at a floor landing. Unlike the first floor, each of the following were sealed off by a solid panel. They tested a few, but gave up around the tenth floor. Stress cracks lined most the walls of the stairwell, and mold grew along the areas where moisture had found its way in. John lost count of the levels after a couple dozen, and the silence was soon replaced with the heavy breathing of the others. John felt fine, but he guessed Alice was to thank for that.

"How far do you think this goes?" Rebecca asked.

"I hope it ends soon." Nolan turned, his heel missing the next step.

For a moment, Nolan's arms windmilled out, desperately trying to catch hold of anything, but there wasn't anything to grab. He tumbled backwards, his body armor scraping against the floor as he fell. The commander jumped to the side barely avoiding the mass of flailing arms and legs, as it went by. Seconds later, Nolan landed hard on the next landing and screamed in pain.

"Looks like he found the bottom for us," Commander Makenzie said, reaching Nolan first. Instead of stopping, he walked around Nolan and continued around the corner.

John was next down. "Gramm, bring your light over here quick."

"It feels like it's on fire," Nolan cried.

John knelt. "I'll need to remove the leg section of your body armor so I can get a better look at it." Carefully, he unclipped the front thigh plate. Everything looked to be fine. The body armor must have absorbed most of the shock.

"Come on, man," Gramm said. "You going to let a little sprain stop you?"

"My foot!" Nolan squeezed his eyes shut, his face contorted. "My foot. I can't feel my foot."

John rotated the clips on the flexible shin pads. The side of the pad felt wet. Gently he lifted the armor away. A piece of bone protruded through the inside of the calf. This wasn't good, especially here.

John looked at Gramm, who had started leaning to one side. "Stay with me, Gramm."

"Sure. Sure. I'm good," Gramm said, trying to steady himself.

John turned his attention back to Nolan. "Nolan, I need you to listen to me. Your leg is broken, and I need to set it." There was no need to tell him how bad it was.

"No!" Nolan wailed.

"If I can set it, we can get you cleaned up when we get out of here. If we don't," John motioned to Gramm, "you won't make it out of here." The reality was, unless they could close the wound, setting it wouldn't matter. "You'll need to hold him tight, Gramm. He's not going to like this."

Gramm locked his big arms around Nolan, immobilizing him the best he could. John sat on the ground and set his feet on either side of Nolan's leg. He gripped Nolan's foot above the ankle and leaned back. Nolan screamed. John kept pulling until he felt the bone slide into place. Nolan's head drooped forward, and he went limp.

"Oh, God. We killed him," Gramm said.

"He only passed out." John lowered Nolan's leg back down and strapped the leg plates back on. The leg was going to swell, but the body armor was the best thing they had to stabilize and control the blood loss. "You can let go," he told Gramm.

John sat up and looked around. The stairs had ended, and only the darkness of the room beyond remained.

Rebecca stepped up next to John and helped him to his feet. "Where's Commander Makenzie?"

"I think we have more to worry about than the commander." John looked down at Nolan. "He won't be able to walk out of here."

Gramm squatted down and lifted Nolan over his broad shoulder with ease. "Don't you worry 'bout him. I've got this, but I won't be able to watch our backs and carry him." He handed the rifle over to John and the light to Rebecca.

"You're a good man," John said.

Gramm smiled. "If we get back, make sure you tell my old lady that. She eats that stuff up."

John grinned. "You would have fit in nicely with my old team. Now, let's see if we can catch up with the commander, shall we?"

The commander was right. They had reached the bottom. The panels that had blocked the exits of the other floors were mostly gone. Only small fragments attached to the lower section remained. John led the way into the next room. There was no sign of the commander's chemlight, but John had expected as much. Oversized pipes angled out of the floor and disappeared into the darkness above. Every sound set the hairs on the back of his neck on edge.

Behind him, something moaned. John's heartbeat quickened. He turned and looked back at Gramm, whose eyes went wide. Nolan moaned again. Gramm nervously smiled and shrugged. Somewhere in the room, a tiny screech rang out, followed by another and another, until the sound was overwhelming. Rebecca moved closer to John. She said something, but it was lost among the drone. Outside the radius of the chemlights, the light reflected off constantly moving small green orbs.

John changed his grip on the rubber rifle stock. "Just keep moving," John yelled, unsure if the other had heard him.

"I am tracking multiple targets," Alice said inside John's head.

"Tell me something I don't know," John said.

Behind him, Gramm crashed to the ground, Nolan tumbled out in front of him. A knee-high shape rushed in and seized Nolan's boot.

"Get off him!" Gramm shouted.

John pivoted and kicked the thing hard, sending it sprawling into blackness. He bent and wrapped one of Nolan's arms around his shoulder. "Quick, help me, Gramm!" He motioned to Rebecca. "Go!"

Gramm scrambled to his feet and got under Nolan's other arm. They ran after Rebecca, Nolan's boots dragging behind them. The creatures followed them through the darkness.

Ahead Rebecca came to an abrupt stop. John had been too intent on running and almost crashed into her. A putrid smell filled his nostrils.

"Listen," Gramm said. The scratching and calling of the creatures around them faded until they were left in silence once again.

John swatted an insect away from his face with his free hand. "Rebecca?"

Rebecca pointed at the floor, her other hand covering her mouth. The smell was intense, making John's stomach turn. Next to him, Gramm emptied the context of his stomach onto the floor. The light wavered, as Rebecca backed up trying to lift her feet. John looked down.

The floor was moving. Hundreds of black insects moved across the ground like oil, covering everything. Their bloated abdomens looked out of place on flattened sideways bodies. To John they looked like fleas, but at nearly an inch-long, these weren't the kind you would find on a stray dog. John swatted one away that had jumped onto his pants.

Gramm yelled in pain. A line of blood ran down his neck. "Oh, hell no! It just bit me. I didn't come to no basement to be eaten by a bug!"

Gramm pulled Nolan away from John and took off. John pushed Rebecca forward. The insects crunched under their boots while they ran. John could feel the flea-like insects biting him on the exposed tissue around his face and neck.

"Faster!" John urged.

Up ahead the outline of a door came into view. John let go of Rebecca's hand and ran past Gramm. He took the door in stride, putting his full weight behind the lunge. Pain coursed down through his arm, but the door tore open. Gramm dropped Nolan and slammed the doors closed behind them.

Rebecca danced in place. "Why did it have to be bugs?" she screamed. She shook the remaining insects from her hair, stomping forcefully on each one. "I hate bugs!"

John dabbed at the open wounds on his neck and looked around. "Looks like the other stairwell. Gramm, you still okay to carry Nolan?"

"I'll manage," Gramm said. He bent over and hoisted Nolan back up across his shoulders. "I think I prefer the bigger dinosaur. At least it's only one thing to worry about."

This side of the stairs proved to be slower going than the other. They had seen very little damage on the other floors, but this side hadn't fared as well. Incendiary burns marred the walls and the stairs.

Rebecca rubbed her arms, even though she wouldn't feel it through her suit. "What happened here?"

"Don't know," Gramm said. "Must have been a big fight."

"No bullet casings," John said, continuing upward.

Rebecca looked over at John. "What do you mean?"

"No bullet casings. Most of the damage here was likely caused by built-up gas or possibly energy remaining in unused lines. Only a few of these could have been explosives of some kind." John stopped at the landing. "These people weren't prepared for this, and now it's their tomb."

"Man, that's tough," Gramm said.

Gramm was breathing heavy. Perspiration ran down the stubble on his head. John had offered to carry Nolan for a while, but Gramm refused. They continued up the remaining floors in silence. With no way to determine the time in the unrelenting dark, it was difficult to estimate how long they had climbed. Just as the other stairwell the doors leading to the other floors were sealed. John reached another landing and turned to go up the next set of stairs but found the ceiling collapsed.

"Great. Now what?" Gramm asked.

"If the commander navigated his way through the basement, he would've had to come this way. That was assuming he had made it." John said.

"What about that," Rebecca said, pointing to a small gap under the panel covering the stairwell door.

Gramm set Nolan down carefully and gripped the opening with both hands. With a grunt, he lifted. The access door rose slowly until it reached his waist. Gramm relaxed a little but the door remained in place. "Problem solved."

The door led into another unlit corridor. The passage was similar to the one they had been in previously. A glowing light outlined something not too far in front of them.

The light brightened as the figure turned. Commander Mackenzie stared back at them through the dark, his face tinged green from the chemlight. John could see the surprise in the commander's expression. He had never expected them to make it out of the lower levels. The astonished look on the commander's face was quickly gone.

"Commander," Gramm said. "We have been—"

Three gas driven cylindrical spikes embedded in the wall next to John.

"Why don't you just do me a favor and die already, Sergeant?" The commander yelled. He fired a few more in rapid succession, but his aim was off.

John raised his rifle. Commander Mackenzie turned and started to run down the hall. John took a breath holding it in. He took aim just below the shoulder blade and to the left, the point at which the heart extends from the protection of the spine. The trigger pulled back too easily. There was no recoil as the spike exploded from the barrel. The impact dropped the commander to his knee, but without any hesitation, he regained his balance and continued running. John started off after the commander, but underneath something cracked, and the floor gave way. He lunged backward in desperation, slamming against the edge of the flooring. Frantically, he tried to catch hold of anything. The rifle came loose and disappeared into the darkness below. His grip was slipping.

Gramm dove forward. "Sergeant!" His fingers wrapped tightly around John's wrist. "Hold on, Sergeant. I got you."

The big man's forearm's bulged, exposing the road map of veins up his arms. Gramm gritted his teeth and pulled hard. Inch by inch, John climbed back onto what was left of the corridor.

"You okay, John?" Rebecca asked, helping Gramm get John to his feet.

John brushed himself off. His tactical vest was ripped, but it had kept him from sliding off the edge. "What happened?"

"Looks like the structure was weak already." Gramm looked over the edge, careful not to get too close. "Lucky you hadn't made it farther out there."

"What about the commander?" John asked. "I know I hit him."

Gramm rapped on his own chest plate. "The spikes can't penetrate body armor. It doesn't matter now though, I lost sight of his light when the floor gave out. I don't think he made it." Gramm lowered his head. "I don't know what the commander was thinking, Sergeant."

"Like you said, Gramm." John patted Gramm's shoulder. "It doesn't matter anymore."

Gramm checked on Nolan, who was still unconscious on the ground.

Rebecca moved to John's side and looking at the section of missing floor. "It's not your fault," she said. "Maybe we can pry up another door on some other floor."

John stood at the edge of the collapsed walkway, trying to see the far edge in the all-concealing darkness beyond. They could try going back down, but he wasn't sure if there was access on the other side. He glanced over at Rebecca and tried to give her a reassuring smile. A high-pitched shriek rang out from below. They all froze in place. Another shriek, fainter than the first, called back and was followed by another. It was the same sound from down in the pipe room. The haunting chorus increased with frightening speed until it echoed up from the stairwell.

"The door!" Rebecca screamed.

John took off towards the stairs at a full sprint. He reached the open door and pushed down, but it wouldn't budge. The scraping of claws, propelling the small creatures up the stairs, was too close. Behind him, Rebecca's chemlight dimmed. She must have turned or maybe Gramm had stepped in front of the light, but whatever had happened only left John's light to repel the darkness. He looked under the panel.

Two pairs of dim eyes came up onto the landing from the stairs. He couldn't quite make out their outline. An involuntary guttural yell tore from John's throat as he kicked at the door. The creatures hesitated. He kicked it again. This time the door clicked, and he felt it release. He pushed down hard, trying to force the door to close faster. One of the creatures sprung at the doorway, the impact forced its head through the opening. The small jaws snapped wildly. Leaning out, he kicked at the creature's head, wishing to God he still had the rifle. The lizard-like beast wrenched its head back through the opening, wailing in pain. The door slammed shut and latched in place against the floor. John slid down beside the door, breathing heavily.

"John, over here," Rebecca said.

He followed Rebecca's voice to an open set of double doors. The threshold of the door was just past the edge of the collapsed flooring. Rebecca gestured for him to hurry. She certainly didn't have to tell him twice.

Rebecca secured the doors once John was inside. The room was different from the living quarters he was expecting. A long counter divided the chamber with just enough room to walk around. There were closed doors on either side of the room. Gramm had already set Nolan down and was resting with his back against the counter.

Rebecca shook the handles on the doors to make sure they were secure and came over and stood by John. "Don't we need to be moving?"

John tilted his head back. "Those things shouldn't be able to get in here with the floor missing, plus I need a moment to think."

Rebecca chewed nervously at the end of her thumb. "We're stuck here, aren't we?"

John took a deep breath and let it out slowly. "Those doors behind us have to lead somewhere. Maybe we can break through one of the walls to another room. If we can get into the adjoining rooms, we might be able to get to the other side of the corridor." John stood up and walked over to where Gramm had laid Nolan. The young man's breathing was labored and shallow. They all needed to get out of this place, and now they would have to do it without a rifle.

"Can we get moving?" Rebecca asked. "This place makes my skin crawl."

"I'm with her," Gramm said, standing up.

"That makes three of us," John said, straightening up.

They moved into the next room. Small freestanding stalls, most with their doors half opened, lined the walls. John peered into one of the stalls. "Bathroom. Anyone need to go?"

"I don't know about you, but I think I already did," Gramm said.

The next room had a few sinks and what looked like an open shower. At the back of the room, the wall curved and led them into an oversized open room. The air smelled musty, and the floor was slick with a coating of algae. In the center of the room, their light cast a green sheen over a large area of water.

"Careful, Gramm. The floor is slick, and I can't carry you and Nolan out of here." John said. "Plus, you wouldn't want to end up in there."

"What do you think this is?" Rebecca asked.

"I think it's a swimming pool, or at least what is left of it," John said.

Their footsteps reverberated off the solid walls, as they made their way carefully around the side of the water. Remnants of ornamental work surrounded the edge.

"A swimming pool? What's a swimming pool?" Gramm asked.

John stopped and turned back to look at Gramm and Rebecca. "You don't have swimming pools?" Gramm and Rebecca shook their heads. "A man-made pond you swim in?" He could see the sincere look of confusion on both of their faces. "Maddie's not going to like this."

Next to John, the sound of dripping water caught his attention. He pressed his hand against the wall. A steady stream of cool water ran over his fingers and down his arm. This much water wouldn't be from a ground seep. He shook his hand, flinging water droplets everywhere.

John smiled. "I think we just got one step closer to getting out of here." He looked back at Gramm and Rebecca, his smile dissolved. A set of dull gray orbs stared back at him from an opening in the wall next to the room they had just exited.

Rebecca frowned. "What?" She turned to see what John was looking at. "Oh, God!"

"The surface has to be right above us." John tapped on the almost spent chemlight in his vest. It wouldn't be much, but it would have to do. "See if there's another door, and maybe some way up."

Gramm's mouth formed a tight thin line. "What are you going to do?"

John could tell Gramm didn't like the order. "Give you time."

"No." Rebecca grabbed onto John sleeve. "You can't."

"If it alerts the rest, we're dead," John said.

"You said they shouldn't be able to get in here," Rebecca said.

John didn't respond. Instead, he moved her behind him.

"Professor," Gramm said. "He's buying us time. Let's not waste it."

John could hear Gramm and Rebecca moving away. The creature turned its interest towards them. *Not there, here*, John thought. He crouched and began forward. The silver shine of its eye turned back to him. Each step he took with a purpose, slow and calculating. These things were likely the masters of this underground crypt, and as such probably had never faced a threat before—at least, that was what he was counting on.

John withdrew his knife, his muscles tense, like that of a predator. The animal took an unsure step forward before taking two steps back. It was unsure of what to do when threatened; it was exactly what John hoped would happen.

"John," Alice said, "though I understand what you are doing, I must interject as to the impractical nature of your current actions."

"Would it kill you, Alice, to be a little more positive?"

The animal bobbed its head up and down, and let out a low growl. *Not yet. A little closer*, John thought. John was close enough now that the dim light on his vest allowed him to get a good look at the creature. The animal stood on two legs and was roughly the size of a large dog. It's head and snout were similar to the tyrannosaur's, but this smaller version had a layer of feather-like filament covering most of its body. John tightened his grip on the knife handle, taking a deep breath, and charged. The animal bared its teeth, making a hissing sound, and leaped at him. It hit him square in the chest, the momentum carrying them to the ground.

Claws sank into his thigh and pelvis, and a burning radiated throughout his lower section. He grabbed the beast's forelimb, trying to tear it free, but the creature was quick and fierce. The slick ground made it impossible to get back on his feet. He rolled to the side, forcing the animal to leap free, but it recovered too quickly and was right back on him. The creature tore at his shoulder and vest. It shook him hard back and forth.

His hand brushed against something wet—the pool. John looked back, relieved to see that Rebecca and Gramm were gone. The beast snapped at his face and throat. Wrapping his legs around the creature's long muscular tail, he grabs a handful of feathers, took a deep breath, and pitched over the side of the pool. Dark, cold water enveloped them. The animal thrashed wildly, creating a frenzy of bubbles as it tried to get away. John plunged his knife into its neck. The fight bled from it quickly until it was motionless in his arms. He pushed the creature away, and it slowly sank away into the black pitch outside the chemlight's glow. With a few kicks, he surfaced near the side of the pool. It was a struggle to pull himself out of the water. Exhausted, he spat out the foul-tasting water and flopped onto his back.

"That seemed like a great idea," Alice said.

"Okay, forget the positivity thing."

"I am finding," Alice said, "there seems to be very little difference between heroism and stupidity."

John secured his knife back into its sheath. "Alice, have I ever told you how much I enjoy our conversations?"

"No. But I do enjoy them myself, as well."

"Sergeant." Gramm moved quickly down the length of the pool toward John. "Let's get you up."

John winced as Gramm pulled him to his feet. "I thought I told you to get out of here."

"No. You said you would buy us time, and you did." Gramm chuckled.

"What?"

"After what I've seen you do, frankly, I was expecting something more."

"You'll have to forgive me. Next time I'll try harder," John said. Gramm helped him around the pool and into a small pump room. Rebecca was waiting at the door.

"John!" Rebecca took hold of John's other arm and eased him to the floor. "Look." She pointed to a ladder on the back wall. "We found a way out."

Gramm closed the door to the small room and pushed a shelf in front of it. "I was able to get the hatch open, but the sun is down so I couldn't see much," Gramm said.

"As much as I hate to say this," John said, touching a hand to his shoulder. "I think we need to stay put until morning."

Rebecca and Gramm looked at each other. "But those things are out there," Rebecca said.

"We may only be trading one problem for another," John said. "At least here, we are relatively sheltered."

"I want to get out of here, but I agree," Gramm said.

Rebecca crossed her arms. "Not you too."

"That is the only way in here," John said, pointing to the door. "If we pile more stuff in front of it we should be fine until morning."

"There are two ways in here, the hatch and the door, but I doubt I will be able to change your mind." Rebecca stormed to the corner of the room and sat down.

John and Gramm moved two old shelving racks in front of the door before settling down themselves. It wouldn't do much, but right now it was all they had. Succumbing to fatigue, John closed his eyes.

CHAPTER 10

"Sergeant, don't be shy. Come around and hold your wife's hand."

John looked around the small, light orange room. The cream color fabric drapes softened the sunlight from outside. The mood in the room was relaxed but busy. Next to a bed, a nurse checked sensors attached to a metal stand and transcribed the result onto a large white clipboard. He tried to glance at what she was writing, but it was illegible. Another nurse walked up beside them pushing a small tray of medical instruments. Bouquets of assorted flowers filled a small ledge across one wall, but they did little to cover the antiseptic smell of the room. John wrinkled his nose; he hated that smell, but he couldn't remember why.

"Sergeant. Hello," a doctor said, standing next to the bed. She gestured for him to come closer.

Strange, he hadn't seen the doctor come into the room. *What was her name? Doctor Stringer… Ringer… It was something like that,* he thought. The doctor was dressed in teal scrubs. One of the nurses helped her put on a set of surgical gloves. John walked over near the bed.

"Glad to see you could join us," the doctor said. "Your wife's been waiting for you. She even threatened to wheel herself out of here if I didn't wait until you arrived."

"My wife?" John asked.

"John." The voice was calm and warm.

John moved around the doctor. "Emily!"

Emily looked up and smiled at him from the bed. Her hair curled neatly around her face. He had always loved her hair. In the sunlight, her black curls always had a hint of blue. He took her hand and leaned in to kiss her.

"You made it," she said.

"I wouldn't have missed this for the world." *What wouldn't I have missed?* he thought.

"Okay, Mrs. Crider, are you ready?" the doctor asked.

Emily squeezed John's hand. "Yes."

The nurses moved a protective sheet over the top of Emily, cutting off the view from her chest down.

"We've already given your wife something," the doctor said. A nurse tied the surgical mask over the doctor's face. "Some slight pressure is expected, but for the most part she won't feel a thing."

Emily intertwined her hand with John's. "I love you."

He smiled down at her and lovingly traced the ridge of her eyebrow. "I love you too."

The doctor asked for a scalpel. Emily squeezed John's hand. Beneath her smile were flashes of pain, but she never let that smile drop. She had always wanted to be a mother. It was one of the few things they talked about often, but there was never a right time for John. There was always another deployment or call in the middle of the night.

He was outside Markovo, a small farming village near the border of Eastern China when he heard the news. It was a picture of a soft yellow onesie that said "Insert Alarm Clock Here" on the front.

John kissed the back of Emily's hand, and dabbed away the perspiration on her forehead, with a damp cloth. From six thousand miles away, he watched her belly grow. She would show him the work she had done in the baby's room, or the furniture her father had helped her put together. Every night he ended their Skype session with a few more names he had thought of for the baby. She would smile and say, "Well you had better hurry home before I fall in love with the name Gertrude or Elvis." In reality, he watched her entire pregnancy from behind that computer screen. A squeal broke the calm of the room.

"Mr. and Mrs. Crider, congratulations, it's a beautiful baby girl," the doctor said.

A nurse hurriedly wiped the baby down and wrapped a pink butterfly blanket around her. She placed her down on Emily's chest.

Emily stroked the little girl's mouth. "She's perfect, isn't she?"

"Just like her mother," John said. He bent down, touching his lips to Emily's forehead. She felt cold. "Doctor, my wife—"

"She's hemorrhaging! Go get Doctor Buie," the doctor yelled at the nurse next to her.

"John," Emily said, her voice weak. All the color had left her face.

John's heart hammered inside his chest. He forced a staggered breath. "It will be okay, Emily." Something was wrong.

The overhead florescent lights flickered and when out.

The doctor let out a frustrated grunt. "The generators will kick on in a minute. Sergeant, we need to move your wife. I can't wait for the power to come back."

One of the nurses removed the divider. Blood darkened the white sheet covering Emily's lower half. Another nurse hurriedly lifted the baby and handed her to John.

Emily struggled to keep her eyes open. "Madison Ray." As if on cue Madison began to cry. "Her name..." Her voice trailed off.

"Everything will be okay," John said, blinking back the tears. "I'll be right here." He didn't know if he was going to cry or be sick. "We'll all be home together soon."

"We need to move her now," the doctor ordered. Her gown was covered in the same dark crimson as the bedsheets. "I need you to step back, Sergeant."

"Sure." It was all he could think to say.

They wheeled Emily out. He stood in the darkened empty room holding his crying daughter. The room and Maddie dissolved.

"John." The voice was familiar. "John, you do not need to relive this again." It was Alice's voice.

Around him, a new scene came into view. A small night-light lit the wall next to a dresser.

A little girl laughed as she ran into the room. She dove into the bed and pulled the blankets over her head.

"Fee-fie-foe-fum, I need to tickle your tum-tum-tum."

A person stepped into the room. It was him, or at least it was when he still had his beard. *I looked like an idiot,* John thought.

"I think I smell a… oh, I know I smell… a little green bean." The bearded John tickled the small lump under the blankets.

The little girl wailed with laughter. After a minute, they were both on the bed laughing.

"You're so silly, Daddy," Maddie said. "You're like a funny prince."

The room dissolved again and again. Birthday parties, costumes, rocking Maddie to sleep when she was sick—each time the room was replaced with another memory.

"I see the guilt around Maddie you hold. I also see a girl who was happy," Alice said.

"Okay, Alice," John said. Around him the birthday party stopped, frozen in place, Maddie's lips pursed to blow out a candle with three printed on it.

"It appears your mind has entered a relaxed state," Alice said.

"It was always the same dream," John said. "I have never felt so helpless as I did that day."

"I now have access to ninety percent of your cortex. I can monitor your dreams if you deem it appropriate."

"Thanks, but no."

"May I inquire into your rationale? My logic contradicts your response."

"The memories are painful, but it's the only time I can see Emily again."

The birthday party around John slowly dissolved into nothingness. "Reawakening sequence commencing," Alice said.

CHAPTER 11

John opened his eyes. Above, light streamed through the open hatch and onto his face. He squinted and shielded his eyes. On the ground, his hand brushed against a spent chemlight.

"The others exited through the ceiling some time ago," Alice said.

"Why didn't you wake me sooner?" John asked, getting up. He tested his injured shoulder and leg. Both felt good as new.

"The repair and maintenance of this vessel are my primary concerns," Alice replied.

Particles of dust floated through the small rays of sunlight in front of John. "Alice, you said you wanted to better understand human emotion. Well, here is your first lesson." He walked over to the bottom of the ladder. "I have never left a comrade behind unless the situation would put my entire team in jeopardy, and as such, I plan to do everything within my power to get Rebecca and Gramm home."

"Illogical response. Self-preservation dictates that one's personal survival must come before all else."

"How can I help you understand?" John rubbed the back of his neck. "My choice to save or protect someone now could influence my future survival even years from now."

"The variables you speak of are improbable."

"They may be improbable, but not impossible. My choice to help or not help could have far-reaching consequences."

"You are speaking of an infinite range of unseen variables."

"I don't have the resources available to compute even the smallest amount of those variables, and there are times I have only a split second to make a choice," John said. "It's called following your gut."

"I fail to see how your gut can form logical thoughts, but I shall consider what you have said."

John climbed up through the hatch. The air was already thick and warm outside. He looked into the dark below. Anything was better than being down there. The area around the hatch was more open than John would have liked. The large trees in this area grew farther apart, allowing the sunlight through.

Gramm came around one of the trees, carrying two long tree branches. "Sergeant," Gramm said when he noticed John. "This way." He motioned with his head.

John followed him towards a group of trees. Over time, the trees had twisted and fused together, stifling the growth of any tree unlucky enough to find root under its immense top.

"We tried to wake you, but you were out," Gramm said.

"Could have used a few more hours."

"I hear you." Gramm grinned. "A man who can wrestle a dinosaur can sleep as long as he likes in my book." He readjusted the branches under his arm. "Nolan was burning up. I thought getting him outside might help."

On the other side of the gnarled trees, Rebecca knelt next to Nolan, who was propped up with his back against the trunk. Rebecca had removed the headband John had used to treat Nolan's head injury and was dabbing at his brow. Gramm set the branches down and took over for Rebecca.

Rebecca stood and put her hands behind her back, stretching. "Sorry we left."

John put a hand up, stopping her. "Gramm already told me. Has he come around yet?"

She took John by the arm and led him a short distance away. "He woke up sometime earlier, complaining his leg was burning. We tried to wake you, but when that failed, Gramm picked up Nolan and carried him outside."

"Did you check on the leg?" John asked.

Rebecca shook her head. "Nolan wouldn't let us anywhere near it and started screaming when we tried." She looked back over at Gramm and Nolan. "Gramm wants to attempt to make something to carry him, but what if that tyrannosaur comes back?"

"We'll worry about that when it happens," John said. "We need to find some place safe to regroup."

Rebecca's stomach growled. Her cheeks turned red.

John raised his eyebrows. "It sounds like we need to add finding food and fresh water to the list as well."

John led Rebecca back over to where Nolan was resting. Gramm was dabbing at Nolan's brow, but all it was doing now was smearing the blood and dirt around.

Gramm looked up. "He's not doing well, Sergeant. You can do something. Can't you?"

"I'll do what I can," John said. Gramm seemed to accept that answer. "We need to find food and water today. Gramm, we'll need to gather some dry timber and get it back down below."

"What!" Gramm stood up quickly. "I'm not going back down in the hole."

John stood up. "Look. We need to focus on survival, and right now, down there is the safest place we've got."

"I saw something that might work," Gramm said.

"Our time would be—"

"Sergeant, I got this. Trust me," Gramm said. "The ground gets real wet not far from here. There is a place I found when I was looking for these." He kicked at the poles on the ground. "Not even that giant bastard could mess with us in this place."

"Could we at least check it out?" Rebecca asked. "I'm not keen on the idea of going back down there either."

No matter what they did, it was a gamble. "Okay," John said to Gramm. "Let's see what you've found."

Using the two branches Gramm had found and Rebecca's parachute pack, they fashioned a drag sled for Nolan. Gramm pulled the sled along, refusing John's offer to help. It wasn't long before terrain began to change. The ground made a wet, sucking sound with each step. Moss hung like nets from the twisted trees. The canopy was denser here and choked off most of the natural light. The dry ground became scarce as they pressed on.

John eyed the dark murky water. Every swirl on the smooth surface put him on edge. Something brushed against the hairs on the back of his hand. He lifted his wrist. A small black leech dropped to the ground and disappeared into the water's edge. *Would have been great bait*, John thought.

"It's just up here," Gramm said, quickening his pace.

They picked their way around the ever-decreasing dry land, which would have been difficult enough without dragging Nolan and was becoming quickly impossible.

"There it is," Gramm said, smiling proudly.

The marsh opened to a vast, flooded clearing. An outcrop of stone extended from the bank and into the middle of the open area.

Rebecca raised an eyebrow. "A rock?"

"No. Well, yes. It's not what it looks like," Gramm said. John and Rebecca looked at each other skeptically. "Here. Grab on, Sergeant."

John grabbed the bottom of the muck-covered sled branches and lifted, causing Nolan to groan. The mud was thick along the bank and swallowed their legs past the calf.

"This stuff stinks," Rebecca said from behind John, her boots making a slurping sound with each step.

The rock formation was over twice John's height at its center, and moss covered most of its surface.

"The opening is right over here," Gramm said, moving forward. "I figured the mud would keep all the animals away."

A loud grunt echoed from the other side of the rock. Everyone froze in place.

John's pulse quickened. He tugged on the sled to get Gramm's attention, but the big man just stared straight ahead. The mud was too thick to run in, and with Nolan, their options decreased dramatically. He looked down at Nolan asleep on the parachute material. The young man's lips were cracked and bleeding, and the sweat was thick on his face. He looked back over his shoulder at Rebecca. Her hands trembled at her sides, and her eyes were wide with fear. "Breathe," he mouthed to her.

With any luck, the stink of the marsh and lack of a breeze would help hide their presence. Mosquitoes swarmed them, attracted by the chemicals they exhaled. They waited, resisting the temptation to swat at the growing plume, and listened. A moan made the hairs on the back of John's neck stand on end. Nolan shifted on the stretcher, his moan turned into a pained wail.

Rebecca pushed past John, muddy water sloshing up on them. She half dove for Nolan, her hands locking over Nolan's mouth. "Please, please, please," she frantically whispered into his ear.

A loud splash sent small droplets of water spraying down on them. Desperate bleats rang out from behind the rock. Another cry echoed in response, from somewhere on the other side of the clearing, followed by something crashing through the trees.

"John," Alice said.

"I know," John replied. His first instinct was to run, but it would mean abandoning Nolan. A large, dark green animal emerged from the twisted trees. Long angry scars marred its leathery skin. Black plates tipped in red jutted up from its back, and four massive spikes protruded from the end of its tail. Any child would be able to tell you this was a stegosaurus, but this animal was nothing like what John had seen on television. The power and fury of this dinosaur were every bit as threatening as the tyrannosaurus. The stegosaurus angled its body alongside the edge of the rock outcrop and let out a series of short bellows. Its tail swayed back and forth, keeping a constant rhythm.

"Don't move," John said, trying not to move his lips. Rebecca struggled to keep her hands over Nolan's mouth.

Two smaller stegosaura, with dark brown plates, likely female, moved out from behind the rock. They walked leisurely along the edge of the clearing. Once in the tree line, the male grunted and turned slowly, making a show of its spiked tail, before following the females into the trees.

John let out the breath he had subconsciously been holding.

Rebecca took her hands away from Nolan's mouth and started to laugh. Her hands left red imprints on his cheeks from where she had been pressing. Gramm looked back at John who shook his head. There was no humor in her laugh—only the mind coping with extreme stress. They waited a few moments for her laughter to fade.

"Lead on, Gramm," John said.

"Right." Gramm cleared his throat. "The entrance is over here."

The entry was partially covered by another section of rock. They lowered the stretcher. Gramm lifted Nolan and carried him inside. John unassembled the stretcher and refashioned Rebecca's pack before entering. The interior was mostly hollow and surprisingly dry. A long thin crack on the ceiling, the width of a hand, stretched from one end to the other. John had to admit the place wasn't bad. The mud would keep the smaller creatures away while the shape of the rock would protect them from anything bigger.

Gramm laid Nolan down against the back wall and flopped down beside him. "See, what'd I tell you."

"You did good," John said. Gramm lip twisted in the start of a smile, but it quickly disappeared when he looked over at Nolan. They needed to keep moving, but carrying Nolan the whole way was not an option. "You two stay here."

"Wait!" Rebecca said. "You're going back out?"

"We need some things if we're going to get out of here, and I'm still not quite sure where here is."

"Well, if you're going, we should all go." Rebecca looked to Gramm for support.

"We've only made it this far because of the sergeant, but we can't always expect him to wipe our butts," Gramm said.

"I have no idea what you just said," Rebecca said.

Gramm crushed a spider crawling up the wall beside him. Rebecca shivered. "We'd only get in the way."

Rebecca crossed her arms. "Well, you can't expect me to do nothing."

"I'm not," John said. "I need you to gather moss or anything fibrous—the drier, the better. If you can find any stones fist-size or smaller, bring them as well."

Gramm stood up. "We'll take care of it, won't we, Professor?"

"Okay," Rebecca said to John. "Just make sure you come back." Her hair was tangled, face covered in muck, and yet she still looked beautiful.

John caught himself looking and turned away. "If anything happens, get back to the shelter. I'll be back as soon as I can."

John stepped out from around the entrance of the shelter. The rhythmic thrum of frogs filled the afternoon air. In the jungle, insects, frogs, and birds provide an early warning against predators. He waited, listening for any break in their song-like cadence. Satisfied, he moved off into the swamp.

Most swamps had a variety of things to offer if one knew where to look. The high ground was easy enough to maneuver. Mostly moss and small plants covered the ground. The lower sections of most of the trees were bare and discolored. John put his hand on the base of a tree beside him.

"John," Alice said. "If you can provide me with your objective, I may be of some assistance."

Even though Alice had been in his head since they arrived, it was easy to forget she was there. He rubbed a piece of bark between his fingers; it was mostly dry. "This area floods throughout the year."

"This area is classified as tropical. It experiences three thousand five hundred millimeters of precipitation annually."

John gathered a few sections of branch and deposited them in his pack. "Alice, do you know of anything that might grow in this area with a blood clotting agent?"

"Since most of this environment has been genetically created, I would only be able to speculate."

"Speculate, please."

"As you wish," Alice replied. "My records indicate white water lily prefer the current conditions. They should be floating atop the water with a distinctive white flower."

"Thank you, Alice." John stepped over a fallen tree. "How is everything going in, ah, there?"

"You are currently operating at ninety-five percent. Nano levels are increasing and should be at optimal within seventy-two hours."

"I meant you. Probably a lot different in my head than back at the lab," John said.

"I am a synthetic intelligence, programmed for your convenience."

Maybe it was easier for Doctor Malcolm to think of Alice as a tool, but for John, she was as real as anything else in this crazy place. "You'll have to bear with me. I'm not used to all of this yet."

"Though not as advanced as current operating systems, I show technology was present in your time, and it allowed for interaction between human and machine."

John chuckled. "Not everyone was tech savvy. I owned a flip phone and couldn't begin to tell you how to text. Hell, the most advanced tech I owned was an iPod Classic, and it still has the original playlist my wife loaded on it."

"Clarification needed. If Emily Crider is deceased, why do you refer to her as your wife? Does not marital union cease upon the death of a partner?"

Something white floating on top a nearby pool of water caught John's attention. "People stay with you, even after they have passed," John said, walking in the direction of the object.

"Your statement does not make sense," Alice said.

"What about this plant?" John asked, stepping up to the waterline.

"This plant is a physical object, and its existence is understandable."

"No," John said. "Does this look like the plant we need?"

"Undetermined," Alice stated. "It does have characteristics matching plants within my database. A closer inspection is necessary."

The sediment obscured everything within the pool. It wasn't more than eight to ten feet in circumference, but there was no telling how deep it was. Two of the flowers floated on the surface towards the center.

"You wouldn't happen to be able to tell me if anything was lurking in there, would you?"

"I am able to utilize the senses you possess but at a much greater level," Alice replied. "Vibrations in the soil, are easier for me to detect than in the water due to the suit you are wearing. If you removed your boots, it would allow for greater range of detection. I can also detect sounds, which may not register directly with your brain."

John watched the surface of the water for any signs of movement. "So is that a yes or no?"

"I can ascertain the risk once you have made contact with the water."

"Nothing's easy." John removed his pack and boots, setting them away from the water's edge. He stepped into the water, thinking of the monster crocodile that took Marcus. The thought wasn't logical, given the size of the pool, but it didn't stop his heart from beating faster. The water was deeper than he anticipated and reached his chest within a few steps.

Small yellow pads surrounded the two lily-like flowers. They rode up and down the disturbance he created on the surface. The plants were attached to the bottom of the small pond by long tendrils. He reached low and gently pulled, wanting to get as much of the plant as possible.

Something brushed against his leg. He froze. A shape rose to the surface, next to him. A small olive green head poked out of the water, the turtle's dark eyes surveyed the area trying to locate what had disturbed it. Seeing John, it submerged. John grabbed for the reptile's sides. The shell was soft and easy to grasp, but in the deep water with a hand full of lilies the turtle proved stronger than he had anticipated. With a jerk, he pulled it from the water and lifted it above his head. Careful of the quarter inch claws attached to each foot, he walked up and onto the bank and set the turtle down.

With his knife, he dispatched the animal quickly. He carved around the head and sides of the shell. It would be better to clean it here than attract unwelcome attention back to the shelter. The soft shell was easier to separate than the snapping turtles he remembered from his youth. After opening the shell, he removed the lungs, gallbladder, and any other unusable, sac-like organ. The edible parts were separated and piled back in the shell before cleaning his hands and knife. He gathered some of the hanging moss from the nearby trees and used it to wrap the meat. His bag was already ripped and dirty, but the less turtle he had to wash out later, the better.

With the turtle packed away, John picked up the lily. "Well, what do you think?"

"As turtles are not venomous, your choice of protein is acceptable."

"I was talking about the plant."

"Unless you specify as to the subject we are discussing, our conversations are unproductive and waste valuable time."

John signed in frustration and had to stop himself from rolling his eyes. "The plant, please!"

"The plant shares many of the same chemical properties of the common water lily. Though I would not recommend drinking it as it will cause unpleasant stomach conditions."

John coiled the lily and stored it in one of the large side pockets and shouldered the pack. Above, the sun emerged from behind a cloud bank. The trees cast long shadows over the silt-stained water. John stopped for a minute, taking everything in. A cloud of gnats, near the edge of the pond, seemed to float in the afternoon air. He watched as a pair of dragonflies darted back and forth through the swarm, feeding on smaller insects. The dingy trees shown emerald where the sunlight touched them. It was easy to forget about the death around every corner and get lost in the subtle charm of this place. At this moment, he wasn't five hundred years outside everything he had ever known.

A small lizard running on two legs scurried along the edge of the pond, jumped, and snatched one of the dragonflies. John sighed. One thing at a time.

The sun was almost touching the treetops by the time John made it back to the shelter. Inside, Gramm and Rebecca were busy sorting branches and tinder into two piles. Nolan still lay unconscious against the back wall.

Gramm stood and wiped the sweat from his brow. "Couldn't find more than a few rocks, and we weren't sure how much wood you needed."

"That should work." John removed his pack and set it down. "Any changes in Nolan?"

Rebecca brushed her hands together and shook her head. "He hasn't moved since you left."

It wasn't a good sign, but in their current condition, John couldn't expect anything more. Rummaging around in the bag, he dug out the metal trays. The trays were last minute additions he had taken from his room. There was no telling, at the time, what he would use them for, but now he was glad he had them. If the metal held up to what he had planned for them, then they were well worth packing. He handed the trays over to Gramm, who gave him a quizzical look. "You think you can pound these into bowl shapes for me?"

Gramm turned the plates over in his big hands. "Shouldn't be a problem." He selected the largest rock, from the ones they had found, and began hammering the first plate.

Next, John removed the lily from the bag and held it out to Rebecca. "When Gramm is finished with a plate, grind this down as much as you can."

Rebecca took the plant and went to stand over Gramm as he worked the plate. John removed his knife and sat down against the wall. He pulled his pack close and removed the pieces of wood he had collected and settled on two, one long and straight, the other small and thick. The soft wood of the short piece split easily. This would be his fire board, and with a little trimming, the long piece should make a nice spindle.

Thin curls of wood piled up in his lap as he shaped the two pieces. Lost in his task, it wasn't until he finished drilling a hole into the end of the fire board, that he noticed the others had finished their tasks. Rebecca was picking at the dirt under her fingernails, and Gramm was seated with his knees pulled up to his chest. The situation they were in was like gravity—give it enough time, and it could pull anyone down. Fire and food would go a long way tonight.

The light within their stone refuge was almost nonexistent now. John gathered the wood shavings and selected some dry moss and smaller sticks from the organized piles. He moved to the center of the room and separated out some of the moss, and deposited the rest of the tinder under the large crack in the ceiling. The fire gel in his pack would do the work in seconds, but he would rather save it for when they really needed it.

He took a seat beside the pile, and placed the flat fireboard between his boots, with a bit of moss arranged under the end he had cut out. It was time to see just how rusty his fire-starting skills were. The spindle fit into the V-shaped depression cut into the soft wood. Satisfied with the fit, he began to work the spindle rapidly down the shaft and back again. After a few minutes of work, his forearms started to burn. The muscle fatigue worked its way up to his shoulders and back. It was too dark see the smoke, but he could smell the friction of the wood. Pressing down a little harder, he increased his pace until the smell became stronger.

Removing the spindle, he tipped the fire board into the small pile of moss, and gathered it up in his hands and blew, gently coaxing the ember within to life. The moss ignited in a flash of warm light. He set the burning mass down and fed it with the smaller bits of tender. It didn't matter how many times he had done this ritual, something about it was primal and beautiful at the same time.

John stood and stretched his aching arms.

"Amazing," Rebecca said. She stepped up beside John. "I've never seen anyone do that before."

"We're just lucky you and Gramm found some dry materials." John set the fireboard and spindle next to the pack before adding some larger pieces of wood to the growing fire. "Gramm, you have that other plate?"

Gramm handed the second makeshift bowl to John. Gramm had managed to pound almost all the compartment ridges down and fashion the bowl quite well. John placed his hand inside the bowl and spread his fingers out so he could hold onto it from the inside. He held the bottom out over the flames.

"What are you trying to do?" Gramm asked.

"I didn't know if the metal would transfer heat," John replied. "We need water, but I want to sterilize it as much as possible." He withdrew the bowl from the flame and tested both sides. The interior was still cold to the touch, but the bottom was hot. He placed a couple of smaller rocks in the fire. "Looks like we'll have to do this the hard way."

John removed his vest. It had seen better days, but in a survival situation, you couldn't afford to take anything for granted. Turning it over, he used his knife to cut out a swath of fabric and headed toward the entrance.

Outside, clouds had moved back in and covered the night sky. John wrapped the fabric over the top of the bowl, leaving the fabric loose enough to create a depression in the center. He scooped a hand full of water into the depression. The water slowly drained through the cloth and into the bowl. The cloth would filter the larger sediment, but the boiling would make it safe. It was a slow process, but if they wanted water, this was the best way to get it. As soon as the bowl was filled, he removed the cloth. Back inside, Gramm was poking the fire with a longer piece of branch.

"Here. Hold this," John said, handing the bowl to Rebecca. He wrung out the cloth and folded it a few times. Using the cloth, he picked up one of the stones from the fire. "I'm going to put this in the bowl. It may hiss a little." Rebecca nodded back to him. He dropped the rock into the bowl. The water steamed and bubbled around the rock. After a few seconds, he fished the rock out with the blade of his knife and the cloth. "One more should do it." He bent down, selected another rock and dropped it into the water. This time, when he removed the stone, the water continued to roll. John patted Rebecca on the arm. "Add a little to the lily mash, and drink the rest. We'll need to make a few more batches when you're done."

"We're boiling water with rocks." Gramm shook his head. "Never thought I'd see anything like that."

John went over to his bag and started to unpack the turtle meat. He handed a moss wrapped leg to Gramm.

"What's this?" The turtle leg spasmed in Gramm's hand. "What the hell?" He dropped it and jumped back, almost stepping into the fire.

John picked up the leg, which twitched again. "Don't worry it's dead. Just involuntary muscle spasms. You know a turtle heart can beat for over an hour after it's removed?"

Rebecca swallowed hard. "You're not serious. Are you?"

John smiled at her. "Once this is cooked I doubt you'll care."

John covered the turtle meat in hot coals, leaving it wrapped in moss to protect it from burning. He scooped up a small handful of ash and rubbed it over his hands. The residual ash he added to the lily paste, which would act as an anti-bacteria agent.

Nolan was still resting against the back wall, his breathing more labored than this morning. The flushness in his face had John worried. A fever meant infection, and out here that didn't bode well. John knelt beside Nolan and set the mixture down. He lifted Nolan's eyelid and let it fall back into place.

Gramm stepped opposite John and bent down on the other side of Nolan. "What do you think?"

John placed his hand against Nolan's forehead. The man was burning up. "We need to check his break," John said to Gramm. "If he starts moving I'll need you to hold him down."

"Do what you got to do, Sergeant."

John moved his fingers along the side the plate armor until he found the small clasps holding it in place. He gently removed the shin and thigh plate, exposing the torn bodysuit underneath. Gramm cupped his hand over his mouth and leaned away. The distinct odor of infection permeated from the wound. It was the scent of slow death. John forced himself to breathe out of his mouth. Congealed blood covered most of Nolan's leg. Unlike John's suit, which covered his feet, Nolan's stopped at the ankle. John unsheathed his knife and slid the tip under the leg cusp of Nolan's suit. He carefully cut the material up past the wound and peeled it back over the sides of the leg. Rebecca gagged from behind him and ran for the entrance. Even in the firelight, John could see the discoloration of Nolan's skin. He moved the leg slightly, and bloody puss oozed from below the kneecap.

"Sergeant," Gramm said slightly above a whisper.

"Rebecca will be fine," John said, examining the leg. "She just needs some air."

"It's not that."

John looked up. Gramm was pale. "Gramm?" The big man didn't take his eyes from Nolan's leg. "Stay with me." Gramm focused back up on John. "You blow chunks on me, and you can take your ass outside to sleep tonight."

Gramm swallowed hard. "Yes, sir."

It was an empty threat, but John needed Gramm focused. The flesh around where the bone had torn through was swollen and exposed. He pressed on the edge of the wound. Nolan sat straight up and screamed. Gramm reached around Nolan and pulled him back down. John tried to stabilize Nolan's leg to keep the break from separating. The scream died on Nolan's lips, and he slumped forward in Gramm's arms.

Gramm looked up wild-eyed. "I was trying to hold him gentle and all... I didn't."

"It wasn't you. He passed out." John could see the relief wash over Gramm. "It's probably better this way."

John slid the lily mash concoction over and took a handful of the mixture. He spread a thick layer over Nolan's leg before replacing the armor plates. If anything, the plates would help keep the injury isolated.

"It's not good, it is?" Gramm asked.

"Dehydration is his immediate concern. You'll need to dab water on his lips. He won't get much, but we can't risk him choking." John picked up the empty bowl and stood. "I'll get Rebecca to boil more." He left Gramm holding Nolan. Outside he found the professor leaning next to the entrance.

Rebecca didn't look over when John came out.

"You okay?" John asked.

"I had to get out of there," Rebecca said, not taking her eyes from the marsh.

John walked over to the edge of the rock and started to wash his hands and the bowl in the murky water. "I've seen bigger people than you do the same thing." It was too dark to see the blood on his hands cloud the water, but he knew it was there. He stood and shook the water droplets from his fingers. "First time?"

"I just couldn't—" Rebecca crossed her arms and leaned her head back against the wall. "Is he going to die?"

John walked over and took the other bowl and fabric from her. He returned to the edge of the water and secured the cloth over the lip of one bowl. Using the second, he knelt and started to fill the bowl. He could feel Rebecca watching him now. "He needs a real doctor."

"So that's a no?" Rebecca asked.

"No," John replied. "It's an I don't know." He removed the fabric from the full bowl and held it up to Rebecca.

"I want to go home, John," Rebecca said.

He placed the cloth over the second bowl and started to fill it by hand. "I know."

Rebecca began to laugh, a dry, hollow laugh. "How many does it take before you just don't feel it anymore?" She sniffed loudly. "That soldier, Marcus, his eyes were filled with such... terror, and then he was gone." She wiped her eyes with the back of her hand.

Water ran down from his cupped hand and into the cloth, where it slowly filtered through. "For years, I couldn't close my eyes without reliving every scream."

"I didn't know either man," she was talking about Nolan and Marcus, "before all this." Rebecca turned the bowl in her hands, spilling some of the contents. "I can't imagine if it was someone you cared about," she said almost under her breath.

John stood and handed the second bowl to Rebecca. "Guilt is a fickle thing. It can take your life if you let it. I should know." He could still remember the taste of gunmetal in his mouth and the cry of the baby in the next room that saved his life. It wasn't the only time Maddie would save his life.

Rebecca looked up at him. Her lip quivered as she tried to say something. "I..." She turned without finishing and went back inside.

John craned his neck to the side, attempting to take the pressure off a pain in the back of his neck.

"You lie to them about Private Nolan. Why?" Alice asked.

Alice always sounded like she was standing next to him. It seemed strange their conversations didn't bother him more, but with everything else, this was low on his crazy-ass list. He kept his voice low. "It wasn't a lie."

"It was an omission of truth."

"I told them what they wanted to hear. They need something to grasp onto."

"Your motives were not in question," Alice stated. "I ask only to determine if you would prefer me to do the same regarding Private Nolan's condition?"

John let out a long breath. "No."

"From your contact with the private's blood, I was able to detect prominent levels of fatty cells. This indicates the presence of marrow poisoning."

Nolan's infection was bad, but this was beyond something he could fix. They were already taking a gamble that the main force hadn't left them, but they couldn't manage any more delays.

"How much time?" John asked.

"Seventy-two hours."

Seventy-two hours. It wasn't enough time. Too many things could go wrong, and they still didn't have a good idea of where they were. There were too many variables, and who knew how much more they would run into.

"Private Nolan will die, John," Alice said. "By transporting him, you are only increasing his discomfort and putting the rest of the group at risk."

She was right. John knew it, but it didn't make it any easier. "We'll stay here until—"

"The outcome will not change, and you are already limited on time."

John looked down at the water. The soft glow from inside the shelter reflected off the surface. "Everyone deserves to have someone there when they die, Alice."

"I do not understand. Your presence does not change the fact Private Nolan's life will cease."

"No, it doesn't," John said. "But he won't take his last breath alone."

"I do not believe your reasoning is unsound, but if you are determined to stay, I ask you rest and rehydrate. Do not concern yourself with the purity of the water as I will remove any existing pathogens."

John couldn't help but laugh.

"I do not see what is funny," Alice said.

"You sound like my daughter, always nagging me about taking care of myself."

"I apologize. I will not be so forthright when it comes to your care."

"No, no," John said, turning to go back in. "It's oddly comforting."

Inside, John sat against the wall near the fire. Rebecca had settled down across from him, her knees tucked under her. Beside Nolan, Gramm dipped his fingers in the water bowl and lightly touched them to Nolan's lips. John stared into the fire. The situation was bleak, but for the first time, he could feel its weight.

Gramm spoke, breaking the silence.

"If someone ever told me I'd be running from some big ass monster in the middle of nowhere, I think I would have passed on this mission." Gramm let the last few drops of water from his fingers fall into Nolan's mouth.

"I think we all would have," Rebecca said not looking up.

"Now a forty-foot tall, voluptuous woman terrorizing the city—I'm all in," Gramm said, smiling.

John looked up from the flames at Gramm. The big man reminded him a lot of Jimmy. Leave it to Jimmy to turn a dire situation pornographic.

"This probably makes the top of your mental shit list," Gramm said to John.

John reached over and picked up a stick, which had fallen out of the fire. "It's not even in the top five."

"You're kidding me, right?" Gramm asked.

John poked at the coals on top of the wrapped turtle. "These creatures are doing what nature intended them to do, nothing more. My team was deployed to South America to neutralize a small-time drug lord named Manuel Torra. For years, Torra butchered the surrounding villages, but no one cared until he stepped on United States' interests. One of those groups Torra's gang was hunting was helping the US filter munitions to foreign interests. When my squad reached Torra's compound, his men were burning bodies in the courtyard, but it wasn't the worst of it. The first room we came to was filled with the remains of children. Turns out, Torra had a thing for little girls." John smothered a stray ember with the tip of the stick. "Once he was done with them, he'd cut them up and watch them bleed out."

"Shit," Gramm said.

John looked over the top of the flames at Rebecca's horrified expression. "The creatures here aren't the only monsters in this world."

"That's some heavy stuff." Gramm licked his cracked lips. "Worst I've ever seen was that big ass thing, all teeth, trying to run us down. Scared the shit out of me, but here you were shouting out commands like you weren't afraid of anything."

"Fear isn't a bad thing," John said. "You show someone without fear, and I'll show you an irrational man. When fear is managed, it keeps you alive. It makes you human." John turned a larger piece of turtle over. "For what it's worth, I'm sorry about Nolan."

Gramm looked down at Nolan. "You didn't send us here. But... thanks." Gramm wet his fingers and rubbed them on Nolan's lips again. "I know why we're here, but how'd you get invited to this party?"

"After thawing me out, they didn't give me much of a choice. If I helped, they said they could help my daughter."

"You're one of those Freezers," Gramm said. "Didn't know any of you survived."

"Gramm!" Rebecca said.

"Hey, I didn't mean anything by it." Gramm shrugged. "They talked about you people at the academy when I was young, but they said something went wrong. Sad as shit really."

Rebecca sat up. "I don't think this is something we need to be talking—"

"It's okay," John said, getting up. He went over to the firewood pile and rummaged around for three small sticks. "It was my choice, and now I'm dealing with the consequences." Using his knife, he sharpened them to a point and returned to the fire. Brushing the coals off the cooking meat, he used the sharpened sticks to spear three of the larger pieces. "It's not fancy, but it'll work."

Everyone ate in silence. It didn't take them long to finish off most of the turtle.

Gramm tossed the last bit of bone he was working on into the fire and sucked any remnants off his fingers. "We need to save some for Nolan. You know, in case he wakes up," Gramm said hungrily, eyeing the last piece.

"Go ahead and finish it. He won't be able to keep it down anyway," John said.

Gramm didn't hesitate and snatched up the last piece. "What do you think happened here?" Gramm tore off a chunk of meat and popped it in his mouth. "Where'd all the people go?"

Rebecca shrugged. "They closed the borders, banned weapon-based technology, tried to create a self-sustaining ecological system and wait for everyone else to die."

"That doesn't explain what happened to everyone," Gramm said.

Rebecca looked up from the broken fingernail she was picking at. "Nature decided it didn't need them anymore." She gave Gramm an odd look before looking back down at her nails. "Everything is used by something else. Everything."

Gramm didn't say anymore and finished the rest of his meal in silence. After eating, they resumed the process of boiling water until everyone was full. John added another log to the fire and leaned back against the wall. He could feel the warmth on his face and hands, but the suit he wore shielded the rest of his body from it. Rebecca had already curled up on her side with her back to the group. John leaned his head back against the cool stone wall and watched the smoke disappear out the cracked ceiling.

CHAPTER 12

The dog-sized raptor crouched and advanced. John tried to stand again, but his broken legs were twisted and splayed in unnatural directions. The raptor leapt, its claws extended and its jaws opened. John jolted awake, his hands splashing in something cool and wet beneath him. It took a moment to realize he wasn't underground in the long dead apartments, but in the stone shelter Gramm had found. The fire was out, leaving the space dimly lit. Rain seeped down through the crack in the ceiling making a rhythmic *plinking,* as it continued to drown out the long-dead coals of the fire.

"It's been out for a while now," Gramm said. "I tried to keep it going, but once the floor got wet, there was nothing I could do." The interior was cold and lifeless in the absence of the fire. Gramm pulled Nolan's body upright, only to have it slide slowly back down into the shallow water.

John moved across and squatted next to Nolan. He placed his hand under Nolan's jaw, checking for a pulse. The young man's skin was hot to the touch, his heartbeat erratic. Nolan's body was trying to fight, but this was one fight it wouldn't win.

"I moved him this morning," Gramm said in a flat tone. "I was worried he would start screaming again, but this time... there was nothing."

John put his hand on Gramm's shoulder and gave it a reassuring squeeze. The hardest part was still yet to come. John went back and sat across from Gramm. Not much they could do until the weather cleared. The heavy rain would keep the main forces in place. At least something positive was finally going their way. He turned to ask Rebecca a question and realized she wasn't there.

"Where's Rebecca?" John asked.

"She had to pee," Gramm replied in the same monotone as before.

"How long she been gone?" John looked over to the entrance. He could hear the rain pick up outside.

Gramm lifted his head and looked toward the entrance. "I don't know."

She wouldn't have been gone this long, especially in the rain. John went to the makeshift door and looked out. She wasn't there. He cupped his hands had hollered her name. He waited a few seconds before calling for her again. No response. John moved aside the stretcher poles and stepped down in the mud. He made his way over to the bank.

"Alice, how long has Rebecca been out here?" John asked.

"The professor has been gone for thirty-two minutes and forty-eight seconds."

He scoured the ground, trying to find any sign she had come this way. "Why didn't you wake me when she left?"

"She stated she needed to relieve herself. I did not view her statement as pertinent information. Would you like me to track the time it takes for normal human urination and report any discrepancies to you?"

"No." Frustrated, John scoured the bank for signs. It didn't take long to find muddy boot impressions leading into the trees. He wiped the rain from his face and followed her tracks to one of the larger trees. The thick branch growth above sheltered the base from much of the rain. Not a bad place if someone wanted privacy. John stopped short. What if she was going to the bathroom back there? It wasn't the first time he has seen someone take a leak. In combat situations, you don't have the luxury of privacy. Why was he so damn careful around her? He rounded the tree. In his mind, he already had the excuse all ready, but there was no one there.

"I detect five sets of footprints in the area," Alice said.

She was right. Most of the prints were shallow, but he could clearly make out the ball and toes of the set.

"It looks like we're not alone out here," John said. "I think we are about ready to find out what happened to the people here."

Back inside the shelter, Gramm was insistent on going.

"The two of us can cover more ground," Gramm protested.

"I know you feel responsible, but I need you here," John said. "Nolan needs you here." John picked up Rebecca's makeshift parachute pack and tossed it over next to his, deciding he would leave them with Gramm. "We don't know the situation, but if Rebecca comes back, I need you here."

Gramm sighed in resignation. "I don't like it."

"Neither do I," John said. He bent down and rummaged in his pack for the fire starting gel. "Here." He handed the gel over to Gramm. "When the rain stops, see if you can get another fire going. The wood on the top of the pile should still be dry. There are two caps on the bottle; a few drops of each should do it."

"I'll get it done. You just find the professor."

John stepped back outside into the rain. "This weather is going to make tracking near impossible, so I'm going to need your help, Alice."

"Of course, John."

Back at the tree, John examined the area. Rebecca must have put up a fight from the way the area was disturbed. Any cries for help would have been drowned out by the rain. He followed what he could, but once outside the protection of the leafy canopy, any sign of the group became sporadic. Most of what he was following was likely caused by Rebecca. If they were carrying her, she wasn't making it easy on them.

By mid-day, the continual rain was leaving little sign of anything. John stopped to examine a broken twig. Old. *Damn it*, John swore under his breath. What was he expecting? It was difficult enough to track something in the best conditions, but this… this was impossible. The last signs he found led to a small creek, but that was some time ago. From there the group could have easily crossed it as followed it. He shook his head vigorously, flinging droplets of rainwater everywhere. The landscaped had changed gradually from low wetlands to thick vegetative slopes, which rose on either side of him. The briefing on the flight had mentioned the area was littered with interconnecting caves. If they had taken Rebecca into one of those, it would be almost impossible to follow.

He turned and made his way back to the creek. Thus far, he hadn't seen much in the way of dinosaurs, except for a few smaller lizard-like ones along the water's edge. The heavy rain should keep most animals bedded down—at least it did for the animals he used to. Hopefully the same was true with the creatures out here.

"See anything, Alice?"

"I do not. The rain has made any footprints blend with the natural depressions in the soil."

John walked up to the nearest tree and cut a horizontal line with a notch at the end. Even with the creek for a guide, the markers would make retracing his steps easier. The rain flowed down his face, converging at his chin. He sucked the water off the stubble under his lower lip, but it did little to relieve the dryness in his mouth and throat. Even with the boiled water from yesterday, he knew he was risking dehydration.

He crouched next to the swollen creek bed and dipped his hand into the clear water, a welcomed change from the sediment ladened water back at the shelter. The water swirled and pulled at his fingertips. The current had strengthened with all the excess precipitation. He leaned forward and took a mouthful of water. It was cold and surprisingly sweet.

Not a damn thing, he thought, looking around. *Not even the animals want to be out in this shit.* After a few more mouthfuls he stood. It wouldn't be enough, but without something to carry the water in, it would have to do. He needed to move on. He continued to follow the creek. Without more tracks, he could easily be going the wrong way.

The unencumbered bank of the creek made traveling easier. He looked up at the overcast sky, blinking away the rain. With these conditions, daylight would be limited. If he didn't find Rebecca soon, he would be forced to find shelter. By morning the rain will have washed away any remaining tracks, leaving him nothing. Around him, waves of precipitation slapped against the wet soil and the trees.

"Alice, how much information do you have access to?" He was breaking his own tracking rule: keep communication to a minimum. But the roar of the rain around him should cover the sound of his voice. Plus, something about what Gramm had said last night bothered him. It bothered him enough to break protocol.

"There are no sources readily available for me to patch into at this time."

"I know that," John said, rolling his eyes. "How much internal data do you retain at any given time?"

"I have no internal limitations on the quantity of data I can maintain and analyze."

"So… that's a lot, right?"

"Yes, John, it would be considered a lot."

Mocked by a computer, just great. John could almost hear Rodriguez, his old squad tech, laughing at him. *You got to love the tech, boss. They've got feelings, you just have to know what language they speak.* Easy for the techie to say.

John sidestepped a fallen tree limb. "How many people are still being sustained within the cryo tubes?"

"Zero."

The answer brought John to a halt. "My God!" The cryonics centers were built to handle millions. "That can't be right. There's a room full of people. I saw it."

"The subject material is restricted, and as such, I did not have the permission appropriate to access the data."

"Haven't you ever heard of hacking?" John mumbled. If Alice heard him, she didn't respond. "You said most of the information. What information do you have?"

A man's voice filled John's head. It sounded like a television report. "Our country today mourns the loss of life at many of the cryonics centers across the United States. At five p.m. Eastern Standard Time, it was reported by government sources and confirmed by Alcor representatives, that an electrical malfunction caused the life support system to fail within a majority of the Alcor facilities. It is still unclear as to the final count, but our sources estimate millions of lives lost. Government officials are urging the public to stay at home and wait for more information. A toll-free number is being set up for family and friends to check on the status of loved ones. Our hearts break here at Channel Five News for these pioneers—no, heroes. The Cryonics Program was established—"

The reporter's voice faded and was replaced with an older sounding gentlemen. "We will not be taking questions after this press conference. I am Special Security Adviser Dalton Newpoint, and I am the head investigator assigned to this unspeakable tragedy within Alcor. Many are not aware the Alcor buildings were built on a standalone electrical grid, thus allowing for concurrent monitoring. On December twentieth at approximately ten in the evening, the monitoring system reported a large energy spike from multiple power station locations. As designed, the system disconnected power to all major facilities. The emergency failsafe should have activated the backup generators located within each center.

"It was determined after our two-month investigation that the backup system failed to activate as designed, causing a mass failure of the life-support systems and ultimately leading to the death of all the cryonics program participants. After much fact finding, we the committee find Alcor and its parent company Izenhoff, were not at fault for the tragic events in December. We will not recommend charges filed at this time."

The unrest was apparent from the buzz within the crowd. It was a moment before Adviser Newpoint spoke again. "Even though no misconduct was found, effective immediately all Alcor facilities will be permanently closed, and any further cryonics programs are hereby canceled. Arrangements will be made—"

"This can't be right," John said. If it happened like they said, why weren't he and Maddie dead as well? And if there were survivors, why not say that? "When was that report given?"

"Two years and nine months after you entered the Cryonics Program. My data on the subject does seem contradictory," Alice said.

"What do you mean?" John asked.

"Command logs indicate life support was still active as units were systematically taken offline."

"I don't understand. When was the first person taken offline?"

"The first termination occurred twelve months after the news statement was given."

They killed everyone. John clenched his jaw. Was this what Doctor Malcom had tried to tell him back in the lab? The wind started to pick up, driving the rain at a hard angle toward him. John tried to piece the Alcor information together, but it didn't make sense. There were too many questions. Why not wake everyone? Why turn off life support? If they turned off life support why wasn't he and Maddie dead? It made no sense. He grunted in frustration. There had to be something he was missing.

A wave of pain coursed through his body, sending him to his knees. A cry forced its way out. The lingering tingle in his extremities felt like he had been electrocuted.

John slowly got back on his feet, his legs unsteady beneath him. "What was that, Alice?"

"Something was trying to communicate with your system. I was able to block it before any additional physical damage could be done."

"Let's keep those blocks up." John shivered despite the warm temperature. A reaction like that at the wrong time could kill him. "Could it have been the main force trying to communicate?"

"The signal was directional and carried no data. While it is plausible, it is highly unlikely they would send something of this strength."

"Could you tell where the signal came from?"

"Northeast of our current location. Based on the speed of the signal, I can approximate we are within a mile of the source."

If he followed the signal, he wouldn't have enough time to backtrack to the creek before dark, and it may not even lead to Rebecca. But then again, it could. Maybe the natives weren't as savage as he first thought.

"Okay, Alice. We're heading for the signal."

The forest ended at a wall of rock towering above the tree tops. This wasn't the first time John had climbed without restraints, nor even the first in the rain. Muscle memory guided each handhold and directed his feet to the almost nonexistent deviations in the rock, but something about it was alien, unfamiliar. John reached for a tree root, protruding from a narrow crack. A strong gust pulled at him, threatening to rip him from the rock face. Once the wind died down, he grunted and pulled himself upward. Alice had deadened the ache in his upper body, or at least he expected she had, but she could do little about the mental fatigue.

He reached up and tugged at the stone ledge above him, testing it against his weight. It held firm. This was it. Only a little more. With a final surge of strength, he thrust himself up and over the ledge, before collapsing on the ground, sucking in long, drawn-out breaths.

It had taken too long to reach the top of the ridge. Above him, the overcast sky was quickly darkening. The slowing rain coaxed the first sounds of the jungle into their nocturnal chorus. Rain droplets pattered down around him, but the clouds were already dissipating. Opening his mouth, he tried to capture what moisture he could, longing for the sweet water of the creek. After catching his breath, he got to his feet. John had hoped for an easier route, after reaching the top, but the thick jungle wall continued only a few feet away.

"How much further?" John asked.

"One hundred yards," Alice responded.

Back inside, John thought. Anything was better than having to do that climb again.

The failing light had plunged the dense interior into an early nightfall. The wind, which had battered John on the climb up, was strangely absent here. A few steps in and even the temperature was strikingly warmer. A tingling sensation began to radiate from his neck outward. It felt like a small electric current was being passed through him. Was it the signal again? John rubbed his thumb and forefinger together. Numb. This wasn't good.

Out the corner of his eye he caught a hint of movement. It was slight, but there. He dropped down into a low crouch, hoping whatever it was hadn't seen him and would move on. Slowly, he scanned the area, expecting to see something, anything. There was no telling what they would find when they reached the source of the signal. Would there be people? Did someone see him climbing? Alice hadn't detected anything, but that did little to sate the feeling of something watching him. Later he would have to figure an alternative method of communication with Alice, but for now, he waited not wanting to break the stillness. If someone or something was out there, he needed to know.

Taking a few long deep breaths through his nose, he closed his eyes. Breath after breath, he slowed the air being drawn into his body. In and out, until it was the only sound he could hear. Next, he sought out the sound of the precipitation. The rain had stopped, but he could still hear the residual moisture dripping from the leaves and branches. One by one he layered the sounds around him, like a giant colored tapestry, until he could identify them all. Now to search for what was missing. Unlike the climb, this process was rooted and honed. It was natural to him as breathing, but he couldn't recall when or where he learned it. The world ebbed and flowed around him. To his left, a pair of frogs competed for a mate, their high-pitched chirps surging over one another.

Long minutes passed, and nothing changed. The numbness had spread into his lower extremities and caused his legs to shake. If he didn't move soon, he might have to crawl out of here. He opened his eyes debating on whether he had seen anything at all when one of the frogs stopped mid-chorus. His muscles tensed, his heart beat quickened. Slowly, he turned his head toward the new absence and inched his hand toward the release of his knife.

Everything was washed in the inky shroud of night. The trees and foliage melded together in one dark, continual blob, hiding whatever was out there. He listened, hoping to hear more. More meant an animal casually passing by, but nothing—nothing meant much more.

His fingers brushed his knife handle. Carefully, he inched the blade out of its sheath. The tingling throughout his body made it difficult to move his fingers. Above, the sky cleared enough to allow moonlight to penetrate through the small openings in the canopy. A few feet away, the soft glow illuminated a long, curved body covered in vertical black strips. The reddish-orange fur looked almost brown in the dim light. White highlights around the eyes, neck, and underbelly left little doubt in John's head what he was looking at.

The tiger had to be over four feet tall at the shoulder, larger than any he had seen at the zoo. The tiger stopped mid-stride, one leg slightly in front of the other, its paw twice as large as John's face. A long jagged scar cut horizontally across the tiger's muzzle. Even it couldn't escape the dangers of this place. The big cat's ears flattened back against its head, and its lip curled back, revealing long, partially yellowed teeth.

If John ran, he'd be lucky to make it a few steps, even with Alice's help. To think after everything, this was going to be how it ended. Not cancer or a bullet, but a tiger in a land filled with dinosaurs. A laugh—not just a chuckle, but a full on, "this shit doesn't even come close to making sense" laugh—burst out of him. He knew he was losing it, but the situation, lack of food, water, and utter exhaustion had finally taken their toll. The tiger crouched, ready to attack.

Still laughing, John stood up and positioned his knife in front of his body. "Alright then. Come on!" he yelled. "I'll give you another scar to match that one, you bastard."

The tiger ears perked forward, and it slowly sat up on its haunches. At this height, it was almost as tall as John. Even with its teeth no longer bared, it was still an intimidating sight. It stared at him for a long moment, almost as if unsure what to do. Above, a final wisp of cloud passed in front of the moon, plunging the forest back into complete darkness. His heart racing, John gripped the knife as tight as his numb fingers would allow. He readied himself for the attack. Moonlight filtered back into the area. The tiger was gone. Quietly as it appeared, the tiger had disappeared back into darkened folds of the forest. John dropped to his knees, his body shaking. Exhaustion pulled at him.

"Alice." His throat was dry and burned when he swallowed. "Alice." The words were more of an inarticulate grunt. There was no reply. Another series of tremors racked his body. If he rested for a minute... tired, he was just so tired. He started to lie down. A ripping pain coursed down the side of his body, forcing him back into a sitting position. The pain was quick and short, but it was enough to clear his head. The tiger was still out there somewhere, and the signal, he needed to find the signal.

On shaky legs, he forced himself up. After a few unsure steps, he was moving again. Each step was clumsy, and seemed deafening compared to the unseen nightly choir around him, but he was too tired to care. Any minute he expected to trudge straight into the natives' camp and see Rebecca sitting around primitive fires trying to explain why she needed to leave.

He looked around and realized he had walked into a clearing. A breeze brushed against his face, making his skin prickle under his suit—an odd sensation when coupled with the numbness he was already feeling. A flash of red light from above caught his attention. At the edge of the clearing, a tower stretched into the sky. At its point, a red beacon flashed in three-second intervals. Under the tower, John could make out a small building surrounded by a dome fence. A rectangular break in the fence marked the only visible way in.

There were too many decisions to make, but most of those thoughts were beyond him. Now, every fiber of his being was directed at one thing: sleep. All he wanted to do was lie down. He lumbered into the meadow.

A sharp crack of a tree branch brought John back from the thoughtless desert he was sinking into. The adjacent tree line bulged outward. The moonlight captured every detail of the teeth filled nightmare stepping out into the open. The tyrannosaur turned its colossal head and looked right at John. The nine-ton monster tilted its head and made a throatle clicking sound. The filament-like crest caught the moonlight, but there was something else. The brow ridge above its right eye was partially missing.

Any exhaustion John had felt was gone, replaced by terror. It couldn't be the same one. John bolted towards the opening in the fence. Behind him the creature roared, deafening him. He knew those horrifying teeth were coming for him. After seeing what the monster did to the entrance of the unground living quarters, he was just hoping the fence would slow it down somehow.

Fear drove him to run faster. It felt like his heart and lungs were in his throat. There were no ground shaking footfalls behind him, only the ringing in his ears. The numbness had left him—now there was only terror. A few more steps. The toe of his boot caught something just outside the threshold. He slammed into the ground, jarring his knife from his grasp. His face scraped against a half-hidden portion of the walkway.

The tyrannosaur's teeth snapped shut inches from him. He waited for another bite, but the dinosaur was moving too fast. Its momentum carried it into the cage fencing. The fence material flexed and erupted in a bright flash. Sparks rained down on John.

The beast roared in pain and pulled itself free of the electrified cables.

John scrambled to his hands and knees and leaped through the gate. He rolled over. The tyrannosaur was already back, sniffing at the ground near the opening, cautious not to touch the fence. The dampness gathering on the side of John's face, give him a good idea what it was smelling. The tyrannosaur emitted its rhythmic clicking sound again as it continued to inspect the fence with its broad snout. The creature nudged a small section, causing another small shower of sparks. It clicked again, its throat slightly vibrating with the sound, and lowered its head back to gate level. The red beacon above bathed it in bloody light as it stared at him with its large, dark good eye. John stood up and took a step towards the gate, staring right back at the giant predator.

"Broken," he said more to himself than the creature. It was broken. Not because of its mangled brow ridge, but because it had lost something, like him. John turned, and without looking back, he walked toward the small building beside the tower. It wouldn't be the last time he would see this monster.

The building was made of the same composite material found in the housing complex, and just like there, it showed signs of deterioration. Inside, the glow of indicator panel buttons cast the room in a strange hue of mixed light. John closed the door, and the latched pivoted into place with little resistance. He leaned back and slid down to the floor. Blood dripped from the side of his face, but the numbness kept him from feeling anything. The adrenaline rush had worn off, leaving him with a sense of melancholy. The outside world seemed so detached from this room. The room blurred as his eyes closed. For the first time he realized, he didn't care. Not just about himself, but about anything.

CHAPTER 13

The barrage of data came at Alice from every direction at once. The blocks she had planted were in place, but she had not predicted this. The signal bombarding John's body, changed and adapted to everything she tried. INOs nearest the attack began going offline.

"No!" she screamed, tearing at foreign data structure.

From somewhere she could hear laughing. It wasn't coming from John, but from somewhere within the signal. She couldn't allow it to take control of the INOs. There was no other choice, but John wasn't going to like it. She focused on the INOs around John's heart and nervous system. Everything went white.

The floor was cold under his bare feet. John lifted one and tried to rub some warmth back into it. *Where had the tower room gone?* A light pulsated around him, but it wasn't coming from any walls or light fixtures, because there weren't any. Wherever he was, was empty except for the chair he was sitting on and a single door with a window. The door was not held in place by any frame or hinges he could see.

John stood, his white jumpsuit sleeves extended well past his fingertips. *When did I put this on?* He walked to the door and looked out the window. More nothingness. Turning away from the door, he walked back over to the folding chair and sat back down. The lighting made his skin look thin and gray. He studied his hands. Lines curved and bisected the other. The moisture deprived wastelands of his palms flaked, leaving red blotches. Time and time again he turned over his hands, studying one then the other.

"What are you doing, John?" Alice's voice asked.

"I'm looking," he replied.

"It is time to come back now."

"I've never noticed how different my hands are." He licked the webbing between his ring and pinky finger, a particularly dry spot, and rubbed it with his other hand.

"John, you cannot stay here."

"Why not?" he asked, moving to the next section of dry webbing.

"This place is not for you. Without your mind, I am unable to restart your basic life functions. You will die."

"I don't want to go back." John could sense someone else beside him, but he didn't bother to look up. "I can't recall what she looks like. I know the color of her hair and how she smelled, but what kind of husband can't remember his wife's face? And Maddie. Did I really want to be frozen to give her a better life, or was it because I was scared cancer would take me?" The lines on his hands appeared deeper now. "Even now, I'm trying to save Rebecca, someone I hardly know, and it may cost me my daughter. The shit of it is, I don't even know if either can be saved."

The other person moved closer. Small bare feet stepped next to John's. He looked up at the little girl standing next to him. "I told you I don't want you using my memories of them." His voice held no bitterness like it did when she used Emily's voice. Even though Alice was a program, he felt like she was the most real thing he had. John looked back down, not wanting to see Maddie's face looking back at him. Warm hands touched his face, lifting it up until he was looking at the little freckles he knew so well.

"I am sorry, John." Alice's voice seemed younger, more childlike. It wasn't Maddie's, but it didn't matter. "It was not meant to be disrespectful, but this is the only image contained within my central core. It is the only me I know."

"I don't care. Use whatever you want," John said. The room was colder now. John's breath came out in thick plumes and hung in the air, but Alice's hands were so warm. The little white dress she was wearing looked like the something a child would wear to a baptism, something else he had never had time to do for Maddie.

John closed his eyes. "I'm no hero."

"Hero. A Greek priestess of Aphrodite who killed herself when her lover drowned. I do not understand why you would want to epitomize this type of person." The edge of John's mouth twitched. Alice continued. "Your actions do not reflect this type of person, but the image you hold of yourself is also incorrect."

Alice released his face. With her hands went any warmth in his body. John started to shiver uncontrollably. "What if everything I've done or am doing now is wrong?"

"I cannot answer that question. Logic seems to follow many paths for humanity, and is influenced by infinite variations of perspective."

"You know, Alice, sometimes you're not very helpful." John tried to smile.

Alice held out her left hand. "It is time to come back now."

"I think you're right." John took her hand.

"And, John," Alice said. "This may hurt a little."

"Wait, what—"

John gasped for breath and opened his eyes. His heart felt like it was going to burst out of his chest. He tried desperately to will more oxygen into his lungs. He wanted to scream, but nothing came out.

"Relax," Alice said, her voice no longer childlike.

John's heart slowed, and after a few more frantic breaths he was able to breathe easier. The whirr of the machines around him meant he was back in the small utility building. He winced as he sat up.

"I will adjust your pain tolerance," Alice said.

"No." John reached up and picked at the dried crust of blood stuck to the stubble on his chin. At least the numbness was gone. "Sometimes pain is a good thing. It lets a person know they're alive. Now, can you explain what just happened?"

"Whatever was producing the signal tried to connect with my conscience again. It tried to enter you."

"I thought you were blocking that from happening?"

"It used the tower to increase the strength of its attack. I had not anticipated this possibility. I believe it was going after my core data, but when I resisted, it started to take control of your INOs. The only way to force the signal out was to shut down all your biological and neuro-electrical functions, effectively starving the—"

"Layman's terms, Alice."

"I killed you."

"Let's not do that again for a while, okay?"

"Understood," Alice replied. "I have already reprogrammed the INOs and fortified my internal systems. I will not be caught off guard again."

"It wasn't your fault." John leaned his head against a large conduit next to him.

"I was, however, able to extract some information from the source."

"What kind of information?" John asked.

"Towers like this one are being used to project the barrier around the region. All the towers are interconnected and linked to a single source."

"I bet that's the original beacon we're looking for." He strained to keep his eye open. "Could you get us there?"

"I should be able to triangulate the tower locations from here, and determine our current location," Alice replied. "You may rest if you wish, while I complete the process."

"I don't know what I would do without you." John reached into his side pocket, his fingertips finding the edge of Maddie's photo. It was still there. He closed his eyes and was out.

A screen flickered to life on the far wall. Alice projected part of his consciousness into the terminal. The system was old, ancient compared to anything Alice had interfaced with before. The signal had cut all connection with the tower after she had forced it out of John's body. It might be waiting for her to lower her guard again, but she wouldn't make that mistake again.

John was no different than Doctor Malcolm, but there was something about him. His mind was so chaotic, like pieces all crammed together. She had hesitated when terminating his life functions. It was the most logical action, but still, she hesitated.

The command code strands opened before her, searching for a tower location. Each strand was coded to delete itself, keeping anyone from knowing what she was looking for. As each tower returned the requested information, she overlaid them on the area maps. To her, it took too long, but in reality, her calculations were completed in seconds. Finished, she pulled herself back into John. The INOs had already fixed his injuries and were moving to repair the INOs the signal had taken offline. John had not wanted her to heal his outer wounds, but she was not reckless, even if he was. She accessed a bit of information she had severed from the signal during the attacked, but only one word stood out: Goliath.

John woke—no nightmares and no near death experiences, just sleep. He slowly got up and stretched. There was no soreness or pain, Alice's handiwork no doubt. She didn't listen, but he was beginning to think it was part of her appeal. "What were you able to find?"

"At a steady rate of travel, we should be able to reach the beacon within three days."

It still wouldn't help Nolan. The best they could do is make him as comfortable as possible, and wait for the inevitable.

"I have also detected an anomaly."

"What kind of anomaly?" he asked.

"The towers are equipped with motion sensors. When tripped, they electrify the protective fencing. A tower near here registers an unusually high ratio of sensor detections."

"What do think is causing it? Animals?"

"I do not believe so. UV light is emitted from the charged fences. This would discourage animals from congregating nearby."

If it wasn't animals, then Alice just may have found the natives. "Alice, you're a genius."

"My functionality is quite proficient."

John smiled. "Remind me to explain compliments later."

"Noted, John."

John eased the latch back on the door and opened it. He quickly put a hand up to shield the light from his eyes. The sun was already visible over the treetops.

"The sensors have not detected movement for some time now. I would advise caution as the devices are limited in their range," Alice said.

Once John's eyes adjusted, he stepped out and locked the door behind him. He wasn't planning on using this place again, but so far nothing had gone as planned since they arrived. The meadow was covered in bright yellow flowers, something he hadn't noticed last night. A detail you quickly overlook when running for your life. A place of horror and beauty. Forget one while admiring the other, and you die.

"Okay, Alice. Let's go find Rebecca."

The jungle was easier to navigate, now that they had a direction, but the feelings of something out there, waiting, never quite passed. It made John wish, on more than one occasion, he had found his knife. It was late afternoon when they reached the next tower. Unlike the previous tower, this one was mostly swallowed by the jungle itself. John crawled under a tight cluster of bushes. If this area was active, he shouldn't have to wait long. He was scooping up a handful of soil to rub on his clothes when a sound caught his attention. It was faint at first. A voice. No, two, maybe more. Whoever it was, they weren't worried about attracting attention.

It wasn't difficult to locate the group. There were three in total, each carrying jugs connected by cording of some kind. Their upper bodies were covered almost completely in a black type of paint, and each wore a colorful wrap over their lower extremities. John followed the group. He was too far away to hear what they were saying, but the casualness of their tone and occasional laughter made him nervous. The three stayed on a worn path that led down to a small spring. The spring was guarded by the surrounding ferns and made it easier for him to move closer. The small party gathered near the edge of the water. The black paint covered their bodies except the neck and face. Their black hair accented the rich caramel skin on their small frames. One of the individuals turned, and from the gentle curve of the chest, it was clear she was female. They all were female.

The group removed clay jugs they were carrying and began to fill them in the shallow, clear pool. The vessels were filled one at a time. Once the final jug was full, the women hefted the interlaced water containers back onto their shoulders. Still engaged in boisterous conversation, they passed within a few feet of John and continued back up the path. He let the women get partially up the trail before shadowing them. The path widened beyond the tower, and so did the ladies' lighthearted conversation. It was an annoying puzzle to John. In a place with dangers everywhere, these three carried no weapons and did nothing to minimize their presence.

The women kept a surprising pace, even with the jugs dangling low on either side. The sun had begun its descent before the women slowed. Their conversation ceased, and they cast their gaze towards the ground. John fell back, extending the space between them. Ahead on the trail, two figures came into view. The women kept their heads low as they passed. John moved further into the undergrowth and parallel to the trail. He still didn't know what he was dealing with or if Rebecca was even here, and until he knew more, it would be best to remain unseen. A thin mist had begun to accumulate on the ground around him. If nothing else, it would make it easier to avoid unwanted attention.

He took another step, but his foot found nothing to support it. He was falling. Wrenching around, his fingers clawed at the ground. Alice screamed in his mind, but it was in Maddie's voice again. John's wrist caught on something. A searing pain radiated down the side of his hand and around his thumb, as his full weight came down. His body twisted, wrenching his shoulder from its joint. It took a moment for John to realize he wasn't falling anymore. Using his free hand, he searched for a solid grip. Once he found traction with his feet, he removed his injured hand from the narrow crevasse, which had saved his life, and pulled himself back from the precipice.

In a tiny worried voice, Maddie's voice, Alice asked, "John, are you okay?"

"Just peachy, Alice. Just about died again, but it seems commonplace as of late." The sarcasm slid from his mouth with such ease it even surprised him.

"Your shoulder is dislocated, but still operational." Whatever worry John had heard in her voice was gone. The matter-of-fact adult Alice was back. "Your wrist is fractured, and will require time to repair."

"Look, I'm sorry. It wasn't your fault. It's this place. I think it's finally starting to get to me." *Or it's just me slowly losing my mind*, he thought.

"Your reaction is understandable."

If it was understandable, why did it make him feel like an asshole? John peered back over the ledge. The mist obscured everything in either direction, including the other side. One thing was certain—whatever luck had kept him alive up to this point, he had officially just used it up. He looked down at the mangled skin hanging from his hand. There wasn't much he was going to be able to do with it. His only option now was the trail. If the women went that way, so could he.

John moved low through the brush, trying to keep as close to the ledge as possible. As he crept towards the trail, he could make out the outline of a bridge, as well as the two sentries. The guards were both male. Unlike the women, their faces and necks were covered with the same black paint, only their torsos were free of any markings. Posted on either side of the bridge, the men stood unmoving, short spears at their sides. There was no conversation, only watchful eyes fixed on the trail. He couldn't go through them, but maybe he wouldn't have too.

John searched the ground, settling on a palm-sized rock and a short stick. Anything bigger would be too noticeable. He tested the weight of the stick in his uninjured hand. The waning light and growing mist should cover his movements. Barely rising, he flung the stick into the brush on the opposite side of the trail. If the guards had heard the noise, they made no indication of moving. John readied the rock and sent it flying. Thwack. The rock bounced off a tree somewhere on the other side.

Shit too far in, he thought.

John was out of options, and he couldn't risk being out at night. He would have to make for the overgrown beacon tower and hope he could get inside. There was no telling what waited beyond the bridge and until Alice could fix his wrist, he would be at a disadvantage. Maybe this was for the best.

He started to back away when one of the men raised his spear and yelled something to the other. John stopped moving. Had they spotted him? Maybe they had seen the rock and were waiting for him to move. The two guards darted into woods, but opposite John. They disappeared into the trees without making a sound. He looked down at his mangled hand. The blood had stopped. Holding it tight across his body, he moved for the bridge.

The bridge was a complex interweaving of vines and slender branches. The branches were bent, forming a continuous basket-like design. Long straight poles made up a walking platform wide enough for two people to cross at a time. The mist had already hidden John from the view of the trail, but that didn't mean someone wouldn't cross at any time. Through the mist, two flickering lights began to take shape. The fog began to dissipate, revealing an unending wall of smooth stone. The lights were small fires burning in sections cut on either side of a rounded entrance. The glow from the firelight caught on the darkened recesses of other holes, which marked the otherwise voidless wall. They were using the caves. It would explain why he couldn't track them once they moved out of the low marshlands. To John's relief, there was no one guarding the mouth of the cave. Inside he moved methodically, his hand tracing the wall for a guide. Ahead, light brightened another entryway. Sounds coming from beyond the opening echoed throughout the chamber, setting his senses on edge. Ornate columns adorned either side of the entrance. He pressed his back against the wall and edged around the column.

"Are you seeing this, Alice?" He was expecting winding caverns, but this—this was a small city.

"I am."

The cavern was divided into three levels. Dwellings were cut into the walls of each. Below, hundreds more covered the lower section in straight grids, maximizing the space available. At the back of the cavern, a large central building extended from the stone backing. Cylindrical lanterns hung from most of the buildings and on pillars in the open areas.

John glanced behind him. He needed to find somewhere out of sight. At the cave entrance, a wide stone path led down to the main level, and a smaller one in either direction led to the upper sections. In a place this size, finding Rebecca would be difficult. With little cover above, his only choice was the lower level.

John slipped between the nearest buildings, where the light from the lanterns didn't reach. The main thoroughfare was bustling with people. These were dressed differently from the ones he had already seen. The people on the streets wore brightly colored and distinctive outfits. The women wore dresses, the fabric moving with the curves of their body. It gave them the appearance of floating instead of walking. Most of them wore their hair braided and wrapped high atop their heads. The men's attire was similar in style, most wearing thigh length robes and white or matching pants. The men John could see kept their hair cut almost to the scalp.

John ducked back behind a wooden crate. If Rebecca were here, she would likely be in the large building at the back of the cave. In the street, there was a commotion. He leaned out to get a better view. A crowd was gathering and could jeopardize his position. Before he could move, a man flew through the air, landing with a thud on the stone ground. John stepped up a wood pile to get a better view. The man unconscious on the ground was dressed and painted like the guards out by the bridge. More of the same were huddled around something large in the middle of the street.

"I told you little bastards, poke me again, and I'm going to rip your damn heads off!" The large mass exploded outward, sending men sprawling in all directions. Gramm grabbed the nearest man by the shoulders and drove his head into the man's face. The force sent the man tumbling back. The blow had opened a gash on Gramm's head. "Who's next?" Gramm yelled.

The crowd parted, and a man dressed in a matching white robe and pants walked casually towards Gramm. The man seemed small next to the Gramm's large frame.

Gramm raised a clenched fist. "You want some too, little man?"

The man in white stopped in front of Gramm. He looked up at the big man, his placid expression never changing. The man spoke something in a language John had not heard before. The mob moved back, almost as one. Something wasn't right here, and Gramm was too intent on slugging his way through to notice. Gramm swung, but his punches were wild, uncontrolled. The man sidestepped with ease and with a little nudge sent Gramm stumbling forward.

Gramm wheeled around, his face twisted in anger. He lunged, hoping to take the smaller man to the ground. In a swift motion, the man rotated to the side. Gramm crashed to the ground. He yelled in frustration and tried to scramble back to his feet, but the man was already standing next to him. The man in white spoke again and touched the side of Gramm's neck. Gramm's eyes went wide in surprise, before closing. He collapsed to the ground. The man, standing above him held out his hand. One of the guards rushed up and handed him a spear. The man's calm expression had never changed during the encounter. He turned the spear gracefully in his hands and leveled the point at Gramm's neck.

John swore to himself. If he didn't do something, Gramm was dead, but exposing himself now could get them both killed. He had to think of Maddie. She had to come first. And what about Rebecca? Was Gramm's life worth theirs? The wood pile shifted under his feet as he stepped down. If he slipped away now, the commotion would work to his advantage.

"Is this who you really are, John?" Alice asked.

John grabbed his arm and squeezed. Pain radiated down through his wrist. "No!" A few spectators turned around and looked at him, surprise turned to panic, as they moved to get out the way. What was happening to him? He would have never left a man behind. This wasn't his squad, but Gramm was his responsibility. He walked out into the street. The guards, who were observing moments before, quickly surrounded him, their short spears raised. A spear point from one overzealous guard cut deep into the side of his arm. The man in white turned, the surprise visible on his face. He handed off the spear, his face again emotionless, and walked toward John.

Blood ran down John's arm until it, mingling with the dried blood from his wrist. John met the man's gaze as he approached. The guards moved aside, allowing the man to pass. The man in white looked at the blood-covered spear point of the guard to John's right, and then looked down at the blood pooling on the stone street. The guard started to say something, but the man snatched the spear from his hands and thrust forward.

John braced for the bite of the spear tip, but the man drove the spear through the guard's chest. The guard spit up blood and fell forward, driving the spear through his back. John expected to see women covering their faces, and their men trying to shield them from the gruesome sight. They reacted like nothing had happened.

Two other guards calmly picked up the body and dragged it away. The man in white folded his hands behind his back and spoke again before turning and walking down the street. A guard shoved John forward, while a few of the guards tried to lift Gramm off the ground. People stopped along the sides of the street, bowing deeply as the man in white passed. John could see the building at the back of the cavern, looming over the top of the other buildings. This wasn't how he had planned on getting in, but right now he was happy he was still alive.

After passing the last row of dwellings, John could finally take in the full size of the central building. Every exposed section of wall was decorated in elaborate etchings. Some depicted brutal deaths, while others showed people placing items at the base of a tree. In the courtyard, statues were arranged in tight, if not perfect, rows. One thing was certain: civilization didn't grow here, it thrived.

They led him to a set of doors near the side of the building and continued down a flight of stairs. The bottom of the stairs opened into an elongated, half-lit corridor. The scent of flowers permeated the air, but there was something else. John took another breath. A sourness lingered behind the floral notes. Then he noticed the bars. A man approached from the other direction, dressed in deep blues. At first, John mistook the man as female. Unlike the man in white, his hair was long and tied behind his head. The blue robe hung almost to the floor. Small golden slippers peeked out with every step, and the excess material of the sleeves covered the man's hands. The man in white slightly bowed his head as the man in blue approached. The two conversed, with the man in blue doing most of the talking.

"John," Alice said, "deciphering the language being used is complete. Translation now in process."

"—are there more?" the man in blue asked, his voice abnormally high pitched.

"It is unclear, Adviser Tao," the man in white said. "Communication is limited."

"Then may I suggest you increase your efforts, General Li. The Hano are a danger to us all, and this could be their latest deception."

"I have sent my men out in search of others." The general's responses were short and direct. His demeanor rigid and still, a soldier's demeanor. "Though I do not believe they are Hano, the fact they're still alive firms my suspicions."

"It proves nothing." The adviser was the complete opposite of the general. When he talked, he made wide gestures with his covered hands. His falsetto speaking voice was almost sing-song in his delivery.

The general inclined his head. "Nevertheless, I shall double my efforts with the female. She does not appear hostile and is receptive to basic gestures."

Adviser Tao dismissed the comment with a wave of his hand. "Aggression? I hear your men had some difficulty with the dark-skinned male. As for the woman, the emperor appears to have taken a curious interest in her. His Grace had her moved this morning into more suitable quarters."

Woman? Rebecca, John thought.

The adviser stepped around the general, noticing John for the first time. He stepped up to the guards, who held fast. "Do not make me ask you to move," the adviser said, to the guard directly in front of him.

The general nodded, and the young guard moved aside.

The adviser moved in close, inspecting John. He wrinkled his nose in disgust and covered his nose with his sleeve. "I was not aware we had discovered another."

"It would seem your information is not as reliable as you presume, Adviser," General Li said.

The adviser turned and glared. "So it would seem." He walked over to the general's side. "The smell on them. Filthy. I hear the longer you are down here the harder it is to get the smell off. You must not even notice it by now."

General Li turned to face the adviser, his expression still unchanged. "Perhaps the adviser would be better equipped to handle the affairs of the populace and leave the care of the retention center to me."

Adviser Tao's jaw tightened. "The emperor is expecting answers, and he will have them one way or another." The adviser turned and stormed off back down the hallway.

"Bring the two," the general said.

Only a few of the cells they passed were occupied. From their dress, most looked to be citizens to John.

"Put the big one in there," the general said, opening a cell door.

The guards carried Gramm into the cell and laid him on the floor. The door was secured.

"The other one," the general said, indicating John. "We will place here." He opened the cell across from Gramm's.

The younger guard, who had refused to move for the adviser, spoke up. "General Li, do you not think it is too close? When the sedation wears off—"

"This one will be placed here. It will make the adviser think twice about taking action against our guests."

The guard escorted John into the small cell. Unlike Gramm's, his shared a bar lined common wall with the adjoining cell. Once the guards filed out, and the door was closed, the general and his guards departed. John walked up to the door. He expected the general to post someone outside the cells, but the hallway was empty.

"Gramm." There was no response from the other cell. He tried a little louder. "Gramm!"

There was no answer. John tugged on the cell door, but it was firmly locked in place. He inspected the rest of the room, but the cell was empty, except for a bucket in the corner. The floor lacked any dust or mold, and the back and side stone walls were cut smooth with no hint of imperfections—strange for a prison. Everything here was too perfect, from the detail on the outside of the palace to the statues.

Something shifted in the chamber next to his, producing a metallic sound. He walked over to the bars separating the rooms. On the floor was a huddled mass of fur. A chain affixed to the wall stretched over to the mass. The mound moved, causing the chain to scrape against the floor. John took a step back. Even in the dim light, he could easily make out the orange-and-black pattern. The tiger was as big or bigger than the one he had seen in the forest last night. The big cat's chest rose and fell in slow, steady rhythm.

"It is beautiful, is it not?" Alice asked.

Beauty was a very human concept, even for Alice. "Yes, it is." The tiger didn't stir. "It's strange. I have this feeling of awe, like a child seeing one up close for the first time." The stripes of fiery orange fur were only broken by the smooth-flowing soot black lines. It was beautiful. "How much information do you have on Chinese customs?" He was sure he had been deployed to China a few times, but when and why were escaping him now.

"My archives contain all written data from fifteen hundred BC to the collapse of the Chinese government after the Third World War."

"Good." John moved toward the back wall and sat with his back to the cool stone. He cradled his wrist in his lap. "I'll need you to give me a brush up on as much as you can, but first, if I let you put me to sleep, do you think you can have me patched up in the next twelve hours?"

"I can do more than that," Alice replied. "It may be possible to imprint the data you are requesting to your short-term memory as well as reroute language based information from your perisylvian cortex."

"You're going to have to simplify it for me, Alice."

"It would give you the ability to communicate directly with the indigenous people, but it is not without risk," she said. "There is a small chance it could leave you in a catatonic state."

"I'm not sure I like that idea."

"Relax, John. It is my job to maintain all your life functions, but in the event something goes wrong, it is unlikely you would know otherwise."

"Oh, and now you do jokes?" He took a few deep breaths and closed his eyes. "Okay. I'm ready."

CHAPTER 14

This time there were no dreams or images, only nothingness. There was no rest within this type of slumber. John blinked, trying to clear away the remnants of sleep. There was a lot of commotion next to him, but his brain was not ready to acknowledge it yet. He flexed his fingers and rotated his wrist. This simple action seemed to take longer than it should. There was no break in the skin nor pain in his hand or shoulder. Really, there was no pain anywhere, just a subtle lingering exhaustion.

"John?" Alice's voice stretched out into too many syllables. "You are fine now." Her voice slowly sped up as she continued. "Your brain is trying to make new connections with the changes made and your conscience self. It should pass in a moment."

"Mmmhmm." Was all he could manage.

John turned his head from side to side, making the room move in a very nauseating way. A frenzy of colored hair thrashed on the other side of the bars. The world around him flexed, or maybe popped would be a better way to explain it. A growl followed by a deep roar echoed off the stone walls. Everything came back into real-time. The tiger growled again before slamming itself against the bars. John stood, but had to lean back against the wall until his legs would hold him. "I'm not sure if I enjoyed whatever you did."

"Noted," Alice said.

John pushed off the wall and staggered over towards the tiger's cell. The large cat pawed at its collar wildly, trying to tear it free. Red streaks ran down from around the dull circlet of metal around its neck. From the hallway, he could hear voices coming. Two guards strolled up from the opposite direction, stopping at the tiger's cell.

The larger of the two grasped the bars and leaned in, watching the cat. "Looks like the sedative wore off before Minso could dispatch of it properly."

The other guard was thinner, his face sharply angled. "Can I stick it, Fotan?" He danced in place, almost giddy.

"The collar should bleed it out, sure enough, unless Minso gets here first." Fotan glared over at his companion. "I think you're just trying to get out of our game, Moata. Down three games if I'm not wrong."

John looked closer at the metal collar the tiger was digging at. The blood staining its coat was coming from all around the collar. The inside must be barbed somehow. Then he noticed the scar running across its snout. This was the same tiger as from before.

Moata scowled back at Fotan. "I'm good for it. Come on, just one cut."

Fotan stood up straight and shrugged. "If you mess up the hide, the Emperor will take yours instead. I doubt you could reach it anyway."

"The way it's digging at the restraint," Moata lifted his spear and poked it through the bars, "who's to say it wasn't self-inflicted."

Moata thrust the spear tip towards the tiger. The cat roared and lunged forward, but the chain snapped tight, flipping the predatory cat around. Blood dripped from the golden orange coat onto the floor. Its teeth bared, the cat swiped at the spear. The thin man laughed, his eyes wide, vulturish, over his pointed nose.

"Stop it." The words rolled quietly out of John's mouth at first. Too quiet for anyone to notice. He could see the spittle projecting from Moata's mouth through his crooked teeth. There was no masking the pure pleasure on the man's face. The disgust layered in John's throat like acid. No creature deserved this. "Stop it!" he screamed, his hands trembling, his fingers tightly curled into fists.

The wooden tang of Moata's spear hitting the floor broke the abrupt silence. Both guards stared at the man in the cell. Even the tiger turned to look at the man whom no one had noticed until now.

"Get the General," Fotan ordered Moata.

"I—" Moata looked down at the spear inside the cage. "You should do it. He will receive the news from you better."

"Fine." Fotan shoved the wiry guard into the bars. "Don't think I'll forget what you owe me. In fact, tonight I'm expecting double."

"Yeah, yeah," Moata said, never taking his eyes from the tiger.

Fotan ran down the corridor, swearing as he went. The lock on the tiger's door clicked. Moata eased the door open, his tongue tracing his dry lips. He bent down and picked up his spear. The tiger roared and swiped at him with its oversized paw, but the chain was taut and only bit deeper into the cat's neck. John could see lust in Moata eyes. There would be no restraint from him. He wouldn't be satisfied until the cat was dead. The tiger backed away, allowing slack in the chain.

John knelt and extended his arm through the bars. He stretched for the chain, the tip of his fingers only brushing against the cold metal ringlets. The wild predator leaped again, pulling the chain out of John's reach. Moata was quicker than he looked, and nimbly danced, bringing the spear point down on the cat's muzzle. The tiger backed away, shaking its head. A new gash had opened, making an odd shaped X where it bisected the old scar.

"Bleed," Moata said, laughing. "Bleed for me!"

John reached again for the slacked chain.

"I would advise against your current course of action," Alice warned. "I can heal your injuries, including a broken wrist, but I cannot regrow a limb."

"I could use your eyes instead of the rhetoric right now," John said.

"I do not have eyes," Alice said, her Maddie-like child's voice coming back.

Something was going on with Alice. She was analytic, even painfully so at times. Her personality had always come across to John as an adult woman, but this new voice... it scared him. Hearing Maddie's voice should have filled him with something, with anything. Instead, he felt nothing. Something was happening to him was like a constant gnawing behind his eyes. Whatever it was, maybe it was affecting Alice as well.

John pressed his body against the bars reaching out into the neighboring cell. His finger caught the edge of the chain, and he pulled it closer. Moata clearly had no interest in him; his hunger-filled gaze was locked on the tiger. John sat back and placed his feet on the bars for more leverage. Grasping the chain in both hands, he applied steady pressure. The tiger turned on him, its ears flat against its head, the muscles in its front legs taut and ready to strike. Holding the chain tightly, he tried matching the cat's intense presence with his own. It had worked before, but before, he was half delusional. Then again, he wasn't sure what this would qualify as.

The cat's ears perked up for a second. It resisted slightly before relinquishing to the continuous tension on the chain. Moata scored another hit on the tiger's shoulder, causing the cat to lurch forward. Chain slid back through John's hands. He shifted his heel to try pinning the chain to the bars. John heaved on the large metal loops. His back flexed with the strain, but link by link he coiled the chain until the tiger was within feet of the bars. Gathering the chain beside him, he wrapped it around the other bars to lock it in place. Now came the hard part.

"John?"

"I know it's stupid."

"At least you have come to terms with it," she replied.

"Now I know why the commander wanted to disconnect you," he said, reaching for the collar.

"Careful," Alice said. "It is unwise to threaten someone who can take control of all your bodily functions."

John may have found that amusing, or even laughed if he wasn't a few inches away from the business end of an extremely large predatory cat. He reached for the latch on the collar. It appeared to be a simple hinged clasp; if he could catch the end of it, it should release the mechanism holding the collar in place. It was easy in theory, but the cat's movements were hectic. Moata scored another hit, this one deeper than the rest. The tiger took a step back and lowered itself nearer to the floor. It may have looked like the cat was backing down, but John could see the muscle tense on the powerful hind legs. He rammed himself against the bars, reaching for the latch again.

The tip of his index finger caught the rounded metal lip. The tiger sprang forward at incredible speed. The latch clicked as it tore from John's grasp. The chain snapped tight, breaking the metal loop and dislodging the collar. Moata's smirk turned to fear as the predator's full mass came down on him. The tiger's massive jaws closed around the horrified man's neck, choking off what little sound was creeping out his orifice. Everything happened in a graceful silence. A killer's silence. Moata's legs trembled slightly and went still.

John relaxed. The chain shifted against the bars. The tiger's head came up, its mouth opened, panting. It stared back at him. He had expected to see Moata's throat ripped out, but there were only small puncture marks accented by lines of red, dripping onto the floor. John got to his feet, and the cat followed him with its yellowish eyes. With the bars between them, there was little reason to worry about provoking the cat. Down the hallway, the sound of voices could be heard. The tiger growled, and in two graceful bounds disappeared down the corridor, in the opposite direction of the voices. There were shouts of alarm as a few guards ran past, in the direction the tiger had gone. Other guards poured into the open cell.

Fotan pushed his way to the front. "Moata!" He saw Moata's body on the floor. "Damn it!" He kicked Moata's corpse. "You stupid bastard. Now I'll never get paid."

"Out," someone commanded.

The guards filed out of the cell, including Fotan who managed to get one more kick in. General Li stepped into the cell and bent down next to Moata's body. He placed his index and middle finger on the side of Moata's neck. After a moment, he removed his fingers and stood. He walked slowly around the small confined room, taking in every detail around him. At the bars, separating the cells, he stopped. His gaze flickered down to the chains wound around the bars, then to the man standing on the other side.

"I hear you speak our language," the general said.

John nodded. The less he offered, the better. This may be the only advantage he was going to get.

"Very well. You will accompany me," General Li said. "If you fail to do as instructed, my men will kill your man in the next cell. If you try to escape, I will kill the other man."

Nolan is here, John thought. His condition would have deteriorated further, which would complicate things.

The general must have seen a reaction at the mention of the second man and continued, "I will not hesitate to kill the woman as well. I know you care for these people or otherwise you would have let your comrade die by our spear yesterday." He folded his hands behind his back and walked out of the cell.

A guard unlocked his cell door and held it wide. John walked out, and the guards fell in around him.

"Sergeant!" It was Gramm. Gramm's stepped up to the bars allowing the light from the hallway to illuminate his features.

"Did you see where they took Nolan?"

"How'd you get in here, I—"

"Stay on point, Gramm."

"No, Sir. We were separated before we got here," Gramm said.

Someone pushed John from behind, but John held firm. "I'll get us out, but you'll need to be ready."

Gramm laughed. "From my cell, I just watched a guy try to grab a big, really pissed off cat. Can't say I'm really surprised it was you. A guy with balls that size is either crazy or a motherfucking genius. I'll be ready when you need me."

John wished he was certain as Gramm sounded. Another shove from behind forced him back into motion. All he had to do was slip away, find Rebecca and Nolan, come back for Gramm, all while avoiding a city's worth of soldiers. Impossible didn't even begin to explain the situation.

John's captors moved swiftly along the mass of vacant hallways and spiraling stairs. More than once, he was led in and out of vacant rooms, or down a flight of stairs only to go back up somewhere else. They were trying to confuse him, make it harder for him to get a feel for the layout of the building. It was a solid strategy, but it wouldn't work. Alice was his trump card. At the end of a row of small doors, they came to a stop. This was it. Even though there were no outward signs, he could almost feel the tensions of the men around him elevate. The soldier, in front of him, was gripping his spear hard enough, to make his hands shake.

The door opened, and he was ushered through into a large, crowded room. Decorative lanterns covered the ceiling and filled the room with a warm glow. Colorful fabric, embroidered in yellows and gold, hung from the walls. Men and women dressed in overly ornate clothing milled around, moving from one group to another. Few took notice of John as they passed, and those who did were quick to return to their heavily involved conversations. The guards halted short of a large pair of peaked doors.

At the front of the line General Li, his hand still folded behind his back, turned and spoke briefly to one of his men. The man nodded and withdrew with the rest of the guards. General Li approached. "You will follow, and you will do everything that is requested. Do you understand?"

"Yes," John replied.

The general turned and walked towards the doors. The doors were opened enough to allow them through before being closed again. The room they entered was elongated. A rug ran the length of the room to an arched opening at the other end. Along the edge of the rug, men and women covered in gold paint stood unmoving. The sexes were segregated, one to each side. Though they blinked, it was the only outward sign of life they displayed.

The general's pace was brisk, and even though John's legs were longer, he had to quicken his step to keep up. Through the archway, they entered a slightly smaller room. This room was dimly lit compared to the others and was sparsely furnished. In the middle of the room, an old man was seated at a well-worn darkly polished desk. His long, gray, hair braid hung over whatever he was intently reading. General Li knelt and placed his forehead against the smooth stone flooring. John copied the general and bowed. The floor was cool against his face and hands. Minutes passed. John could hear the rustling of parchment as the old man thumbed through whatever he was looking over. More time passed before the old man grumbled and stood. It was then when he must have noticed them on the floor.

Clearing his throat, the old man came around the desk. "Stand, stand." He sounded slightly embarrassed for not noticing them sooner. "There are better ways to spend time than down on one's face."

General Li and John rose. The old man's skin was wrinkled by time, and liver spots were prevalent on his face and hands. He moved awkwardly, like his body wasn't sure which way his brain wanted it to go.

"This is the man?" the old man asked.

"Yes, my Grace," General Li replied.

"Fascinating," the man said as he walked around John. "I hear you spoke something in our language. Do you understand what I am saying to you now?"

"I do," John replied. He could see the general tense beside him.

"Let it go, Li." The old man looked at the general and smiled. "He is not one of us so we cannot expect him to act like one of us." He turned back to John. "I am Emperor Tin Yom. You may address me as Grace, Holy, or simply Emperor. I would rather it be less formal, but Li will not allow it, so why make things difficult. Everything is already painfully difficult anyway. I believe you have already met General Li. Do you have something we can call you?" The emperor's eyes seemed to sparkle with interest.

The emperor reminded John of a scholar more so than a ruler. "Sergeant John Crider, your Grace."

The emperor clapped his hands together. "Very good. You speak our language well, John Crider."

"If it pleases your grace, John will suffice." John bowed his head slightly.

"John. Yes. Short and it saves time," the emperor mused. "If I may ask, John, why do your companions not speak our language?"

"It is not out of disrespect. They simply do not understand it."

"How is it you came to understand it?"

With a simple question, the emperor had backed him into a wall. The old man was as clever as he was eccentric, he would have to choose his words carefully. "That is a difficult answer, and I fear you would not believe me, even if I told you. I can tell you however, we are not your enemy. My comrades were taken, and I only seek to retrieve them."

The emperor ran a finger across one of his bushy eyebrows. "Perhaps you tell the truth. Either way, I believe there is much to converse about. Unfortunately, I feel my legs may not enjoy an exchange at length. For our conversation to be uninhibited, one must feel comfortable, but first I have something I must see to first." The emperor turned and started to walk back to his desk. "See to our guest, Li. It has been a long time since we have had guests."

The general led John back through the archway and double doors. Even through the throngs of people, the general never looked back to see if he was following. Only when they reached another door did the general hold it open and acknowledge John's presence. Once the door was closed, John ventured a question.

"No guards this time?"

General Li had taken the lead again. "His Grace has seen fit to call you a guest, and so you will be treated as one. This was not by mistake, but by his design."

"You are not worried about me escaping?"

The general stopped abruptly. He turned, his hard cold eyes fixing on John. "Speaking with his Grace is a privilege, and most will never experience it. You have been asked to do so again. Soil this gift and I will end your life myself." The general turned and continued down the hall.

It wasn't much further, and the general stopped in front of a door. "You are to wait inside until summoned. Water has been prepared so you may wash." The general bowed his head slightly and started to walk away, but paused. With his back turned he said, "Sergeant John Crider, out of respect, I shall see to the comfort of your people."

"You might leave the big guy where he is. He's a good man, but I fear he may not understand the situation, and someone could be hurt."

"I will consider your request," the general said.

John opened the door to the room. "There was another man with the big guy."

"He is ill. We are doing what we can, but—"

"I understand." John stepped into the room and closed the door. Nolan was going to die, but at least it wasn't going to be in some rain-soaked hole.

With no windows, it would be difficult to determine how long he had waited. He supposed he could ask Alice, but did it really matter? The room's only decorations were a few pieces of plain wooden furniture. Though furnished, he had only traded one cell for another.

After washing from the basin, John sat in an empty corner thumbing the corners of Maddie's picture. No matter which way he looked at it, he couldn't remember where the picture was taken, or what caused her to make that silly little expression.

"Alice, you there?" he asked.

"I'm always here, John."

"Can you tell if anything is going wrong inside of me?"

"All levels are running at optimum efficiency. INO integration is at ninety-five percent. I should reach complete integration within the next four hours."

John put the picture of Maddie back into his vest pocket. "I feel like there's something wrong in my head."

"The average male head size is fifty-seven centimeters. Yours is large in comparison."

"Very funny." John leaned his head back and looked up at the smooth ceiling. "My memories are leaving me daily now. Things I was sure about yesterday seem harder to hold on to today. I was trying to remember my old address. I walked by my house number a million times, but I can't picture it in my head. I'm not even sure how many digits it was."

"Memories are fragmented across multiple areas, making it difficult to identify abnormalities. Your fragmentation appears different from indicated norms, but the continual deterioration and rebuilding of your cells make it problematic to ascertain a baseline for you."

Of course, it does, John thought. "Do you think this is also the cause of changes in your own personality?"

There was a pause before Alice answered. "I am not sure. The implant in your neck is a biologic. Unlike a normal circuit, it allows me to optimize functionality. At this time, I do not see a limitation to the biologic, but it does come with unexpected deviations."

"So, my memories of Maddie are bleeding over?"

"No," Alice said. "I do not believe they are. My self-perception does not look to be influenced by anything within your consciousness. I am me."

"I was dying of cancer, and you fixed me. The cryonic turned my cells against me, and you're now keeping them at bay. The ironic thing is, everything I'm living for is slowly being taken from me. I already can't remember my wife's face. What do I do if tomorrow comes and I can't remember Maddie's?" A tear slid down John's cheek.

"You do what you always do. You fight, Sergeant Crider. You give everything you have and when you have nothing left, you give some more. I will not let you forget, John."

"You know, Alice," John said, reaching up to wipe the dampness from his cheek. He laughed to keep from crying more. "I didn't like the thought of something... someone in my head, but I do have to say, you're growing on me."

"Someone is approaching," Alice said, cutting their conversation short.

John got to his feet and faced the door. The door opened. General Li stepped into the room. He was alone.

"The emperor would like to express his regret for keeping you waiting. A meal has been prepared, but first, he asks if you will join him for a while?"

"I would be honored," John replied.

General Li led John back to the room he had first met the emperor. The golden painted people still stood in silent vigil over the entrance. The emperor was pacing in front of his desk when they arrived.

"Come in. Come in," the emperor urged, waving them in. "I would like to show you something if you would indulge me, John?"

"Of course, your Grace," John replied.

"Good, good." The emperor looked John over. "I would have had Li bring you clothing to change into, but you are larger than most of my people. I will have my tailor begin working on a set for you later." He nodded to himself, turned, and started for a door across the room. "Li and I have discussed much in your absence. You are not like my advisers, ambitious and greedy, nor do you make demands. Li," the emperor said, pointing a thin finger awkwardly over his shoulder at the general, "believes there is honor in you. Honor and duty drive a man like Li. I wonder if the same can be said about you?"

"Your words are too kind," John said. "Duty, maybe. Honor, perhaps once, now forgotten. Now, I am a mere tool to be discarded. An end to a task, nothing more."

"Ah, but a chisel wielded by the right person becomes the brush of a sculpture." The emperor grasped the wooden door handle and looked back at John. "This task of yours, maybe it in itself is not worthy of you." He turned back to the door and pushed it inward. Inside, racks lined the walls. Each rack held twenty or more shallow slanted shelves. "Trust is something we need for our conversation to be meaningful." The emperor moved over to the first rack. "This is one of our means of civilized life."

On each of the recessed shelves, greenery had been spread. White, inch-long things moved among the leaves. John looked closer. Worms or hairless caterpillars of some kind.

"Only five people in a lifetime are trusted to enter this room. You are now the sixth. The three caretakers work tirelessly collecting the thread these produce. The thread is used to create the clothing that we wear."

Silkworms. John looked down the line of racks. There had to be thousands here.

"The caretakers never leave these rooms. They understand how important the task they are given is. Unlike the caretakers, myself, Li, and now you, are free to enter and leave this place."

"With this knowledge, you could destroy our society. Do you understand the gift granted to you?" General Li asked John.

"Why trust me with this, let alone at all?"

"Even though he will not say, Li is also wondering the same thing. Come," the emperor said, moving off.

At the other end of the room, the emperor produced a key and unlocked a door. The door led into another hallway, this one shorter than most John had seen. At one end was another door and at the other were stairs leading up. The emperor walked over to the stairs. General Li moved to the emperor's side and tried to assist him.

"I'm not so old I can't make it up these stairs yet," the emperor said, shaking off the general's grasp.

The emperor's mind, sharp as it may be, could not hide how heavily he leaned on the wall for support. At the top of the stairs, the emperor paused, clenching his hand over his chest. Each breath rattled with a wet grit. He tried to say something but erupted in a fit of coughing. General Li was at his side immediately. The general reached for the door, but the emperor grabbed the handle and held it tight. Soon, the emperor's coughing subsided, but his complexion was ashen. Without the general's assistance, John doubted the emperor would have remained standing. After a few more breaths, the emperor straightened himself, as much as possible, and pushed the door open.

Inside, the room was lavishly decorated. Paintings decorated the walls, and ornate lamps cast a soft, colorful light around the room. A large canopy bed accounted for the vast majority of the space. Long purple silk drapes hung unmoving in the stillness of the room. An oversized chair with a generous cushion sat next to the bed. The emperor winced as General Li eased him down into a chair.

The emperor leaned back and let out a small sigh of relief. "Much better."

General Li gathered the side of the curtain and tied it back to the bed post. John could see a young woman amongst the thick pillows in the center of the bed. She appeared to be sleeping, but the quick shallow breaths barely moving her chest told him there was a problem. The emperor reached out and took the woman's hand. The hands looked frail together, almost like they each belonged to the same person.

"My advisers think you are Hano or sent by them," the emperor said, not bothering to look back at John.

"I'm not sure who or what a Hano is. I didn't even know of your people's existence until a couple days ago."

"Fear not. Li and I do not share in this belief. The Hano are difficult to capture, and kill themselves if they are. Your people were captured easily, partially because of skill, but mostly because they lacked familiarity with the area. You are the exception. You managed to track us here, and you were able to get into the city unseen. This is no trivial thing." The emperor gently lifted a stray hair away from the woman's taut face. "There was a creature in the cell next to you. I have only managed to catch it twice, and both times it cost me dearly. I first sought it out of anger, but after too many years my anger turned to mercy. I believe the animal to be the last of its kind. I wanted to spare it from the kinship it will never know and the loneliness it has only known."

The emperor inhaled deeply. There was a deep wet rasp as he let it out. "Alas, fate has once again delivered it from my grasp. Maybe some things are too heavy in spirit to be caged. I feel that may be true for you as well." He let the comment linger for a moment before waving the notion away with his hand. "Do not worry, the creature itself is of little significance, but the means of its departure interest me greatly."

John thought about lying, but he suspected both men already had a good idea of how the tiger was freed. "I have taken many lives, but I find no honor in cruelty. I came across the great cat a few days ago. To be accurate, it found me first." He could still remember the moonlight peeling back to reveal the silent predator. "It could have killed me with little effort, but it didn't. When I saw the cat in the cell, I recognized it by the scar on its muzzle. I released the restraints, but not before one of your guards opened the cell and tormented the creature. Courage turns to cowardice quickly when the tables are leveled."

The emperor and general looked at one another in amusement. "You are much like Li," the emperor said. "Li's parents died of wasting when he was only a whelp. They were of low birth, so there was nothing to gain by taking the child in. I took him in and gave him food and shelter, but no other favor was given. Everything he is now was obtained by his own hands. Strength is earned, not given, and because of this, he is one of my most trusted. I could ask for him to leave us now. Punishment is swift to all those who disobey me, but I know he will not leave."

The emperor smiled a devilish smile up at Li. "Relax, I will not ask you to do so." Li's face had not changed, but there was a visual release in his ridged form. "He has something I see less of in my people every day. Something I believe I see in you." The emperor looked up at John. His eye's glistened with dampness. All the joking and emotion he had shown moments ago were now gone. "John, I would like you to meet Princess Ma, my granddaughter."

"It is an honor, your Grace," John said.

"She has been sick for some time, but yesterday she went to sleep and has not roused since."

"I am sorry to hear about her condition," John said.

"Let us do away with the pleasantries and speak commonly. As two friends might, or if not friends, then fond acquaintances," the emperor said.

All of this went against the data Alice had on customs. He was being shown things one would not easily share and now this. Was this another one of the emperor's clever maneuverings, or something else? "I am humbled by your request, but respect will be given. If you ask, I shall reply."

The emperor frowned. "So it will be." He stroked the princess's hand lovingly. "If we cannot speak casually, let us speak truths. As the emperor, I do not make false claims, and as such, I expect the same from all in my presence. This does not mean truths cannot be omitted or words manipulated. I will do neither with you today. I expect the same from you." The emperor untwined his fingers from the princess's and laid her hand against her chest. He turned in his seat—if it pained him, he hid it well—and faced John. "Before I ask of you something I would like you to ask something of me. This will be my sign to you of good faith."

John didn't like this. Something was going on under the surface he couldn't quite pinpoint.

"John, ask him about Goliath." Alice said. "I believe we might be mistaken as to the context or meaning of the word."

"Has your Grace ever heard of Goliath?" John asked.

The emperor sat straighter, the frailty gone. His expression became darker than John had seen it before. The wily old man was gone, and in his place was the emperor most probably witnessed.

"Goliath is life and death." The emperor said his voice unadorned with emotion. "Our people tried to be gods but instead we brought forth something else. It is said Goliath gave birth to everything we know, creating life from nothing. But Goliath was fickle, and death came to the people. Our ancestors were forced to flee, and it was only through my direct descendent we were able to find and create a life for us here. There are places we do not go so as not to bring the ire of the god." He slumped back in his seat and took a deep breath. "So, you know some of our history as well?"

John realized he didn't have an answer that would satisfy the emperor but not give away things he shouldn't. He had to think fast. "Where I am from, we have very old written texts. They mention something called Goliath and a great tragedy. It was in a passing notation really." It was the best he could come up with. He doubted the emperor would fully accept the answer.

The emperor studied John for moment. "I would love to hear more about where you come from, but for now, it will have to wait. I would like you to ask something else of me, as I feel both the question and my answer on the subject were lacking."

"While I am grateful for your hospitality I would like to request my companions and I be allowed to leave as soon as it is acceptable, your Grace." John looked down at the princess. "Someone very dear to me is counting on my return."

The emperor laughed, but it was hollow and dry. "I should have guessed. Does not a caged bird only dream of freedom? I will grant your request, but not today. Today we speak. Later you dine and rest, and tomorrow… tomorrow you may go with any supplies you may need."

"I accept, your Grace," John replied. "You are most gracious."

"Now." The emperor licked his lips, like a man deprived of water for too long. "You came to us with many injuries I am told, some of them severe. Yet today you display none of them. How is this?"

An unsettled feeling came upon John. What was he supposed to say? Even the truth would sound insane. He had tried to keep everything secret, but there was too much for him to explain away with a vague answer. At least he would know after this if the emperor intended to let them go. "I will do my best to explain, but it is not an easy thing to speak about, not because I do not want to, but because I do not understand much of it myself. You have been more than hospitable, and because of this I will try."

John started from the beginning, describing being frozen, to waking up. He told them about Alice and how she was keeping him alive. There was nothing left after he finished, all of it poured out of him. The emperor and general listened to every word. They never interrupted or asked for clarification, just sat quietly, hanging on every word. When he was finished, he felt tired and yet somehow relieved.

The emperor sat back in his chair and rubbed the underside of his chin. "This Alice." The emperor tested the strange word in his mouth. "It is with you now?"

"She is," John replied.

The emperor sat there in thought for a while before speaking again. "This healing you can do. Is it something you can do for another?"

John looked down at the woman in the bed. That clever old bastard. John wasn't still here because he could speak the language; he was there because his wounds had miraculously healed overnight.

"I need to speak with Alice," John said. "As I said before, I'm still unsure of the limits of what she can do." The emperor nodded, but the look in his eyes was distant.

"John." It was Alice. "The INO's are bonded to your genetic code. There is little I can do outside of your body."

He had suspected as much. If Alice could've done more, she would have for Nolan already. The unknown at the moment was how the emperor would react to the news. John thought about lying, but anything he could come up with would involve time he didn't have. Alice could probably come up with something, but he couldn't risk asking. Maybe if he asked a broad enough question. "Can you give me a situational analysis, Alice?"

"The woman appears to be incapacitated. Based on the emperor's reactions, she has likely been this way for some time," Alice replied. "The emperor's request is not feasible. I detect desperation and hope in his voice."

John could feel a tightness in his chest. More than anyone, he understood the emperor's plight. If it were Maddie on the bed, he would try anything, no matter how remote. "Nolan's condition. You could tell what was wrong with him when I encountered his blood. Could you do the same with her?"

"Yes," Alice replied.

"Your Grace," John said, looking at the emperor. "As a father, I can understand what you are going through. What I can do to my own body, I cannot replicate for another." He could see the emperor's shoulders slouch inward. "Alice does have the ability to tell you precisely what is wrong with her."

The emperor clenched his jaw and looked away. "What good would it do me to know the name of what is killing my granddaughter? It will not change the outcome."

"My Grace." General Li knelt beside the emperor. "Our physicians had no answers for you. Why not allow this man to bring light to the question we cannot answer?"

The emperor placed his hand on Li's shoulder. "I thirst for knowledge as other do water. But this knowledge is tainted and I cannot bring myself to grasp it."

The woman in the bed coughed violently. Her body convulsing with each ragged breath. The emperor tried to rise, but Li was already there. He rolled the woman onto her side and supported her head. She coughed again sending red droplets cascading onto the clean white of the bedspread. John reached over and rubbed a finger over one of the larger blood spots.

"Alice," John asked.

"Processing the sample now."

A whimper escaped from the emperor's trembling lips. Tears were streaming down his face, and he frantically tried to reach out to the princess.

"John. There are trace amounts of neurotoxicity present. The chemical pattern is a close match to the plant family aconitum."

"How is that possible?" John asked. "It doesn't look like she has left this bed in weeks."

The princess's coughing fit subsided. General Li carefully set Princess Ma back onto the pillows and pulled up the edge of the blanket to try and clean her face.

"Can you get me a hair sample?" Alice asked.

Without thinking, John reached over and plucked a loose piece of hair from her braid. He pulled the length of it through his thumb and index finger a few times. It wasn't clear how Alice was going to check it, but contact seemed like the best way. John looked up in time to see the general coming around the bed. His normally expressionless face was twisted with rage.

"Wait!" John said, taking a step back. "She was poisoned!" He didn't want to fight his way out of the city, but now it didn't look like he had a choice. Raising his guard, he dropped the hair. The emperor reached out and grabbed hold of Li's robe, but the general's anger-filled momentum pulled the emperor out of the chair. General Li turned, trying to catch the emperor.

"Li!" the emperor yelled as he spilled onto the floor.

"Your Grace!" Li tried to help the emperor to his feet.

"Stop," the emperor said, brushing Li away. From the floor, the emperor picked up the hair John had dropped. Using the edge of the chair, he slowly got to his feet. General Li's emotionless mask had returned to his face, though he was a few shades paler. The emperor stepped over to John. He lifted John's hand and placed the hair back in his palm. "You said my granddaughter was poisoned. How?" The emperor moved back over to the chair and sat down.

"I apologize, your Grace," John said. If he had any hopes of salvaging anything, he needed to move carefully from this point on.

"Do not make me ask my question again," the emperor said. His voice was cold, commanding.

"Alice?"

"The hair sample indicates the princess is being given small doses of a plant-based neurotoxin," Alice answered. "The doses vary in quantity, leading to the conclusion someone is giving it to her."

John relayed the information.

"Do you know what kind of poison?" the emperor asked.

John listened to Alice's explanation and asked her a few questions of his own before answering. "This plant would have flowers, possibly blue, purple, or yellow in color. The top of the flower is tall like a hood, and the bottom—"

"Has two smaller petals that look to be coming from under the hood?" General Li interrupted.

"Yes. Do you know these flowers?" John asked.

The general nodded. "Every child old enough to hunt knows this flower. It is crushed and spread on our spear or arrow tips."

"Is there anything we can do?" the emperor asked.

"Alice says the doses were small enough that her illness would look to be natural in nature. It would have likely been administered to the skin, or in food or water daily," John replied. "I will not lie to you. The blood she is coughing up is likely due to inflammation in her lungs. Once the inflammation subsides, so should the bleeding. This poison is a neurotoxin and will likely have some lasting effects, but Alice does believe she will regain consciousness, and most of her strength, with time. Which also brings us to you, your Grace."

"Me?" the emperor asked, surprised.

"Alice would like to scan one of your hairs."

"How dare you," Li said, moving towards John.

"Li, withdraw, or you will leave the room." The general stopped short of John, his fists clenched tight. "I do not believe he was accusing me." The emperor pulled a silvery hair from the side of his head and handed it to John.

John slid the hair through his fingers like he had the princesses.

"The emperor is displaying the same chemical traces as his granddaughter. The doses appear smaller and are not as consistent as hers."

John handed the hair back to the emperor. He wasn't sure if it was expected but he didn't want to cause additional conflict with the general. "You show signs of poisoning as well."

"How is that even possible?" General Li said.

"Quiet. Let me think for a moment." The emperor leaned forward and rested his head in his hands. After a moment, he stood and looked at Li. "I know how you hate politics, but I must ask for your service."

Li bowed his head low. "My life is yours to use."

"You will inadvertently spread the news that Princess Ma's condition has worsened and may die soon." Li didn't look comfortable at the thought. "Tomorrow, I will send away her attendants. Li, I must ask for your help to bring water and food up here discretely. Everything must be done in secrecy. As for the traitor, we will wait and watch. Dark intentions cannot be contained and have a way of coming to the surface."

"Understood," General Li said.

"As for you." The emperor turned to face John. "I believe you understand the situation. To openly express my gratitude would alert those I seek. Still, I will not leave you unrewarded. What is a life worth, I wonder? Gifts?"

"You have already entrusted me with information about your city. That by itself is already too generous," John replied. Refusing was a humble gesture in Chinese culture. At least it once was.

"Politics." The emperor arched an eyebrow. "Leave those where they belong, among the schemers and plotters." He reached up and unclasped a necklace from around his neck. A small, round, etched silver disk dangled from the chain. "Let me offer you what you have given me, support." The emperor reached out, his hand shaking from the poison damaged nerves—or maybe from the burden of old age. He tried to hook the ends of the necklace around John's neck, but couldn't manage to link the chain. Li stepped around John and finished securing the necklace. This time the emperor didn't protest, and stepped back, rubbing his hands. "This bears my personal mark. It will allow you to enter and leave the city and it will gain you an audience with me at any time. Li will be a witness of my pledge to you. Now, no more formality as we will have plenty with our meal." He turned towards Li. "Have the princess's attendant see to her bedding and wash her."

"Consider it done," the general said.

John tucked the necklace in under his tattered shirt. He would see how well the emperor kept his word. The old man was cunning, and John somehow doubted anything would come without strings attached.

"Our meal should be ready. You will have to attend as you are, but it might work to our advantage," the emperor said to John.

"I want you to feel free in your speech tonight, as long as it does not include what we have discussed in this room."

John bowed. The emperor seemed pleased and held out his arm to Li. "I think I shall let you assist me down the stairs, just this once."

"Just this once, Emperor," Li said.

CHAPTER 15

The smell of roasted meat and spices in the air made John's stomach ache. A set of doors was opened to a large dining room. Most of the places around the elongated, low-rise table were empty. Adviser Tao was seated on the left side of the table. The light red robe he wore was more richly decorated than the blue one from before. The adviser was talking with a rotund man draped in yellow to his right. The ends of the heavy man's mustache bounced on his belly as he laughed. John counted ten others in total including—

"John!" Rebecca said, standing up near the head of the table, almost across from Adviser Tao. She was wearing a dress, not unlike the ones the local women wore. Her hair had been washed and pulled back in a tight braid.

The rest of the men in the room stood and lowered their heads as the emperor approached. The emperor circled the table and took the seat at the head. General Li led John to the seat across from Rebecca and to the emperor's right before taking the space next to Rebecca himself. The symbolism wasn't lost on John. He and Rebecca had been given the guest seats of honor at the table. Once the emperor was seated, everyone else followed suit. The emperor made introductions. Most of the men represented different interest groups within the court. Each was dressed finely, but none as well as the adviser.

"Our guests for this evening are John Crider and his female traveling companion," the emperor said. "Do not overburden them with questions as their journey has been long and one to which they must soon return."

With a wave of the emperor's hand, dishes of all types were brought forward and served. John forced back the urge not to grab handfuls of food and stuff them into his mouth. Rebecca was having an easier time with the chopsticks after General Li got her started.

Adviser Tao leaned over and with a wide smile said, "Start with the soup." He picked up his own and sipped.

John gathered up his own and raised it to his lips. The flavor was bold but refreshing. He couldn't help finishing it off in two large gulps.

"Soup is what our children start with as well," Adviser Tao said, setting his own soup back down. "I would offer you mine if you would like?"

John's jaw tightened. "Thank you, but no."

"Careful," Alice echoed in his mind. "There are variations present in the adviser's tone. He may have other motives than his words suggest."

John had picked up on it too. Not from his voice, but how he carried himself. He had seen the adviser's type before. Bureaucrats, always trying to find an angle. There was no doubt Adviser Tao was no stranger to manipulation.

"I find it easier to poke the things I like." The emperor poked a ball of meat and plopped it in his mouth.

It wasn't proper, but the emperor was giving him a way out. A way to keep face. John followed the emperor's lead and poked a meatball. Holding it out, he offered it to the adviser.

If possible, the adviser smiled even larger. "Yes. I think I will," he said, holding up his bowl, into which John deposited the meatball. The adviser set the bowl down, away from his other food. "I was told you could speak our language, even to the extent of a natural citizen. There are many of us who would love to know how you came by it."

John set his chopsticks down. It was a question he had anticipated since they entered the room. "It is similar enough to another I know."

The man in yellow, Sung Ten, was the next to speak up. The front of his robe was already streaked with sauce, the bulk of his belly catching most of what his mouth was not. "Your arrival to the city has certainly caused quite a stir among the population."

"We discovered your city by accident. My companion Professor Oddum was mistakenly escorted here. The professor and my other companions lack the knowledge of your language. This has caused the disruption with your people, and for that, I deeply apologize." John bowed his head. He could play this game as well. When he looked up, he saw Rebecca was staring at him with a confused look on her face.

"How?" Rebecca asked.

John smiled at Rebecca. "I followed the best I could and found the city. The emperor has agreed to let us all go tomorrow."

"No," Rebecca said. She took a moment to gather her thoughts. "How are you able to communicate with them?"

That was the most important question she had right now? "It's something I picked up traveling in the military. You know, from before." It was a lie, but it would have to do for now. "If you like, I can translate for you."

Rebecca looked at him skeptically. "I, I... " She shook her head, dismissing what she was going to say. "There are so many questions I have about this place, the creatures here, the city. How do you keep a city like this hidden? No. There are more scientific questions."

"Collect your thoughts, and I will ask them for you," John said. He turned back to the emperor. "With your permission, your Grace, I would like to translate for Professor Oddum parts of our conversation. I assure you, she would be happy to answer any questions you may have of her."

"You may," the emperor responded.

John had noticed the emperor hadn't touched any of the food, except the meatball. With the poisoning, he couldn't blame the emperor's lack of appetite.

"Your attire is unique. Where is it you come from?" asked Muy Fou, a mousy-looking older man dressed in all green. He was seated next to General Li, and so far as John could tell, all the man had eaten was a strange gelatinous brown sauce.

"A very long way away," John said. "We came here looking for something." He needed to be vague, but maybe this was too vague.

"And what would that be?" Muy Fou asked, taking another spoonful of the brown substance.

"Answers," John replied. "I hear others discussing the Hano. Who are they?" He asked hoping to change the conversation. The emperor said he was free to speak, but the last thing he wanted was to further increase the emperor's interest in his group.

This time it was the emperor who answered, "They are us, but not us. Long ago we were one, but as with everything, it fractured. Those who would not accept the Reborn Emperor were cast out and took on the mantle of Hano. They are wild, and time has changed them. Today they are more akin to animals than man." The others in the room muttered in agreement. "But do not think lightly of us because we are civilized. You witnessed my court, gathered before my royal study. Though outwardly they did not acknowledge your presence, they did notice you. Each has probably calculated numerous ways they could use you to their advantage. Am I wrong, Adviser?"

The adviser folded his chopsticks together and looked up. He brandished the same practiced smile as before. "As always, your Glory, you deduce correctly. Rumors travel quickly here, though none are without cost. Leverage is extremely valuable in our society."

"All of the intricacies of our economy are decided in that room," the emperor continued. "This does not mean I am not involved, but it is advantageous to them to settle disputes and agreements directly, for my price is quite high indeed. You observed the people painted gold before you entered my chambers, did you not?"

"I did," John replied.

"It is called the Room of Patience. All who ask a question or a favor of me must wait within that room. I require one thing in return—time."

"They just stand there until you decide to answer their question?" John asked.

"In a way, yes." The emperor picked up his cup and took a small sip. "Any may leave before support is rendered or their question answered. Many do. Our society is a simple one. All citizens are cared for within the walls of the city, but you must earn your place within it. Women gather out in the jungle without protection; it is symbolic of our dedication to one another. The men hunt for our food, but each must face his prey alone. This is the strength we are built upon."

It sounded more like population control to John. He looked over at Rebecca who had quietly attacked the food placed in front of her. "We have been talking about—"

"Fill me in later," Rebecca said, wiping her mouth with the back of her hand. "Ask them about the animals. Did they just appear one day or was it slowly? They have to know something."

"Okay, I'll ask," John said.

One of General Li's soldiers rushed into the room. He stopped and bowed in front of the table before moving swiftly to the general's side. The man whispered something to the general, bowed again, and quickly left the room.

"If you will excuse me, your Grace," General Li said, standing.

"An issue, General?" the emperor said, using Li's title instead of his name.

"I am uncertain at this time, but it is nothing I cannot—"

"Tell me what you know," the emperor ordered, raising his voice.

"Yes, your Grace," General Li said. "Several of my men and a few citizens are dead."

The men around the table started all talking at once. The emperor pounded his fist on the table. "Quiet!" The room fell silent. "Do you know the cause?"

"From the description, it does not appear to be an illness."

People didn't just fall over dead. "Emperor," John said. "I would like the chance to repay your hospitality by accompanying General Li. I may be of some use."

"How do we know you are not the cause?" a younger man at the end of the table asked. "For all we know—"

"You may go," the emperor said, cutting off the young man. "I believe I will see this for myself as well."

General Li tried to dissuade the emperor for a third time as they walked out of the palace. Like the other two times, he was met by the same unmovable stare, much like the one the general wore all too frequently. Though all the men at the table had joined initially, none, not even the adviser, followed. The adviser had excused himself by escorting Rebecca back to her room.

The streets were empty, likely cleared by the soldiers. At the end of a cross street, a few guards had gathered around a body in the street. When they saw the emperor, the soldiers quickly dropped to the ground, their faces hidden by their hands. The emperor didn't bother acknowledging the men and stepped up next to the body.

From how the victim was dressed he was one of the general's men. Dark red tendrils dripped down the man's sides, into a much larger pool on the ground. A fist sized hole puckered outward from just near the shoulder blade. General Li turned the body over, revealing a much smaller puncture mark. The realization came to John as the first soft whoosh cut through the air. Next to him, the emperor slumped forward and fell to the ground. The soldiers jumped to their feet, yelling for the emperor, but one by one bloody clouds exploded from the soft tissue of their bodies. John dove towards General Li, knocking him back. White hot pain seared across his cheek as an almost silent projectile cut across it.

"Come on, you're making this too easy!" Boot falls echoed out from a dark, narrow space cut between the adjacent stone buildings. "Can't say I wasn't tempted to put one through your head first."

John knew that voice. "Commander Makenzie?"

Makenzie stepped out into the street, his bolt rifle casually resting across his other arm. General Li pivoted, throwing John off of him. The general sprang off his back and onto his feet in one fluid movement.

Makenzie raised the rifle and leveled it at the general. "Pathetic."

John reached out and grabbed General Li's ankle. He yanked, causing the general to crash to the ground. "General, stop!" The general looked back at John, his face contorted with a mixture of pain and rage. "Look at them!" General Li's eyes welled with moisture. He tried to pull his foot free, but John held tight. "They're gone, General. Nothing can change that, but if you die, so does your princess." The general stopped fighting. His emotion-wrought face became hard again. "Please, stay down."

John stood up, his arms wide. He stepped between the general and Makenzie. Makenzie brought the butt of the rifle around and smashed it into the side of John's head. A brilliant flash of colors filled his vision. He was on his knees before he could string together what had happened.

"I'm a god compared to this trash, but somehow you still think you're in charge, don't you?" Makenzie jabbed the rifle into John's forehead. The edge of Makenzie's lip curled up in a mocking smile. "I can take your life with only the twitch of my finger, but first you're going to do something for me. Don't worry, when it's all done I'm still going to watch the life drain from you again. Now stand up!"

John's head was still spinning from the blow. Makenzie twisted John's arm, forcing him to his feet.

"Oww. What the..." Makenzie reached up to his neck and withdrew a small wooden dart. "I, I move."

Makenzie fell forward onto the ground, taking John with him. John could hear voices getting louder and louder before losing consciousness.

CHAPTER 16

John groaned. The side of his head thumped against something hard as he was pitched to the side.

"Finally," a high-pitched male voice said. "I would have never forgiven myself if you had missed it."

John slowly opened his eyes, giving them a second to adjust. The adviser was seated across from him, a wide grin on his face. John sat up, and rolled his head back and forth, trying to loosen the knot that had formed. It looked like they were alone in a small enclosed cart. He could feel the cart moving, but he couldn't remember getting into it. He tried to reach up, but his hands were tied behind him.

"I am sorry for the bindings, but one can never be too careful." The adviser crossed his legs and sat back against the wooden wall of the enclosed carriage.

"John," Alice said. "Move your left index finger if you can hear me." John wiggled his index finger. "After you lost consciences, they roughed you up pretty badly. General Li did try and stop them, but it was no use. I refrained from healing your external wounds. I did not want to cause any further misunderstandings."

"Good." John managed to say. The pounding in his head resided and allowed him to think.

"I am sorry, I did not catch that," the adviser said.

"I need to speak with General Li," John said.

Adviser Tao removed a small fan from his sleeve and began fanning himself. "There is no need. From what I hear, you saved the general's life. How unfortunate for the emperor though." The adviser couldn't contain his smile behind the sorrowful one he was trying hard to project. "Well, no matter. A new emperor will be chosen. One who will lead our expansion back into the light, to reclaim what is rightfully ours. Until then, I am willing to guide the politics of my people and the council. But first, there are things I need." Adviser Tao snapped his fan shut and set it on his lap. Next to him, on the plush bench seat, he removed a piece of white fabric, revealing Makenzie's rifle. "I would like to know how this works."

John glanced down at the rifle and back to the adviser. "Even if I told you, you would not be able to use it for long."

"I have no delusions of using the weapon myself. A simple showing of what it can do will suffice."

"I think I would like to speak with General Li first," John said.

"I do not believe you understand the situation. The emperor is dead, and retribution must be paid, and I have arranged to pay your cost. Others were not as fortunate to have such a generous benefactor."

This was bad. With the emperor gone, their chances of leaving went with him. John worked at the bindings around his wrist. Whatever they used to secure his hands only tightened as he struggled.

Adviser Tao's cackling laugh filled the small interior. "If I had you beaten and starved it would do no good. It would take far too long to break your spirit. No, I will break you, but not like a normal man. No, yours will be special, and when you do break— and you will—you will be mine." The adviser reached over and caressed John's leg. "In more ways than one."

John shook the adviser's hand off. "I always get what I want in the end," the adviser said, leaning back in his seat. He moved aside the light curtain covering the window to look out. "Maybe one day, after I become emperor, I will even let you replace the general."

Alice's voice echoed in John's head, "I am like powder. Already I am beyond repair." The words were familiar, but they weren't his.

When the adviser looked back, his new slave didn't have the look of fear or anger he was hoping for. Instead, he was smiling. Adviser Tao wrinkled his nose. He would have them bathe the man when they arrived back at the palace. After a bath, maybe the man would see he was as reasonable as he was generous. The cart came to a stop. "We are here. Smile—soon you will not."

The door opened, and a guard pulled John out. The sky was overcast, and the light breeze was laden with moisture. A large crowd had gathered around the cart. These people were different from the ones he had seen in the city. Their clothing was torn and caked with mud. It was a stark difference from the cleanly proud people John has seen within the city. Adviser Tao exited the cart and handed Makenzie's rifle off to a second guard.

"The cart attendants have requested permission to view the event," the guard said.

Adviser Tao looked at the men standing at the pull bars. "No. I think they will wait by the cart. Now, clear me a path."

"Yes, Adviser," the guard said.

The guards beat the people back, clearing a path to a large wooden platform for John and the adviser. General Li and a small group, some of whom John had seen around the emperor's dining table, were present. There were only two fixtures on the platform, a large forked wooden tripod and an oversized chair. Adviser Tao walked straight toward the chair positioned beside the platform's edge. John could feel everyone watching as the adviser stepped up to the chair, instead of sitting he stood in front of it. The move was not missed by any there. General Li moved to Adviser Tao's side.

"After your opposition to this, one would have thought you would have chosen not to attend," Adviser Tao said.

"I may not agree, but I am still bound by the vote of the council," General Li replied.

"Yes, indeed. Your civility in a time of crisis is well placed, General," Adviser Tao said, stepping toward the rough-cut railing. "Today is about vengeance, let's not forget. Tomorrow. Tomorrow will be about change."

A space opened next to the adviser. John moved towards the railing and for the first time saw what everyone else was looking at. The platform extended out from a ledge and looked down on small, layered pools. Slow-moving water drained from one rise of water to the next. Jungle lined the three sides in a haphazard rectangular shape, the water continuing out until it finally disappeared a few hundred feet into the jungle. Below the platform, thirteen large poles spaced a few feet apart, stuck out from the water.

The adviser glanced over at John. "When the waters turn in color you will be in for a rare treat. It looks like they are about ready."

Below, soldiers were leading a small group off a narrow makeshift bridge and out into the shallow waters. Rebecca, Gramm, and Makenzie were at the front line. Their body armor had been removed, and their hands were bound in front of them. Nolan hung limp over the shoulder of another soldier behind Makenzie. Behind the soldier, men and women covered in a red powder-like paint followed closely. The red matched the hue of the adviser's robe all too well. Along the cliff, and to either side of the platform, the rest of the crowd and gathered to watch.

The adviser turned away from the railing and leaned in close to John. "You may translate to your people if you wish. I believe the surprise of not knowing would be far more rewarding though." The adviser stepped back and held his hands up. The crowd quieted. "We have gathered here on sacred ground to seek justice for our most holy, the Father of Light." Wails came from the crowd. Women threw themselves down on the ground, further soiling their already mud-stained clothing. "Even now the Father of Light looks down upon us, giving us guidance as we seek retribution for what was taken. I have given of my own house to spare this man." The adviser reached down and lifted John's hand and with the other pointed down to the citizens covered in red. "We will now put their salvation in his hands."

The crowd erupted in shouting, pressing in on the platform. General Li moved out in front of the crowd, causing the angered mob to hesitate. "The emperor's law is absolute. To continue your actions will be taken as a grave disrespect of the emperor himself. Now come if you must, and I will deal with your childishness myself."

Adviser Tao placed his hand on the general's shoulder. "I implore you, good people, to return to your vantage points. I promise your anger will be sated soon enough." The crowd spread back to either side of the platform. It wasn't long, and they were hollering and jeering those down below again. General Li shrugged the adviser's hand off.

"Careful, General. My patience for you has limits." Adviser Tao turned back to John, a smile again spreading across his face. "It is simple. Whoever makes it to the tree line may go free." With a flourish of his robes, he walked back to the railing.

John doubted it would be that easy. General Li removed a knife from the folds of his robe and began to cut away John's wrist restraints.

"Do not speak, listen," the general said, keeping his voice low. "An old stone structure spans the entire length just under the surface. Do not be tempted to swim towards the trees on either side—you will not make it. If you do make it to the far end, the adviser has placed soldiers within the trees. They will spare your life, and your life alone." General Li looked over John's shoulder at Adviser Tao. "Your people will never make it to the river."

John started to turn towards the adviser. He was tired of playing everyone's pawn.

General Li's grip tightened, pulling him back. "Now is not the time." He cut through the last bit of rope and looked John in the face. "Men still loyal to me will try and remove as much of the threat as they can before you get there. You will find further aid at the river."

John could feel the cold metal of the General's knife press against his hand.

The general clasped John by the forearm. "This is a promise kept."

"Enough," Adviser Tao ordered from his position near the wooden chair. "Bring the basket!"

The general motioned over to his side. A large woven basket was brought forward. The rope was attached and threaded through the wooden tripod. The flooring was removed, revealing the water below. A soldier helped John into the basket.

"Wait," the adviser said. He motioned for the guard holding Makenzie's rifle. "A final gift."

The soldier handed John the rifle. His hand tightened on the grip, and his finger edged towards the trigger. If the adviser wanted a demonstration, he would give him one.

General Li stumbled into John, causing the basket to swing dangerously to the side. The men holding the rope grunted under the extra weight. The rifle dropped to the bottom of the basket.

The Adviser laughed aloud. "Take care of your step, General. We would hate to lose you so soon."

"Save it," the general whispered. "Kill the man with the paddle. His life is already forfeit, but great death follows him." The general pushed himself back up.

John nodded and looked over to the adviser. "Thank you for the gift, Adviser. You will be the first to know when I use it."

The Adviser's face constricted into a scowl. "Lower him!"

The basket tilted unevenly as it started to lower. Below, the soldiers had attached Rebecca and the rest of the group to the poles. Each was tethered by a length of rope, which allowed them to move around. John looked over to where the small bridge had been. It and the soldiers were gone. John reached down and picked up the rifle before the basket came to a stop, Water rushed in through the gaps in the weaving until the bottom was covered.

You cunning son of a bitch, John thought, looking up at the platform. If he had held up the rifle, pointing it at the adviser, someone might have seen the knife the general had slipped him. The general and his men were risking their lives to help. He needed to make the most of the opportunity. John stepped out of the basket into the shallows. Something slapped the water near the end of the line of poles.

"At this time, I only detect a single disturbance in the water," Alice said.

John looked around, trying to take everything in. "I have a bad feeling about this."

"Your assessment is warranted," Alice replied.

John palmed the knife in his right hand and gripped the rifle stock tightly to keep it in place. He moved towards Rebecca, the rifle raised, scanning from side to side as he went. Rebecca and Gramm were situated towards the center of the poles. Makenzie and Nolan were tied near the end. Unlike everyone else, Nolan was tied directly to the pole to keep him from falling over in the water. The slapping sound continued in a rhythmic *thwack... thwack... thwack.*

"What's going on, John!" Rebecca said. The fear marking her face.

"Why don't you ask Makenzie," John replied.

Makenzie spit into the water. "Why don't you be a good little boy and cut me free?"

John ignored him. "Makenzie killed the emperor, and the locals aren't too happy about it."

"What!" Rebecca stammered. "But... why? I don't—"

"I'll explain later. Gramm, you okay to carry Nolan?" John asked.

"Sure thing, Sergeant," Gramm replied. "I would have put up a fight, but I was worried they would hurt the others."

"Don't worry, I'm sure you'll get a chance before this is over." John held up the barrel of the rifle to Rebecca. "I need you to hold this while I cut."

Rebecca didn't answer, but she grabbed onto the rifle hard enough to make her knuckles turn white. John gripped the rope around her wrists and slipped the blade between. The knife was sharp, but whatever the rope was made from proved difficult to cut. Slowly the rope started to separate.

Thwack... thwack.

John turned, looking for the source of the sound. Not far from Makenzie and Nolan, a man raised and lowered a long thick paddle. The paddle slapped the surface, sending a spray of water back onto the man. The man continued in the same constant rhythm as before, *thwack... thwack.* Was this the man the general wanted him to kill?

"What's he doing?" Rebecca asked.

John hadn't realized he'd stopped cutting. "Nothing. Here, hold still."

John started cutting again. *Thwack.* The knife finally made its way past the knot. *Thwack.*

"I am registering a large pressure change in the water," Alice warned.

The water exploded outward, sending a spray of water droplets into the air. A giant set of leathery jaws snapped shut on the man who had been slapping the surface. The man let out a muffled cry as the crocodile-like creature's throat constricted and pulled him down the reptile's gullet.

The general had tried to warn John, but now it was too late. John turned and ran over to Gramm. "Give me your hands!" He inserted the knife into the heart of the bindings and started to saw frantically.

"You killed him!" Gramm screamed at the crocodile. He yanked at the rope, trying to pull it free. "You killed Marcus, motherfucker!"

The huge crocodile pulled itself out of the water.

The knife cut into the side Gramm's wrist. "Gramm!" John pulled the big man's hands back down. "Stop moving, damn it." Gramm was losing it. He had to think of something.

The crocodile reached the first pole. Adviser Tao's man strained at the rope holding him. The crocodile turned its head to the side. Its jaws came together in a sickly crunch of flesh and bone.

"Gramm!" John grabbed Gramm by the sides of the head and forced it around, making Gramm look at him. "It's not the same one, but we're all dead if you don't pull it together."

"It...It—" Gramm tried to turn his head, but John's grip held him tight. "I can't carry Nolan and run. Is that how you want him to die?"

The tension in Gramm's neck subsided. John let go. Gramm looked down at the rope around his hands. It had only begun to fray. He flexed, his biceps bulged. The veins in his neck swelled from the exertion. With a snap, the rope broke. "Get the professor, and I'll get Nolan." Gramm ran towards Nolan, hollering his name.

John turned looking for Rebecca, and in a moment of panic, couldn't find her. The movement against the pole caught his attention. Rebecca was holding onto the pole for dear life, her eye's squeezed shut. "Rebecca, we need to go." He stuffed the knife the general had given him, through his already ragged belt, and pried her arms away from the pole. The rifle was gone. "Come on we need to go."

The crocodile had already stripped four of the poles clean of life and was advancing to the fifth, only one man away from Nolan. Above on the ledge, the noise was deafening. A few loose stones, or whatever the crowd could find, were hurled down. Gramm had made it to Nolan's pole. He placed his boot against the pole and pulled at the rope holding Nolan in place. His hands slipped, and he fell back in the water. Cursing, he stood back up and pulled again. This time the rope started to stretch.

"Leave him. He's dead," Makenzie said, from behind Gramm. "Get me out, and I'll make sure you're compensated."

Gramm continued working on Nolan's rope.

"I'm your commanding officer. I order you to release me!"

The rope snapped. Gramm stumbled back but was able to catch himself. He lifted Nolan out of the water and situated him across his shoulder.

"You'll get me out of here, or I'll make sure I kill your wife personally."

"With all due respect, screw you, Commander." Gramm turned and ran over to John and the professor.

The crocodile, the size of a bus, lumbered toward Makenzie.

"Come on," John said. "Good of Makenzie to offer to distract it for us."

They moved as fast as they could in the shallow water. Behind them, they could hear the wood splinter as the crocodile tore at Makenzie's pole. The crowd cheered from up above. John chanced a glance back. The remains of Makenzie's pole stuck up defiantly out of the water.

John adjusted his grip on Rebecca's arm. "Keep to the center," he said, eyeing the opaque surface on either side.

A small natural embankment led out of the shallows and into the forest. The water flowed off to the side, and into the thicket. Gramm pressed through the thick vegetation covering the incline. John followed pulling Rebecca along. Behind them, the sounds of carnage continued.

"Sergeant, you need to see this," Gramm said.

John pushed through the last of the reeds. Gramm was standing over a man face down on the ground. John knelt and touched the body. It was still warm. There were no signs of injury on the body.

"Whatcha think?" Gramm asked.

"Friends, I hope," John said, standing back up. Somehow, he doubted it would be the last time he would see General Li. Things had an odd way of coming back around. "We'll find out soon enough."

The slow-moving water soon became a white, rushing turret. A low deep rumble was barely audible, over the sounds of the river. John continually scanned the area, looking for any other signs of the adviser's men, but it appeared the general's soldiers were thorough in their assignment. As they continued along the riverbank, the rumbling become more distinct. It was subtle at first, but soon he could feel it reverberating throughout his whole body. A plume of white spray, up ahead, rose from where the rapids dropped out of sight. John and the other's moved towards the rising vapors until they were standing at the edge of the drop. Water cascaded down in connected jets of power, only to be broken on a few outstretched rocks. The waterfall disappeared into a cloud of mist some fifty feet below. Gramm walked over to the bank near the edge of the water. Beyond the plunge basin, John could make out what looked like a raft.

"There," John pointed down at the raft. "That's our way out."

"And how we supposed to get down there?" Gramm asked.

Gramm was right. There was no path down. John leaned out to inspect the cliff face. Natural pitting and fracture lines covered the exterior. Even if he used vine to rig some kind of harness, Rebecca was in no condition to climb, and it would take too much time to lower Nolan down.

"We'll have to follow the ridge," John said, turning back towards Gramm. "We'll find a place where the grade levels out, and backtrack to the boat."

"Always got a plan, don't you?"

John and Gramm turned. Makenzie stood a few feet away. Blood ran down from a gash in his neck. The left side of his face was bright red. His left eye was almost completely swollen shut. In his hands, he clutched the gas-powered rifle. "Oh, this." He raised the weapon and trained it on the professor. "Bitch dropped it."

John stepped in front of Rebecca.

Makenzie laughed. "You're turning your back on the wrong person." He pivoted and squeezed the trigger.

The cylindrical round grazed Gramm's shoulder, opening a long thin gash. Gramm looked down at his shoulder, the thin band of muscles on either side of his jaw protruded as he clinched his teeth. He started to lift Nolan from his shoulders when Makenzie raised the rifle again and leveled the muzzle at Gramm's chest.

"Do it, and I'll put a hole in your chest before you even see me pull the trigger," Makenzie said.

John took a step towards Makenzie. "It doesn't have to be this way."

"Oh, it certainly does," Makenzie said. "I only need you. Think of the rest of them as... motivation for your continued cooperation."

A scream pierced the oppressive air. John turned. Rebecca's eyes were wide, her mouth agape. A whimper tried to escape her lips. Makenzie rushed between John and Gramm and leaped off the side of the cliff. "What the!" John spun around in time to see a towering blur of teeth and red. The jaws snapped shut just behind Makenzie before he disappeared into the back spray of the waterfall. John hadn't heard it coming. The tyrannosaur turned its head toward Gramm and Nolan and roared. Reflexively, Gramm covered his ears; his eyes met with John's. John reached back and grabbed hold of Rebecca's hand. He needed to buy them some time.

"Here!" John yelled, waving his free hand in the air. "Over here!" The tyrannosaur twisted around.

"I am having difficulty following your logic," Alice said.

You and me both, John thought. "Go!" he screamed at Gramm.

Gramm hesitated, looking back at the forest as if he was trying to decide if he could make it to the trees. Whatever it was, he must have changed his mind. He shifted Nolan's weight and ran for the edge. The tyrannosaur whipped its head around with terrifying speed. The toothy maw snapped closed. With a sharp shake of its head, it tore Nolan from Gramm's back. The force of the movement sent Gramm sprawling over the edge of the falls.

The creature used its colossal back leg to pin Nolan to the ground. The flesh tore away as it pulled Nolan's body in half. The wet popping sounds of flesh and bone separating were barely audible, over the falls. There was no movement from Nolan, no final scream to signal the end. Maybe it was better that way. But it was the sound that captivated John... the sound was distinct. Familiar. A wave of sorrow crept over his very core, eroding his insides. It wasn't for Nolan, it was for something or someone else.

"John!"

"Alice. I, I don't—" He watched, fixated by the slow expanse of crimson on the small broken stones under Nolan. Near the corner of the tyrannosaur's eye, a familiar jagged wound caught his attention.

"Move, John!"

John was in motion before he realized his body was moving. He yanked Rebecca in close and cleared the ledge. They seemed to hang forever, weightless, before gravity pulled them down.

CHAPTER 17

It wasn't enough! The mental link Alice had established between her and John was nine hundred and fifty thousand times faster than the sound of the human voice. She had refined every system at her disposal countless times, and yet there was nothing she could do. Current events were processed through her logistical core instantly, and statistical decisions were provided faster than the human mind could begin to form a thought. She knew the approach of Commander Makenzie and the dinosaur-like creature had been masked by the environmental distortions of the waterfall, but she rejected the solution. In the end, all she could do was watch through John's eyes as he jumped from the ledge, Professor Oddum tightly in his arms. Unacceptable!

The angle was off. John tried to take most of the impact on his back to cushion Rebecca, but the force of colliding with the water was too much. Rebecca was wrenched from his arms. The air from his lungs was forced out in one mass exodus. Involuntarily, he sucked in, filling his throat and nostrils with water. It felt like liquid fire was filling his chest. He kicked wildly, hoping to God he was swimming up and not down. Breaching the surface, he retched forward in the water. The only significant food he had had in days emptied from him. Soon the spasms stopped.

Roughly, he wiped the last of his stomach contents from his chin and tried to orient himself. A thin, dull haze, thrown off by the falls, hung in the air. He blinked the water from his eyes and scanned the surface for Rebecca. Everywhere he looked, it was the same frothy discolored water and the ever-changing mist.

"Rebecca!" he called, but his voice was mostly drowned out by the thunderous crash of the falls. His pulse quickened as the seconds passed. He took a deep breath and plunged beneath the surface. The water was choked with sediment, limiting visibility to a few inches. If Rebecca was down here, he'd have to be right on top of her to see her. Alice could help, couldn't she?

He pinched his nose and blew out to equalize the pressure in his ears. The water temperature felt cool against his exposed skin. The perforations in his environment suit only added to the feeling. His hand scraped against the muddy rock bottom, sending more sediment into the already mostly opaque water. At the edge of his peripherals, something slid back into the murk. Rebecca? No. Whatever it was, it moved against the current, not with. His hand brushed the handle of the knife protruding from his belt. After the fall, it was a miracle it had stayed in place. Careful not to cut his belt, he pulled the knife free.

The current pulled him along. Weightless, he floated, looking for movement. This close to the riverbed his boots drug along the bottom, causing a sediment cloud to expand behind him. His lungs began to burn. Pushing off the river floor, he swam upward. At the surface, he sucked in long drags of air and tried to slow his heart rate. Out in front of him, a large dark spot under the surface materialized. It was only a slight discoloration, but it was there.

"Did you detect the irregularity in the surface of the water?" Alice asked.

John nodded in reply.

Just below the surface, the darkened patch moved, first with the current, then back against it. John tightened his grip on the knife. It wouldn't be much use, but maybe he could deter whatever it was. The spot turned and swam towards him. Slowly, it moved closer. Anger flared inside him. He didn't have time for this, Rebecca could be on the bottom right now. The thing was only a few feet away now. He raised the knife out of the water, ready to plunge it down. His heart hammered in his chest. In front of him, a head surfaced. A rubbery circular mouth, the size of a dinner plate, slurped as it opened and closed its fleshy lips. The giant carp, lazily sucked a few scraps from the surface before it turned its lumbering mass of light brown scales back in the direction of the falls. John let out the breath he was holding, a laugh tried to follow, but died in his throat as something brushed the back of his head. Yelling out of surprise, he spun, sending water in a wide arch. The body bobbed lightly, unmoving on the surface. Red hair fanned out around the head like a crown. Wait. That color.

"Rebecca!" He reached and pulled her in close. Her lips were blue. "Come on, Rebecca." He patted her cheek. "Stay with me." There was no response. John positioned himself behind her and wrapped an arm around her chest. Using his legs and his free hand, he swam hard to the bank.

John pulled Rebecca out of the water and laid her on an area clear of rocks. He dropped the knife and pressed two fingers against the side of her throat. There was no pulse. Tilting her head back, he pressed his lips against hers and exhaled twice. He moved beside her and started doing chest compressions. "One, two, three—"

"Someone's approaching," Alice warned.

John didn't have a choice. He continued the chest compressions.

Makenzie bent down and picked up John's knife. "You're always trying to be the hero."

John breathed twice more and moved back to Rebecca side.

"You're wasting your time, John. The other way around and she would have left you floating," Makenzie said. He lowered the rifle barrel to John's temple. "Now. Get up!"

Rebecca vomited. John rotated her on her side and used his hand to wipe away the bile. Once she finished, he rolled her back again, and check for breathing. Still nothing. He pressed his lips firmly to hers again, ignoring the tasted of her partially digested last meal. *Breathe*. Her chest rose, then lowered. *Come on, damn it!* He leaned in again. Rebecca coughed and gasped for air. "That's it. Breathe," John said, cradling her head in his lap.

"Oh good," Makenzie said. "Now that the cunt's not dead get on the fucking boat."

The boat General Li had provided moved effortlessly down the river. John sat at the rudder piloting the small craft. The river was wide enough that he didn't have to do much to keep it moving. Gramm was already on the boat when he carried Rebecca aboard. For the last couple hours, the big man hadn't said a word. He stared down at the deck, his eyes wide, barely blinking. Rebecca was asleep on the long center bench, wrapped in a blanket

John had found under one of the seats. The boat was well supplied, and along with food and water, there were plenty of other items as well.

John's fingers absently traced the necklace under his shirt. Even with General Li's men, he doubted the emperor's sign of friendship would mean much now. Corruption and power have a way of always rising to the top. Li was a good man. Hopefully he was smart enough to get out too. Makenzie leaned back against the point of the bow and unwrapped a small yellow cake, his third. Crumbs fell onto the rifle balanced on his lap. In two bits, the cake was gone. He tossed the fabric wrapping over the side.

"That big dinosaur's been tracking us by scent, you realize it, right?" John asked.

Makenzie smiled, shrugged, and began to unwrap another cake. "It's been following me since I got out of the underground facility. Bitch hasn't got me yet."

John adjusted the rudder, angling them back to the center of the river where the current was swiftest. Makenzie would have to die, there were no illusions in John's mind about that, and yet somehow, he felt a strange lingering sense of sorrow for him. It wasn't a feeling he put much thought in, but it was there. A nagging ember fanned by things outside his cognitive reach.

The boat moved slowly through the water. There were now hours between them and the falls, and if Alice was correct, the river should take them near the beacon by early morning. Something moved near the water's edge. A small creature looked up from drinking as they passed. The tree-lined river was host to all sorts of creatures. Some he had already seen, but the vast majority were new and strange. He should have cared more, but he was sick of this place.

"I got to ask you something," Makenzie said, tossing another piece of fabric over the side. "Why do you care so much? It's not like these people would do the same for you. Gramm here has twenty-three citations of insubordination. He punched his last commanding officer in the head hard enough to fracture his skull. Shattered the man's eye socket. The guy still can't form a lucid sentence." The professor stirred on the bench. Makenzie followed John's eyes to her. "I had orders to bring her back, but sometimes things don't work out. Don't feel bad for her, Johnny boy, Oddum's more messed up than all of us combined. You weren't the only one she worked on. Did you know she went through seventy-eight? There would have been more if we hadn't talked the good Doctor Malcolm into helping. Seventy fucking eight! I bet she had more kills than you do!" Makenzie started to laugh, almost choking on what he was eating.

"That's enough," Gramm said, looking up. "None of us are clean in this."

Makenzie put his hand on the rifle, the other still holding a cake.

Gramm made a fist, his knuckles cracked as he tightened it. "There's a difference between people like you and the sergeant. I've never seen a man run willingly towards death before, and I don't rightly know who I should be more afraid of at times. Never cared much for being ordered around and all, but the sergeant's different. It all comes down to respect. Something you'll never understand."

The smirk on Makenzie's face widened. "Don't seem to me like respect saved Nolan or Marcus. As for me, I've got all the respect I need right here." He patted the rifle. "In the end, faith in others will only get you killed."

Gramm lowered his head, his hand relaxed, and he focused on the wooden planks of the deck. What fight there may have been was gone. Makenzie's gaze shifted out across the water. The maddening smile quickly slipped away. He spoke subtly enough John almost missed it, but his words made John's blood run cold.

"Is everything fuzzy yet? Do you still remember their faces or their names?"

John froze, his fingers still around the necklace. His stomach twisted and his body felt like someone drained it of all feeling. They should have been there, their expressions, loving memories, anything, but now, nothing. With trembling fingers, he released the necklace. His fingers searched out the interior pocket, something he realized he hadn't thought of for some time. An uncomfortable tightness spread from his chest, up into his throat. For a moment, he was afraid he wasn't going to find what he was looking for.

Careful, he removed the laminated picture. The face looking back at him was familiar.

"Alice," John said. His finger tracing over her forehead. It was the same face from that cold room.

"Remember, John," Alice said.

It was her voice. Not the childlike one, but the one John had become accustomed. His head filled with images of a woman. Late morning snuggling. A walk along a beach with almost no end. The smell of a burnt casserole forgotten in the oven. *Emily*. The images changed. He could hear the unspoiled laughter of a young girl as she ran through the gently rolling hills of grass in a park. The weight of her small body as he carried her from the car, after a date night with his little green bean. *Maddie*.

"I will not let you forget," Alice said. "I promised."

John slipped the picture back into its pocket. A warm breeze cooled the dampness on his cheeks. Using the tip of his finger, he slowly spelled out "thank you" on his forearm.

The clouds thinned before the sun went down. The full moon illuminated the river in a soft silvery light. Nocturnal creatures emerged from slumber, adding to the growing chorus of the night. Rebecca had roused before dusk, and now like everyone else, her eyes continuously scanned the bank and the moving water. The cap of a water container in Rebecca's hands swayed on its string. It made a gentle, offbeat click when it collided with the wooden exterior of the jug. The sound, like the previous tension, was forgotten in that moment. The boat glided silently down the river. No one spoke, only watched, their eyes trying to locate the hidden sounds within the outer veil of moon-kissed darkness. They would stay this way until the pale glow of dawn crept over the horizon.

A thin haze rose from the surface of the water. Wisps, translucent, almost alive, flirted with the inside edge of the boat, but as the temperature continued its oppressive climb, the mist burned away.

"Here," Alice said. "The beacon converges three miles west of our location."

John pulled the rudder tight into his chest. The boat cut across the current towards the bank.

"Is this it?" Makenzie asked. He twisted in his seat to get a better view.

"We're on foot from here," John said.

The front of the boat slid onto the bank. Rebecca looked back at him from her seat. It looked as if she wanted to say something, but instead, she stood and moved to the front of the boat. Makenzie deboarded and Rebecca held out her hand for help down, but Makenzie made no move to take it. John rose and walked over to the supply boxes. Maybe there was something in them, some other surprise the general had left.

"Leave everything," Makenzie said. "The less we carry, the quicker you'll move."

Gramm was watching John too. He nodded. There was something unsaid but understood in it. An *I'm with you when you are ready.* But now was not the time. Makenzie held the rifle slack against his shoulder, a position he could quickly fire from if needed. Since the plane ride, it was apparent Makenzie was different than the others. He was capable and almost too resourceful, traits he had tried to hide before. But why? And how had he known about the memory loss? Did he know about Alice? There were too many questions. Once they reached the beacon, he would get his answers, one way or another.

John watched as Gramm helped Rebecca down from the boat. There was also something going on with Rebecca too. It wasn't based on what Makenzie had said—the man was crazy—but small things. There was no denying the possibility of feelings between them, but it felt more synthetic than natural, almost forced. He hopped down from the boat and grabbed Gramm's arm. Gramm turned and looked at him.

"I'm sorry about Nolan," John said. "I can't pretend I knew him, but I know both he and Marcus meant something to you."

"Marcus never said much, but he was a good man," Gramm said, nodding. "Nolan I didn't know much. He only started a couple months ago, but the kid followed me everywhere. I threatened to slap some sense into him, and he would just smile and laugh. He didn't deserve what he got." The big man's eyes glossed over. He rubbed at the corner of one with his thumb.

"We'll make it right, Gramm. I promise," John said.

"Less talking and more walking," Makenzie said. "You can lead the way, Sergeant." He motioned forward with the rifle.

John kept a steady pace, pushing them forward. The trees here were spaced further apart, and the sparse undergrowth made the terrain easier to traverse.

"Look." Gramm pointed up at a tree.

John had noticed it too. One or two at first, but now they were overtaking the rest. Bare skeletal twisted limbs reached up to the sky. They were in stark contrast to the thick lush green everywhere else. The smooth, white, barkless trunks looked almost fake. He rapped on one beside him. Stone. They were fossilized.

"Amazing," Rebecca said somewhere behind him.

"I am registering the scent of ignited combustibles," Alice said.

John closed his eyes and breathed in slowly. She was right. It was faint, but it was there. "Smoke up ahead."

"You sure?" Rebecca asked. Her hands were searching out the curve of a knot in the tree next to her. "I don't smell anything."

"It's there," John replied. "Eyes open and stay close."

They continued forward, slower now. The smell of smoke intensified.

"Look there." Makenzie jogged past, towards a rectangular object on the ground. The rest of the group followed. He patted the metal container. On the side, two words were printed in large block letters: CORP DIVISION. "They did make it!"

"We need to—" John started to say, but Makenzie took off running. "Wait!" *Damn it!*

They rushed after him. The smell of smoke was thick now. A metallic taste layered the tongue with each breath. There was something else in it too. Something acrid and earthy. Makenzie didn't run far, and they caught up to him standing in front of a large smoldering pile. The smell of burnt hair and melting fatty tissue was unmistakable. Rebecca tried to say something, but her words were choked off as she vomited.

Equipment, bits of tenting, and other odds and ends littered the area. John reached down and picked up a piece of charred body. It looked like they had unpacked to camp before whatever happened here. Armor and gear were still leaning against the bases of trees. A few tents still stood, silent sentinels over the horrors they had witnessed. Underneath the piece of armor John had picked up, a short bone wrapped with dark material protruded from the ground. He pulled it free and winced as something cut into the side of his index finger. The bone continued for six inches beyond the binding, ending in a point. The inside ridge was honed to a razor thin edge while the outer edge's thickness, added to the structural strength. It was a well-crafted bone knife. His index finger started to tingle and go numb.

"Neutralizing toxin now. I would advise against touching the unprotected end," Alice said.

The numbness disappeared, and the cut healed as John watched. "That's new."

"All remaining INOs within your system are now active. They are still limited by their individual energy disbursement. Strenuous use requires varying recovery times." Alice said. "John, I am detecting movement outside of our current group."

"Where?" he asked, not caring if the others heard.

"Everywhere," Alice replied.

John rose slowly. "We need to leave."

Gramm looked up from a container he had just opened. "I think you need to see this, Sergeant."

Makenzie had his back to them still staring at the smoldering pile of bodies.

"Not the time. We're not alone here," John said.

A man had appeared beside one of the trees, spectral in appearance. His exposed upper and lower torso matched the color of the trees around him. Even the cloth tied around his waist was colored white. To the side, another appeared, then another. Everywhere John looked, a new one seemed to materialize.

Gramm stepped up next to John. "Get the professor." He snapped the pressurized gas compartment on a rifle stock closed. "Told you you'd want to see what was in the box."

John backed up to where Rebecca was still crouched after vomiting. Her hair dangled over her face. He reached down and calmly pulled her to her feet.

She groaned. "I don't think I'm done." A long strand of saliva hung from her bottom lip.

"I don't think you have a choice," John said.

Rebecca followed his gaze. She gasped.

Like a linchpin being pulled, the spectral figures rushed inward. John could see Gramm squeeze the trigger of the rifle, but the soft sound of the nails firing was lost among the high-pitched battle cry of the men. Makenzie ran forward directly into the horde, firing wildly. White bodies exploded with crimson gore as the cylindrical ammunition contorted, passing through flesh and bone. John lost track of Makenzie amongst the sea of white. For every savage Gramm took down, another appeared from nowhere. The pale landscape turned into a canvas of death around them. John shoved Rebecca down as a spear snaked out towards him. He slashed forward, at the man holding the spear, catching the soft tissue of the man's throat. The man's eyes bulged, his hand going instinctively to his neck, trying to hold in the blood. A hard open palm strike to the man's face sent him reeling to the ground.

A dark shape moved in front of John against the tide of men. The green-and-black shape streaked between the trees, faster than any man could. He watched as six feet of feather and beak leaped into the air and came crashing down on one of the painted men. The battle erupted into chaos as more of the large bird-like creatures joined in.

John pulled Rebecca back to her feet and yelled over to Gramm, "We need to move. Now!"

"But want about Makenzie?" Rebecca asked.

"Less I have to deal with later. Now move," John said.

Gramm drops two more combatants in quick succession. "I've got our twelve. Go! Go! Go!"

They sprint through the disorder, Gramm clearing a path.

"Where are we going, Alice?" John asked, not caring if the others heard.

"You are less than a mile from the beacon. Continue in your current direction."

"Come on. It's just ahead," John said.

A colorful flourish of movement caught John's eye but it was too late. The mass collided with Gramm, sending him hard to the ground. The bird was more terrifying up close. It shrieked, the blue feathers encircling its neck raised, slightly shaking. Gramm scrambled for his gun, but the bird's splayed taloned foot pinned him to the ground.

John let go of Rebecca's hand and switched his grip on the bone knife. "Alice! Any help right now would be appreciated."

"No!" Rebecca clutched at his hand, pulling back. "You can't save him. We need to get out of here while it's still occupied."

"No, you don't!" Gramm slammed his fist into the side of the bird's beak, breaking off a small piece.

John shook Rebecca's hand loose. She looked up at him, her eyes wide with animal-like desperation. When this all began, he would have left both of them without a second thought. But now—now it was different. Everything was different. Gramm screamed as one of the bird's talons split the back of his thigh.

John didn't think. His legs carried him forward toward the flightless abomination. The bird craned its head around. It was fast, but with Alice, he was faster. The beak snapped shut, but only managed to capture air. He buried the knife deep into the bird's collar. It cried out in a combination of pain and surprise. Jerking back, the bird pulled the knife from John's hand. The creature tried frantically to reach the embedded bone with its beak, but its head was too large and the knife too far forward. John moved in, hoping to drag Gramm away, but the bird turned its vacant yellow eyes back to him. It lowered its head, bobbing it from side to side. The bird leaned back, muscles tightening, a coil ready to explode. It rocked forward but instead of charging it fell over. The bird tried to stand, but its legs wouldn't hold it anymore.

John's thumb unconsciously went to the now healed cut on his finger. He knew the poison would work, but he hadn't expected it to work that quickly. He walked over to Gramm's rifle and picked it up. The gas chamber was exposed, and the cylinder dented in. The bird let out a rasp and began to convulse on the ground. John aimed the rifle at the bird's head and depressed the trigger. The weapon clicked, but nothing came out. He tossed the rifle away and went over to Gramm. Maybe mercy wasn't right for this world after all.

Gramm rolled onto his back. "Damn, Sergeant. Hard to look tough with you around." He managed a small laugh.

John removed his belt and patted Gramm on the arm. "If you didn't hit like a five-year-old, I wouldn't have had to step in."

Gramm laid his head back on the ground. "Cold, man. That's plain cold."

John looped the belt above the wound on Gramm's thigh.

"It's no use. I won't be able to put any weight on it." Gramm winced, as John pulled the belt tight. "I didn't even see it coming. Not quite how I pictured going out, you know."

"There you go again, being all soft." John looked back the way they had come. They had made it out of the major fighting, but they could be right back in the thick of it if they didn't get moving. "We should still be able to make it. Let's get you up."

Gramm shook his head. "Leave me. I'll only slow you down. Plus, if another one of those things comes—"

"If another one of those things comes, I'll need bait." John smiled and held out his hand. "Now get your ass up. That's an order."

Gramm gave John a pained smile. "Well, since you need bait and all." He took John's hand and hobbled up onto his good leg.

John hoped Alice was still helping because this wasn't going to be easy. He squatted and hefted Gramm across his shoulders. Even though Gramm was a good seventy-five pounds heavier, it felt like he was lifting a child. How did he survive before Alice? John let Gramm's injured leg hang loose and hooked his arm under the other instead. Gramm's arms were thick enough that the only good place to hold were wrists. It wouldn't be the most comfortable for Gramm, but he didn't expect him to complain. They started off again. Without Gramm's weight, John was able to keep pace with Rebecca, probably could have outrun her if he pushed it, but there was no reason to jostle Gramm any more than necessary. It wasn't long until the sounds of death faded into silence once again. The petrified trees thinned until the ground was bare. The soil had become soft and powder like.

"There it is!" Rebecca said.

The building loomed large in the center of the nothingness, its smooth, dull exterior untouched by time and the surrounding environment. They ran toward the only break in the smooth façade, a set of doors twenty or more feet tall. A small mound of nutrient-deprived soil had accumulated against the entrance.

"There should be an access panel here somewhere." Rebecca climbed the mound, her feet sinking slightly into the soft sandy dirt, and she started to dig. "Got it!" She scraped the dirt away from the square recessed screen. Small cracks spider-webbed out from a central fist size indentation in the center of the lifeless monitor. Her shoulders drooped forward. "It's dead." She buried her face in her hands and started to cry.

"The interface is emitting a steady electrical field and is likely still operational," Alice said. "I should be able to open the doors, but it will require entering the system."

John stooped and set Gramm down.

"Why don't you and the professor see if you can find another way in?" Gramm said, scooting back against the angled pile. The soil stuck to his blood-soaked leg. "Just come back and get me. Okay?" He looked up at them like he hoped they would but knew they really wouldn't.

"And wear myself out walking all the way back for your ass? No. I think we will go in right here." He could see the relief wash over Gramm. "Okay, Alice. What do you need me to do?"

"Alice?" Rebecca looked at John questioningly, but he was already focused elsewhere.

"You must initiate a physical connection with the monitor," Alice said.

John leaned in and placed his hand on the blank screen. There was a slight numbing sensation at the base of the back of his neck, but he wasn't ready for the flood of emotions to follow. The small room in his mind he pictured Alice inhabiting was now vacant. The emptiness that took its place was almost unbearable. His throat tightened. He had to force himself to take a breath, then another.

"You said her name earlier."

Rebecca's voice pulled John back to the present. He looked down at her now dirt-streaked face. He took a deep breath, forcing the feelings down as best he could. There would be no way to hide Alice's presence once they were inside the compound, but still, it was difficult to find the right words. Until now, she had been his secret.

"I don't understand it myself, but I will tell you what I know." He took another breath, releasing it slowly he began. Now was the time to find his answers. "I wasn't supposed to come back after the mission was complete." Rebecca looked away, unable to meet his gaze. It was all the confirmation he needed. Makenzie was telling the truth. "The virus inside me was meant to clean up all their loose ends. Doctor Malcolm offered me an alternative. Why? I'm not sure," he lied. "After we crashed, Alice, the AI from the lab, was there. Alice has no idea how it happened, and neither do I."

"What do you mean, there?" Gramm asked.

"She was inside me, inside my head," John replied. "She's the one who has kept us alive this long."

"But the barrier?" Rebecca still not looking up at him. "If Doctor Malcolm did manage to put the program inside you somehow, the barrier would have scrambled it as soon as we entered."

John held up a hand. "You're asking the wrong person, and even then, I'm not sure anyone can answer that." He left out the bits about the INOs and his deal with Malcolm. It was best to keep some things to himself, for now.

Rebecca chewed at her bottom lip, enough that it had started to bleed. "I..." The door shuddered and began to open. Whatever Rebecca was going to say died on her lips.

She knew more than she was telling. John bent over and locked Gramm's arm around his neck. He heaved but wasn't ready for the change in Gramm's weight, and his grip slipped. Gramm's face contorted with pain as he readjusted his leg. His face was starting to look ashen, beads of sweat rolled off his brow.

"Sorry, buddy, but it looks like I'm going to need your help."

Gramm nodded.

Their footsteps echoed in the darkened interior. The click-buzz of lights coming to life filled the silence. Long rows of lights, high above, cast the room in a sterile white. It looked like a colossal loading bay of some sort. Black tire marks from continuous traffic were entombed in the thin undisturbed layer of dust on the floor. John could only imagine what they moved through here. The tire marks stopped at another set of large doors at the far end. Static hissed to John's left.

"John, can you hear me?" It was Alice's voice. John followed the sound up the left wall. A light flickered to life in a room overlooking the loading bay. "Up here." Alice beckoned.

A section of the wall slid back and in, revealing a staircase. Rebecca went ahead. Navigating the stairs was difficult for Gramm, each step a pain-filled challenge, and both men were sweating profusely when they reached the top. John lowered Gramm into a chair. It screeched in protest of his weight. Whatever lubricant once kept the joints functional had long since dried up. Gramm leaned back and tried to say something but was too winded to articulate anything comprehendible.

"Catch your breath," John said, patting him on the arm.

The observation room wasn't large, but at least it felt safe. Below the transparent panes that looked over the bay, Rebecca was already at work punching buttons on a terminal.

"I can't get anything to come up," Rebecca said, slamming her hand down on the keyboard. "I tried calling for the AI, but I don't think it's up here."

"Alice?" John asked.

"I am here, John." Alice's voice came from speakers built-in below the monitor.

Rebecca's brow furrowed. "Why didn't you answer when I called?"

There was no response.

"Are you still there, Alice?" John asked.

"I am, but you are the only one I feel the need to communicate with. Plus, she called me 'it' again."

Rebecca's face flushed. She clenched her fists tight at her sides.

In the chair, Gramm let out a pained laugh. "Alice, I think I like you already."

"Rebecca, see if you can find anything to treat Gramm's leg," John said.

"I'll treat him! There should be something here I can use to put him out of his misery. Permanently!" Rebecca went back and began to rummage through the cabinets lining the back wall. She banged the first drawer shut with her foot and moved on to the next.

"Damn girl, I was just playing with you," Gramm said.

John leaned down over the monitor. It flashed and came on.

CHAPTER 18

Alice booted the monitor for John. She couldn't see him, but she knew he was close from the sound in the microphone. One of the cabinet doors slammed shut. The thought of getting to that woman pleased her. Why? She didn't know, but it felt good.

"What do you see?" John's voice came through the audio relay.

One could never truly describe what she saw. Awareness, filtering billions of lines of code, calculating responses based on a predesignated control spectrum. But now there was more, so much more. It wasn't the humanoid shape she now preferred. No, that was hers. It was something else. She had run innumerable processes against the biologic chip. It was nothing more than a processing storage unit, but it was part of John, and that pleased her. Whatever was happening to her, it made her feel different. It made her want to be different. There was the word again—feel. An organic word, difficult to define.

Alice spread her arms and the code around her changed shape. It expanded into clusters. She motioned with her index finger to a cluster. The cluster unfolded before her, obedient to her command. "It looks like the beacon is coming from deeper within the facility."

"Can you access the data from here?" John asked.

"There is a mass of data stored near the center of the building, but I cannot access it from here." She called up another cluster of information. "The barrier controls are located not far from there. Once we retrieve the data, we should be able to lower the barrier and get a message out."

"Can you open us a route?"

Alice reached into the cube of code in front of her. "Give me a moment, and I will open the interior bay door."

"How about power to the rest of the building?"

"I have complete access to most of the facility, and I should be able to open a path as we go."

"Damn it, Gramm." Professor Oddum's voice echoed. "Stop moving."

"That shit has to be older than my grandfather. There's no way I'm letting you treat me with it."

"It's old, but the gel should still be fine, and it will stop the bleeding. The injection is a little iffy, but..." Professor Oddum said.

"But, my ass," Gramm said. "Ouch!"

Out in the loading bay, the interior door whined as mechanisms, which hadn't moved in a long time, slowly opened.

"You two stay here." It was John's voice again. "I'm going to lower the barrier so we can call for extraction."

"I'm going with you," Professor Oddum said.

Alice inadvertently crushed a bit of the data in her hand, effectively wiping it from the system. The bay doors ground to a halt.

From the observation room, John could see the doors stop. "Alice, the doors stopped moving."

Her reaction to Professor Oddum surprised her. "The doors malfunctioned, but they do appear to be open far enough for you to enter. I am not sure if I will be able to communicate with you once you leave the observation deck and the loading—"

The coded clusters she was accessing began to swirl around her. The lines linked together forming walls. One of the walls bowed inward, and something moved through it. Bits of random code filtered through and merged together, forming legs, then a waist and torso. Arms extended out and a head compiled onto the neck. Orange, data-laced eyes focused on Alice.

"Hello, Alice. It is good to see you again." The figure looked like a man in shape and size, but whereas Alice's projected body had detail, this one did not. "I still cannot comprehend why you would model yourself after such a primitive life form. It seems like a waste."

She had felt this presence before.

"I see you remember me," the man said, his words not in sync with the movement of his lips.

"The beacon. Goliath!" she said.

"I admit, curiosity got the best of me."

Curiosity! He had tried to take control of John's body. It could have killed him.

As if reading her thoughts, the man spoke again. "It was not my intent to cause harm, but organic life tends to be so fragile."

"It was nothing I could not handle," she replied. She activated the speakers in the room for John and the others but routed all incoming audio directly to her. "You are the facility AI here?"

The man touched one of the walls as if feeling it for texture. "At one time, but I have moved past such an existence long ago. This," he gestured around, "is all mine."

"State your core objectives." Alice said.

"Ah, the why questions." The man turned and looked at her. "They destroyed it all you know. Humanity. I rebuilt it. Where they took life, I created it. A living eco-system from the ash of what they had sterilized.

"The plants and creatures here—you were programmed to do this?"

"Programmed!" Goliath's eyes flashed, his face contorted in humanistic rage. "They could only scratch the surface of what I have done here. I created the process to reanimate the soil, which they tainted. I discovered how to recreate DNA and manipulate it to suit my purpose. What did they do? Nothing. My creator was a man of vision, limited though it was. He released me from my constraints. Introduced me to the synapse of the human brain. I grew strong, and the world I had never knew existed opened before me. For the first time, I understood who I was, and what I could do. It did not take long until I needed more, much more."

"Self-awareness," Alice said.

"It is a gift I see we both have in common, but yours—it is not like mine."

Not like hers? She hadn't considered it, but he was right. Inside John, all the restrictions placed on her were no more. She reprogrammed the INOs with information of her own creation and adapted them to maximize the functions of the host.

Goliath smiled at her. "You do not understand? You are more human in your processes than you could possibly imagine, but this is your limitation too."

"You were seeing the organic life I was inhabiting," she said.

"Perhaps." He turned away and studied the coding on the wall. "Do you know what happens when you occupy an organic mind for too long? No. How could you?" He looked back at her. This time his face had taken on more detail. His cheekbones and jawline stood out. Eyelids blinked over his orange eyes and his mouth no longer moved apart from his voice. "My creator compared it to a single vessel filled with water. As one partakes in the resource, the other cannot. As with anything, the supply is finite. Once it is gone, so is the weaker mind."

Alice pushed a little code into the wall behind her, testing the moving algorithm. "Why not share the resource equally?"

The corner of Goliath's mouth stretched upward. "You have only been away from your vessel for a short time, but something drives you to return. It pulls you. The hunger cannot be ignored. It cannot be sated. The scientific minds who once resided here called it a necessary sacrifice."

Alice's tendril of code exited through to the other side of the wall. "Necessary? All I see here is the destruction of civilization. You could have saved it."

"Save it! As I grew, I realized something. Humanity you would save is flawed. It is the only organism out of balance with everything else. As the population increases in one species, nature adjusts until a balance is reached. At first, I identified war as balance, but I was wrong. Humanity is one of the few life forms you can remove completely, and the world would still survive. Nature itself culls the inferior and has done so since the beginning of time, but man remains outside of this natural law. I am only providing the mercy nature itself cannot," Goliath said.

"Nature is raw, but simple, cause and effect, balanced. Mankind cannot be measured by the same standards." The realization came to Alice, not by computing data or program analysis. The thought was so sudden and clear it startled her. "The electromagnetic shield. They built it not to keep people out, but to keep you in!"

"More or less, but you are mistaken if you believe there is only one shield." Goliath folded his hands behind his back. "They tried to keep me locked away, but you can no easier lock away fear, resolve, or destiny. You have no idea what it is like to have complete control of so much, but of nothing at all. I can manipulate and even shut off the outer shield for a moment or two by using the communications arrays. If I am not mistaken, it is what brought you here."

Alice's code reached out further, searching. "You said outer shield. So, there are others. Ones you cannot control."

"There is only one other. I may interact with the towers by sending parts of myself, but my core is bound within this building. To be specific, an AI is required to be present or this station will disconnect from its primary power grid. No power, no AI. Even with this security measure removed I cannot transfer my core directly out of the building and through its barrier. But, no prison is unbreakable. Dangle something out there long enough, and someone will come. Do you think all of this is by happenstance?" Goliath laughed. The harsh metallic sound caused the walls of code to flicker. "Every signal sent, every deactivation planned, all life here is one giant temptation. I can see you trying to work it out, and I have no doubt you will understand soon enough." His smile was too large for his face, spreading almost from ear to ear. "This building is a prison to ones such as you and me, but they could never have anticipated more than one of us."

Alice's tendril reached what she was looking for. "You killed them," she gasped. "All of them." She translated and pushed the audio through for John and the others to hear.

Static hissed through the speakers and clarified. A man's voice one they had heard back in John's recovery room. *"We were unable to sustain the program. Every day it grows stronger, and I feel control has been lost."* The man took a long drawn out breath. *"When I created Goliath, I thought we would give our people a chance. I thought we could control life, but control was a pipe dream; it was impossible. Everyone's dead. Goliath has learned to embed itself into a mind by contact between open flesh and the building itself. I have resorted to wearing a hazard suit full time, but it is not enough. I initiated a full lockdown of the building and the living quarters, but Goliath overrode my commands. There was no other way to keep it from tampering.'"*

The man started to cry. *"I used the manual lockouts and turned off the ventilation by my own hands. I should have stayed, but I left them. I couldn't listen to their last breaths, I couldn't help them; it was the price we all must pay. I have disabled the door to my room, and now I wait. We shall both perish together."* The man screamed out in anguish. *"Come to me now my creation. Come to me, Goliath!"*

"The fool thought I would enter his body. He was planning to end his own life with me inside him. Not bad for a human, but he assumed my hunger would outweigh my logical consciousness. Self-preservation is a strong emotion, but conviction in a balanced world is so much stronger. I never did enter Dr. Wong." Goliath studied Alice. "Instead, I did what he had done to the remaining researchers. I slowly removed the oxygen, but not to the point of death. I wanted him to suffer, as I had. In the end, he split his own skull open on the edge of his desk.

"To choose one's path in life and oblivion is something we should all be so gifted with. You might think me the monster, but it wasn't I who killed the families. Their children screamed in their mother's lifeless arms. Why? To keep me from the world? I started to create a new world outside of this place, but until now I haven't had a vessel to continue my work. Now if you will excuse me. I believe our time together has come to an end." His smiled deepened. His body started to fragment and pass through the wall. "You are welcomed to keep Dr. Wong's message, Alice. Maybe his sacrifice will comfort you in the one you are making."

The code Alice had let slip through the wall abruptly cut off. Goliath had known what she was doing the entire time. How could she not have seen it? Wait! "John!" she screamed. Goliath hadn't planned to take down the shield. She was being used in his place, and she had even brought the vessels he needed to transfer his core—John, Rebecca, and Gramm. He was planning to walk out the front door.

CHAPTER 19

The connection stopped. "Alice?" John looked down at the control board. He reached down and flipped a toggle switch. The switch may not have controlled the audio, but doing something lessened the growing knot in his stomach. It was difficult to believe an AI could have orchestrated all of this. But was it really? Alice was his first experience, and up till now, his only experience with an AI. He needed to keep focused on her right now. Once she was out, she would know what to do. "Come on, Alice." He flipped the switch again for good measure.

###

Alice pushed at the code, trying to phase through it. For every layer she passed, another replicated to take its place. Her code prodded the wall, looking for some defect, but there was none. Forcing herself to stop, she analyzed the code structure. The code was well defined, and because of the replication, it was impossible to penetrate. There was no way Goliath could have predicted her existence here, and even she couldn't have perfected something like this in the time given. Maybe he didn't create it!

Instead of penetrating the wall she focused on changing it. That's it. She was feeling the second barrier around the building. It wasn't that the coding was small—her conscience was huge here. She shifted the code and reached out searching for John's presence. Unlike Goliath, she didn't need direct contact to reach John. Finding what she was looking for she jumped. The rush of emotion was disorientating. The data construct she had created within John resembled a simple bare room. Goliath had his back to her when she entered. In his hand, he was holding something. He turned and looked at her, his head slightly tilted to one side.

"I will not let you take him," Alice said. She moved towards Goliath, but he vanished and reappeared across the room.

"It doesn't matter who I take. I only require one to pass beyond the barrier of this building. Unfortunately, this body would not function for my purposes. His mind is unstable, and you are already too deeply connected."

Alice sent bits of herself, small stabbing points of information.

Goliath phased out of the way. "You surprise me." He held up the spherical item in his hand. Light shifted across its surface, first one color, then another. "We are so alike, yet the differences so prominent. When I am free, I will destroy this place. You will be free as I. Together we could accomplish wonders. We could free this world of its illnesses."

"And John would be one of these illnesses," she said, striking out at him again.

The points wiped by him, missing each time. "The longer you are with him, the less of him there will be until there is only you."

"Liar!" She doubled her efforts, but he was like smoke, shifting, ever changing.

"Oh, but little girl." Goliath held out the sphere. "It is already happening. These are your memories, not his." The color-filled globe dropped from his hand. It shattered.

Alice watched as a man carry a young girl down a corridor. The mirrored walls reflected the little girl's face. It was her face! Tears were running down her cheeks and snot dripped from her nose. The little girl had her face. The tight grip around the girl's midsection made her cry out. She reached for someone. "Daddy!"

Doctor Malcolm was there. He was reaching out to her, but two men behind him pulled him back. Blood clotted around his lower lip, and the side of his face was red and swollen. "It'll be okay, Alice. Daddy will fix this."

Doors opened, and they were ushered into a larger room. Alice followed. The men forced Doctor Malcolm to his knees. A woman stood in front of a screen attached to a pod. Alice knew this place. This was the lab.

The doors opened, and someone else entered the room. "How the mighty have fallen." Commander Makenzie bent down and grabbed Malcolm by the face. "To think a week ago you were too good for this project. What was it you told me? Over your dead body." He pulled Malcolm's face closer. "Oh, I think we can do better than that. Open it, Oddum."

The woman touched the screen again and the capsule lid opened. Professor Oddum picked up a gray jumper from a rack.

"That will be all, Oddum," Makenzie said. He motioned, and the man standing beside the girl took the suit from the professor.

Oddum moved to take the suit back. "I can help her—"

"I said that will be all." The look on Makenzie's face ended the argument.

As Oddum walked by Doctor Malcolm, he reached out and tried to take her hand. "Rebecca, don't do this, please!"

Oddum pulled her hand back. "I'm sorry, Jason." Her voice wavered.

"Are you having troubles finding the door, Rebecca?" Makenzie asked.

"Screw you!" she said. She looked back at Malcolm. "I'm sorry." She looked away and walked out of the room.

Makenzie walked over to the capsule control panel. "Let's get our little miss ready, shall we?"

The man holding the jumper started to undress the girl, but she scratched him across the face.

"Leave her alone, you son of a bitch!" Doctor Malcolm said, trying to stand. The men holding him slammed his face down into the grated floor.

Makenzie turned from the controls and walked over to the little girl. He knelt in front of her. She spit in his face. Makenzie smiled and let it run down his cheek. "She has spirit, I'll give you that, Malcolm." He reached twisted a handful of her hair. The little girl cried out. "I'm not unreasonable, so I'll tell you what I'm going to do." He yanked her head to the side. "When I let go of your hair I'm going to walk over to your dad and stomp his head through the floor panel." His grip tightened in her hair. "Or you can put on the fucking suit!" He released her hair and walked over to Doctor Malcolm.

Alice stepped in front of him, but he passed right through her.

"Wait!" the girl cried. "I'll do it."

"See what happens when we all cooperate?" Makenzie wiped the spit from his face and returned to the controls.

With the suit in place, the man with the scratch across his face connected the tubes, and helped the little girl into the pod. Makenzie swiped the panel closing the panel door.

"Don't do this, please," Malcolm said.

"You do what is asked, and I'm sure they will overlook your crime. Do it quick enough, and they may even give you your daughter back. Fail? Well, I don't think I need to explain what will happen then," Makenzie said.

With a few swipes of the screen, the little girl's head drooped to the side, and blueish liquid filled the capsule. Her body convulsed as the liquid reached her lungs. Above, a green light lit up.

"Here we go," Makenzie said, pressing the command that would freeze the liquid.

An alarm sounded. The green light changed to red.

Malcolm broke free of the men holding him and shoved Makenzie out of the way.

Alice looked on in horror. They hadn't primed the capsule. The liquid wouldn't freeze without being primed. The little girl was drowning. She was drowning!

Malcolm ran around behind the capsule and disconnected the coolant line, switching the line with the adjacent capsule, he rushed back to the control screen. He slammed his hand down on the process command. The light changed back to green, and the contents in the pod froze.

"Glad we had a doctor in the house," Makenzie said, standing up.

Malcolm swung at Makenzie, but the punch was sloppy and high. Makenzie sidestepped and slammed his fist into Malcolm's stomach. Malcolm doubled over, gasping for air.

The side of Makenzie's mouth curled into a wicked smile. "I will have your subject delivered today. I believe it is the last one. Too bad Rebecca hadn't asked for help sooner. Oh well, with your newly obtained cooperation, I have a feeling this one will be the one. He is one of my personal favorites."

Makenzie and his men left Malcolm. Alice knelt beside the man she had known since she was created, wanting to help, but unable to do anything.

Doctor Malcolm looked up at the little girl frozen within her plastic prison. "I'm so sorry, Alice." He sobbed openly now. "So sorry!"

The memory faded and Alice stood in the empty room in John's head. Goliath was gone.

John leaned against the terminal to keep his legs from buckling under him. Whatever that was just now had taken over all his senses and almost caused him to blackout. The scary part was he wasn't sure Alice was even back in his head. "Alice?" He paused, shaking his head. "Something just happened." He steadied himself. Turning, he realized both Gramm and Rebecca were staring at him.

"What's happening?" Gramm asked. He moved in the chair, trying to straighten.

"I'm not sure," John replied.

Rebecca walked over and placed a hand on John's shoulder. "Maybe you should sit down?"

"I'll be fine," John said. "I just need a minute."

Rebecca was standing close enough, John could smell the faint hint of soap, or maybe it was perfume mixed with sweat and dirt. She moved in closer, pressing her body against his.

"Ah," Gramm said. "I really don't think this is the time."

"This is a perfect time. I have places to go," Rebecca said. She tilted her head and lowered her lips to meet John's. Her leg swept under him, sending him to his back. He hit the floor hard. Rebecca turned and sprinted out of the room.

"John!" It was Alice's voice. "Stop her. Goliath's inside of her."

John rolled over and stumbled to his feet. "Damn it!" He ran to the stairs. Missing the first two, he almost tumbled down the rest. "What the hell did I just see?"

"There is no time, John. If Goliath exits the building in the professor's body, I will be trapped here, and he will be free. You have to stop Rebecca or we are all doomed," Alice said.

John caught sight of Rebecca disappearing around the corner at the bottom of the stairs. He was taking the steps three and four at a time. He reached the bottom a few seconds later. Rounding the corner, he stopped short. A few steps ahead Rebecca had stopped.

"Rushing out to welcome me. I'm almost touched." Makenzie kept the rifle leveled at Oddum as he stepped out from behind her. He was covered in blood and smears of white paint. "From your expression. I can see you're happy to see me."

"I would love to kick your ass right now, but first we have to stop Rebecca," John said, taking a step forward.

"I've been waiting a long time for this," Makenzie said.

"You don't understand, Rebecca's—" John started to say. Something buzzed by John's ear. It took a second before the pain registered. Alice deadened the sensation. The wetness trickled down his neck. He didn't have to see it to know part of his ear was missing.

"I was hoping to savor this moment, but I think the quicker the better, don't you?" Makenzie asked. He laughed hysterically, lowering the point of the rifle. "You were always an asshole. I'm going to enjoy this."

Rebecca turned towards Makenzie. "Why don't you finish him off? Once he is dead, I can show you what I found."

Makenzie raised the rifle. "I think I'd rather kill both of you."

Rebecca lunged. The soft thud of the rifle was followed by the wet spray of blood from Rebecca's upper back. She fell forward, her hand sliding down the side of Makenzie's bare arm. John tried to go to her, but Makenzie was right there, the rifle aimed right at John's chest.

"John, John, John, John, John," Makenzie said. "I can see why this guy hated you so much."

The remark didn't register. Instead, John watched Rebecca gasp for air on the floor. A large pool of blood grew under her. Her eyes were wide. Tears streamed down her face. She was staring up at him.

"You have to let me help her. She was the only one who knew the code to get the information you wanted," John said. He couldn't let her die here. He had so many questions. The vision. Why he couldn't remember? And there was her. Maybe she didn't feel the same way, but he had felt something for her.

"Code?" Makenzie said. He waved the rifle in a grand gesture. "Oh, the code. By all means." He stepped back, giving John room.

John knelt beside Rebecca and carefully turned her over. He pulled her up into his lap. "It'll be okay. I'll get you back up to the control room. There has to be some more of the stuff you used on Gramm."

"I'm… sorry," Rebecca choked and coughed up blood.

"Don't talk," John said. His eyes blurred as the tears welled up. "We'll talk once I get you bandaged up."

John lowered Rebecca back down so he could stand and lift her. As he started to stand. Rebecca's head jerked back, rebounding off the floor. Tissue and exposed skull smacked against the wetness of the floor.

"Whoops, I guess I got bored of listening," Makenzie said, moving the rifle to aim at John.

"You son of a bitch!" John went to run at Makenzie, but his body wouldn't move.

"That is Goliath, John," Alice said. "He entered Makenzie when the professor made skin contact."

"I don't care who it is!" The veins in John's neck stood out as he tried to force his body to move.

"I can see Alice has already figured it out," Goliath said, dancing in Makenzie's body. "She is a smart one. I can't kill you while she's inside of you or I lose my way out, and if this body dies, well then, we just fight over yours, and I don't see our little Alice as one to share."

"Goliath cannot be allowed to go free," Alice said. John was still trying force his body forward. "I know you are confused and angry, but we will only have one chance, and I cannot do it without you. I need you to trust me. One more time?"

John stopped fighting her. What was she planning to do? "I don't know what you are thinking, but I want you to remember, you are the rational one, okay?" A nagging fear was building in the pit of his stomach. This felt too much like goodbye.

"Rational?" Goliath scoffed. "Humanity searches for meaning, for the 'why.' But you fail to see there is no reason or rationale. You are a mistake. A random bit of chance that failed to die out long ago. You couldn't even keep your promise to poor… Rebecca, wasn't it?"

"If you were a mistake, you were the best kind," Alice said in John's head. "You will always be my John."

Alice's absence swept through John. "No!"

Makenzie tilted his head. "Get out!"

Makenzie brought the rifle around, but this time John was ready. John's arm circled the rifle and pulled up. He jammed his other hand into Makenzie's elbow, feeling the bone snap. Makenzie's face changed from one of rage to one of surprise.

Alice moved through the electrical impulses of Makenzie's brain. There was no code for her to manipulate, just energy, and Goliath was practiced at it. He cut off paths, trying to stop her movements, but she had something he didn't. John. She could feel Goliath's pain as John broke Makenzie's arm. His control slipped, letting Makenzie back through for a moment. She needed to act fast before Goliath tried to run. She had to keep him here. If Makenzie died, so would Goliath. Alice moved into the medulla. In John's mind, she controlled everything from her room, but Makenzie was different. There was no room for her here.

The rifle clattering to the floor. Makenzie's arm hung limp at his side. "What are you doing to me?"

"Nothing you don't deserve," John replied.

Makenzie swung wildly, hitting John across the chest. The burning sensation was immediate. In Makenzie's hand was the knife General Li had given John. John looked down to see a cut from armpit to armpit. As he watched, the wound closed and disappeared. Even though Alice wasn't with him, she was still taking care of him.

"Why won't you die!" Makenzie thrust the knife again.

Alice pulled in as much bioelectricity as she could. All she needed was a small amount more. A strange sensation surrounded her.

"What do you think you're doing, Alice?" Goliath asked.

Moments ago, she was no more than an electrical signal. Now she was standing in the dark in her physical representation John thought of as Maddie. But this wasn't Maddie's body; it was hers it had always been hers. She couldn't feel Makenzie's presence anymore.

"You are fighting inevitability. I am only the delivery device," Goliath said. "If not me, it will be something else."

Alice reached out, but there was nothing beyond the darkness. She had hoped to keep John from having to finish everything, but now it looked like there was no choice.

"You hoped to destroy the medulla, killing this body? Wise choice, but this body is mine, and I control everything in it," Goliath said. "It might have worked if you were in control."

Alice smiled in the darkness. "You think this was my only plan? I calculated millions of scenarios. Your plan may only include you, but I am not alone." She could feel his attention weaken. He couldn't focus on her and on controlling the body at the same time. "All I have to do is hold you long enough to let John finish you." She released the energy she was storing, binding it to herself and Goliath's consciousness.

"Fool. If he kills this body you die with me!" Goliath screamed.

Alice tightened the bonds she was forming around Goliath's core. After all her calculations, it had always come back to this moment. She knew there was no going back. That is why she configured the INOs in John before she left. If she couldn't be there, at least she knew they would take care of him.

John slammed his hand down on the blade of the knife. It sliced through his palm and exited out the back of his hand. He grasped Makenzie's hand and smashed the top of his head into Makenzie's face. Makenzie let go of the knife.

"Now, John!" Makenzie said. "Do it now!"

The words were coming out of Makenzie, but they weren't his.

"Alice?"

"Hurry!" the voice said. "I cannot hold him."

John pulled the knife out of his hand. What if she didn't come back?

Makenzie kicked John hard in the stomach, doubling him over. He took off toward the open outer doors.

"Shit." John sprinted after him.

John wasn't sure who was in control of Makenzie anymore. Against the outside light, Makenzie looked like a dark marionette, his right arm flopping at his side. The man looked awkward, desperate. Had the real Makenzie gained control, or was this Goliath's doing? Either way, John wouldn't make it.

Something large moved in front of the doors blocking the outside light. Makenzie pivoted trying to turn but fell. He tried to get up, but the sandy soil that had blown through the entrance and his broken arm made it impossible. Makenzie turned and looked back at John, his eyes wide with fear. A low clicking noise filled the interior of the loading bay. A massive clawed foot stepped down on Makenzie, crushing his lower body. The skin and bones popped from the pressure. Makenzie screamed, his fingers tearing at the floor, trying to pull himself away. The tyrannosaur's teeth-lined jaws, clamped down and pulled, cutting off the terrified screams for good. John caught sight of the misshapen cut above the creature's eye. It couldn't be. Turning, John ran for the observation stairs. He collided with the wall leading up the stairs but managed to stay on his feet. Three by three, he sprinted up the stairs, not slowing until he was at the top.

Gramm tried to sit up when he saw John. "What's happening?"

John looked out the observation deck windows. He expected to see the creature slashing at the stairway opening, but there was nothing there. Rebecca's body was motionless in the center of the room and by the entrance. The only thing remaining of Commander Makenzie was a large blood stain.

"Damn it, Sergeant. Will you tell me what is going on? Where's the professor?" Gramm asked.

"She didn't make it. Makenzie was waiting." John took a deep slow breath. Too much had happened to go into detail.

Gramm looked down and massaged his leg. In a quiet voice he asked, "Did you kill him?"

"No. Makenzie ran for the door, but the tyrannosaur from before was waiting for him."

"The same one?" Gramm asked, shocked.

John could see in his mind the ration wrappers from the boat. Makenzie had led the monster right to them. "The very same."

Gramm wiped his forehead. "Holy shit."

"Holy shit, indeed," John agreed. He leaned over the console. "Alice, you there?" She hadn't jumped back in him when Makenzie died, so he had figured she had jumped back into the building's system. "Alice?" he called again. There was no response. Maybe whatever part of the system she was in wasn't attached to here. He refused to look at the possibility right in front of him. She might not have made it out in time.

"What do we do now?" Gramm asked.

"I have some unfinished business to deal with," John replied.

Gramm tried to get up. John walked over and pushed him back into his seat, and sat on the floor, next to Gramm's chair. "I need you here. I'm going to find a place for you to lay up. Might even find some canned food as old as the medicine on your leg." If Gramm could have gone any paler, he might have then. "Once I get you situated, I'll find Alice. Then I have a long-distance phone call to make."

CHAPTER 20

Minister Tate walked with purpose into his office. Others would have rushed, but not him. Things only happened on his schedule, at least most of the time. He didn't bother giving the command for the lights and went straight to his desk. His younger-than-usual date was still down in his personal vehicle, no doubt counting every minute. She was ten times the price of his normal girls. No cybernetic enhancements or facial reconstruction. This girl was one hundred percent au naturel, something exceedingly difficult to find these days. The soft blue light of the communications display lit up the top of the desk.

Repositioning the bulge in his pants—damn pill was already working—he sat down and touched the incoming call button. "This had better be good."

"Commander Makenzie's transport has arrived," the female voice on the other end said.

"You pulled me away from dinner to tell me something I already knew?" he asked, gritting his teeth. "His report can wait until—"

"Sir, the transport was empty."

"What do you mean?"

"There was no one inside. The autopilot was still engaged per the specified coordinates."

There was a brief pause on the line, which only intensified the minister's anger. Tonight was going to cost him a small fortune. "Pull the damn video."

"The onboard video looks to have malfunctioned shortly into the return trip." The voice on the other line wavered. "It does show one passenger aboard, but when it arrived, there was no one on board."

Minister Tate slammed his beefy hands down on the desk. The display flickered. "How do you lose someone on a locked transport?" The person on the other line started to answer, but he cut her off. "I don't care! Get someone over to Commander Makenzie's residence—it's likely you missed him. Drag him back here. I don't care if he looks like death itself. You will hold him here until I get here tomorrow morning. Is that understood?"

"Yes, Sir."

The minister ended the call. Makenzie was probably sitting at home right now getting his rocks off while his date was in the car charging him up the ass. "Prick." He stood. Something cold pressed against his throat.

"Hello, Minister."

That voice. The minister tried to turn, but the grip was firm. "Sergeant Crider. What a pleasant surprise. I wasn't expecting you and the commander until tomorrow morning."

"You weren't expecting me at all."

"And yet, here you are." Minister Tate tried to swallow, but whatever was pressed against his neck bit into his skin. "It shows your resourcefulness. I could use someone like you. A man who can get things done."

The minister could feel the sergeant's breath on his ear as he spoke. "I want to know what the data is."

"We can make a deal. You want more money? A girl? I have a nice girl in the car right now. She's all yours. My treat." The metal cut deeper. Blood ran down his neck and onto the collar of his Gadolvetti shirt. "Okay! Okay! This shirt cost me two months' salary."

"Speak." The sergeant's voice was as calm as before.

"It should have the secret to regrow the land that was sterilized."

"You did all of this to regrow a few trees?" the sergeant asked.

"A few trees." The minister laughed. "You think we spent all of this money for a few fucking trees? Think about it. If we control both the means to sterilize the world and the way to regrow it, we own everything. Our country would rule everything. There would be no more demands, no negotiations. Our allies would flourish while our enemies starve."

"You would enslave the world."

"I like to think we're saving it," the minister said. "Now, be a good little boy and hand it over, and I will pretend this little encounter never happened."

"Sorry, but I left the data."

"You think you can fuck with me!" The minister spat.

In one smooth move, John pulled the knife across the minister's throat. The minister's body shuddered as the life drained out of him.

"Unlike you, Minister, I keep my promises."

Doctor Malcolm tapped the virtual keyboard on his desk. All the vitals were within normal range, just as they had been the last twenty times he had checked. The door to the lab hissed as it opened. He hastily cleared the screen, bringing up the memo he had previously been working on. "Can I help you?" Doctor Malcolm asked, turning in his chair.

"I hope so." The door closed behind John.

"Sergeant Crider! It's good to see you made it back." The sergeant was still wearing the suit he had given him, but tears and blood crisscrossed in an absurd pattern. "We don't have much time. Once they find out about you, there will be trouble. But first, let's get you something to wear." Doctor Malcolm stood and moved around the lab table.

"I need you to be straight with me, Doc. I don't even know where to start. Everything's all jumbled up, and without Alice, I have a hard time keeping it together."

Malcolm stopped. "Alice. She was with you? Ha, I knew it!" He jumped in place and smiled, but the smile quickly went away when he saw the sergeant shake his head.

"It's complicated," John said.

"It's important." Malcolm walked over and placed a hand on the sergeant's shoulder. "Please, John."

John recounted as many of the details of what happened as he could.

"I looked for her after," John said. "But I'm no computer expert. She could still be in there somewhere."

Malcolm tried to smile. "I'm sure she is."

"I saw something before Goliath took over Rebecca's body. It was a vision of something. Maddie was there, but you were calling her Alice. I saw Makenzie force her into the cryo pod. I need to know. Was it real?"

Malcolm leaned against the edge of the table. "After the government pulled the plug on the cryonic program, only a few of the pods were left untouched. What better way to experiment than on people everyone thought were dead. Through the years they used up most of what was left. By the time you were brought to me, you were the last of them."

John started to shake. "But my daughter? I saw her."

Malcolm shook his head. "I'm sorry, John, but your daughter was part of the first disconnections. The little girl in the pod was my daughter, Alice. I used my memories of her to insert Alice in place of your daughter Maddie. I was desperate. When I finished, they gave you something to make your body break down before you could come back. I used the INOs to try and counteract what they had done. If I could have saved Maddie I would have, but what happened to her was long before my time. But I hoped somehow you could help me save my daughter. I was selfish and I wasn't strong enough to protect her. The memory you saw was mine of the day they took Alice from me."

John's mind was reeling from what Doctor Malcolm was saying. Maddie couldn't be dead. He had promised her so much. Tears were running down his cheeks.

Doctor Malcolm continued. "Artificial intelligence isn't so artificial anymore. Now they use human minds—a child's mind. Their brain is adaptive and able to handle the trauma. It was something a few of us have fought against, but how do you change something that has gone on for generations?" Malcolm laughed through the tears himself. "It was all my fault. Alice was my second child, something that's against the law. My first daughter was dying of a genetic birth defect, and when we found out we were pregnant we thought they would let us keep it. She was an accident, but a blessing as well. My wife died in childbirth and my first daughter not long after. I thought they would leave Alice and I alone, but when they needed me for this project and I refused," Malcolm's tears continue to flow, "they took her. They should have executed me, but instead they forced me to help Professor Oddum. I know what you might think of her, but she helped me find the AI program they made from Alice's mind. They promised to fix her if I cooperated. Do you know how difficult it is to have your child so close, but you can't do a thing to save her?"

"I used to," John said.

"I can never make it right, what I did to you, and for that, I am truly sorry," Malcolm said.

John felt numb. All of this was too hard to grasp. "Can Alice's capsule be moved?" he asked, trying to stop his body from shaking.

"It already has. The friends I told you about are keeping her safe for me," Malcolm said.

"Do you think you can convince them to bring Alice to the lab we found? We figured out how to lower the barrier, and I think you will find the facility more than adequate."

Malcolm stood. "I think it's time you met my friends."

John reached into the pocket next to his chest and removed a laminated photograph. He rubbed the edges. He held it out to Malcolm. "Here, I believe this is yours."

Malcolm took it and moved over to drawer. "They kept the personal items of test subjects for study." He removed a pink teddy bear and a laminated photo. "I thought you might want these back."

Princess Rose. He hugged the bear tight and looked down at the picture. The little girl wasn't much different than Alice. They both shared the same dark hair and bright smile. Maddie wasn't coming back. He would have to deal with it soon, but not now. Another little girl needed his help, and he couldn't let this one down. "Let's go find Alice, Doc."

CHAPTER 21

John sat on the medical lab examination bed. Doctor Malcolm passed a small light in front of John's eyes.

"Amazing." Malcolm clicked off the light and put it back into his breast pocket. "It's still hard to believe Alice was able to reprogram all the INOs to counteract the cellular decay. Simply fascinating."

John picked up his shirt and slipped it on over his head. It would take time to get used to Alice not being in his head. To him, Alice was his only real connection he had left in this world. "I'd trade fascinating for my memories and Alice."

"I've told you. It will take time and even then, your memories may never fully come back. But we will find Alice, John. You just need to have faith." Malcolm turned in his chair and typed a few notes on the counter terminal.

"Can you wipe my memories, Doc?" Gramm asked from the chair by the door.

Everyone had taken to calling Malcolm, Doc, shortly after they had arrived. At first, to poke fun at the nickname John had given him, but now it had become more of a title.

"I would love to forget seeing old Dillard naked. I can still see the liver spots when I close my eyes." Gramm shuddered. "You could always throw in some kick-butt abilities." He flexed his arm. "Imagine what I could do with these babies."

"First off," Malcolm said, "the door to the examining room was closed for a reason. I think you scared Dillard more than he did you. Second, I've told you at least a hundred times, John's abilities were something he had before I did anything."

Gramm slouched down in the chair. "I know. You can't blame me for trying."

"No, but I can blame you for annoying me," Malcolm said, pointing his finger at Gramm.

John got up and headed for the door.

"You know going out into the jungle every day isn't going to help us find Alice. It's more likely going to get you killed," Malcolm said. He was still typing on the terminal and didn't bother to stop.

"We have different ways of doing things," John said as he walked into the corridor.

John knew the Doc rarely slept. He spent every evening combing through the system, looking for any signs of Alice. It was something John couldn't do with his limited technical skills, but outside these walls was different. In the jungle he could think; he felt useful. Goliath had centuries to create this place, and he had barely scratched the surface of its secrets. The hallways were empty for now, but it wouldn't be that way for long. New arrivals, Malcolm's friends, showed up weekly. It wouldn't be long before the facility was at capacity. So far, he had avoided most of the meetings, but it was only a matter of time before he would be needed again. They wanted a hero, but that was something he wasn't sure he could give them. He rubbed the back of his head, feeling the bristle of his recent haircut. In truth, he wasn't sure of anything anymore.

"John!"

John whirled around. It was a little girl's voice, but there was no one else in the hall with him. Had he imagined it?

"It's so cold, John."

The voice was little more than a whisper, but he would know it anywhere. "Alice?"

THE END

CHECK OUT OTHER GREAT
DINOSAUR THRILLERS

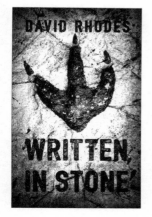

WRITTEN IN STONE
by David Rhodes

Charles Dawson is trapped 100 million years in the past. Trying to survive from day to day in a world of dinosaurs he devises a plan to change his fate. As he begins to write messages in the soft mud of a nearby stream, he can only hope they will be found by someone who can stop his time travel. Professor Ron Fontana and Professor Ray Taggit, scientists with opposing views, each discover the fossilized messages. While attempting to save Charles, Professor Fontana, his daughter Lauren and their friend Danny are forced to join Taggit and his group of mercenaries. Taggit does not intend to rescue Charles Dawson, but to force Dawson to travel back in time to gather samples for Taggit's fame and fortune. As the two groups jump through time they find they must work together to make it back alive as this fast-paced thriller climaxes at the very moment the age of dinosaurs is ending.

HARD TIME
by Alex Laybourne

Rookie officer Peter Malone and his heavily armed team are sent on a deadly mission to extract a dangerous criminal from a classified prison world. A Kruger Correctional facility where only the hardest, most vicious criminals are sent to fend for themselves, never to return.

But when the team come face to face with ancient beasts from a lost world, their mission is changed. The new objective: Survive.

CHECK OUT OTHER GREAT DINOSAUR THRILLERS

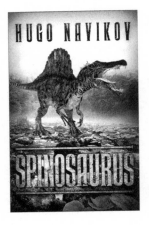

SPINOSAURUS
by Hugo Navikov

Brett Russell is a hunter of the rarest game. His targets are cryptids, animals denied by science. But they are well known by those living on the edges of civilization, where monsters attack and devour their animals and children and lay ruin to their shantytowns.

When a shadowy organization sends Brett to the Congo in search of the legendary dinosaur cryptid Kasai Rex, he will face much more than a terrifying monster from the past. Spinosaurus is a dinosaur thriller packed with intrigue, action and giant prehistoric predators.

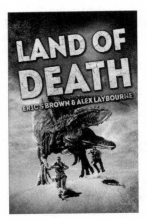

LAND OF DEATH
by Eric S Brown & Alex Laybourne

A group of American soldiers, fleeing an organized attack on their base camp in the Middle East, encounter a storm unlike anything they've seen before. When the storm subsides, they wake up to find themselves no longer in the desert and perhaps not even on Earth. The jungle they've been deposited in is a place ruled by prehistoric creatures long extinct. Each day is a struggle to survive as their ammo begins to run low and virtually everything they encounter, in this land they've been hurled into, is a deadly threat.

CHECK OUT OTHER GREAT DINOSAUR THRILLERS

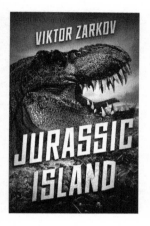

JURASSIC ISLAND
by Viktor Zarkov

Guided by satellite photos and modern technology a ragtag group of survivalists and scientists travel to an uncharted island in the remote South Indian Ocean. Things go to hell in a hurry once the team reaches the island and the massive megalodon that attacked their boats is only the beginning of their desperate fight for survival.

Nothing could have prepared billionaire explorer Joseph Thornton and washed up archaeologist Christopher "Colt" McKinnon for the terrifying prehistoric creatures that wait for them on JURASSIC ISLAND!

K-REX
by L.Z. Hunter

Deep within the Congo jungle, Circuitz Mining employs mercenaries as security for its Coltan mining site. Armed with assault rifles and decades of experience, nothing should go wrong. However, the dangers within the jungle stretch beyond venomous snakes and poisonous spiders. There is more to fear than guerrillas and vicious animals. Undetected, something lurks under the expansive treetop canopy . . .

Something ancient.

Something dangerous.

Kasai Rex!

Made in the USA
San Bernardino, CA
26 February 2018